SCIENCE
FICTION

EDITORIAL DIRECTION **JOY LITTELL**

DESIGN **WILLIAM SEABRIGHT**

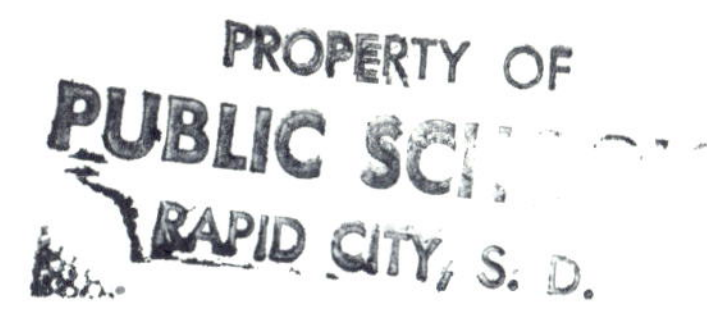

Revised Edition

SCIENCE FICTION

EDITORS SYLVIA Z. BRODKIN

ELIZABETH J. PEARSON

McDOUGAL, LITTELL & COMPANY

EVANSTON, ILLINOIS

Acknowledgments: See page 255

ISBN 0-88343-164-5

Box 1667, Evanston, Illinois 60204
 Printed in the United States of America

CONTENTS

OTHER CREATURES, OTHER WORLDS

INVASIONS

NEW HORIZONS

OF MISSING PERSONS

JACK FINNEY

Walk in as though it were an ordinary travel bureau, the stranger I'd met at a bar had told me. *Ask a few ordinary questions—about a trip you're planning, a vacation, anything like that. Then hint about The Folder a little, but whatever you do, don't mention it directly; wait till he brings it up himself. And if he doesn't, you might as well forget it. If you can. Because you'll never see it; you're not the type, that's all. And if you ask about it, he'll just look at you as though he doesn't know what you're talking about.*

I rehearsed it all in my mind, over and over, but what seems possible at night over a beer isn't easy to believe on a raw, rainy day, and I felt like a fool, searching the store fronts for the street number I'd memorized. It was noon hour. West 42nd Street, New York, rainy and windy; and like half the men around me, I walked with a hand on my hat-brim, wearing an old trench coat, head bent into the slanting rain, and the world was real and drab, and this was hopeless.

Anyway, I couldn't help thinking, who am I to see The Folder, even if there is one? Name? I said to myself, as though I were already being asked. It's Charley Ewell, and I'm a young guy who works in a bank; a teller. I don't like the job; I don't make much money, and I never will. I've lived in New York for over three years and haven't many friends. What the heck, there's really nothing to say—I see more movies than I want to, read too many books, and I'm sick of meals alone in restaurants. I have ordinary abilities, looks, and thoughts. Does that suit you; do I qualify?

Now I spotted it, the address in the 200 block, an old, pseudo-modernized office building, tired, outdated, refusing to admit it but unable to hide it. New York is full of them, west of Fifth.

I pushed through the brass-framed glass doors into the tiny lobby, paved with freshly mopped, permanently dirty tile. The green-painted walls were lumpy from old plaster repairs; in a chrome frame hung a little wall directory—white-celluloid, easily changed letters on a black-felt background. There were some twenty-odd names, and I found "Acme Travel Bureau" second on the list, between "A-1 Mimeo" and "Ajax Magic Supplies." I pressed the bell beside the old-style, open-grille elevator door; it rang high up in the shaft. There was a long pause, then a thump, and the heavy chains began rattling slowly down toward me, and I almost turned and left—this was insane.

But upstairs the Acme office had divorced itself from the atmosphere of the building. I pushed open the pebble-glass door, walked in, and the big square room was bright and clean, fluorescent-lighted. Beside the wide double windows, behind a counter, stood a tall gray-haired, grave-looking man, a telephone at his ear. He glanced up, nodded to beckon me in, and I felt my heart pumping—he fitted the description exactly. "Yes, United Air Lines," he was saying into the phone. "Flight"—he glanced at a paper on the glass-topped counter—"seven-oh-three, and I suggest you check in forty minutes early."

Standing before him now, I waited, leaning on the counter, glancing around; he was the man, all right, and yet this was just an ordinary travel agency; big bright posters on the walls, metal floor racks full of folders, printed schedules under the glass on the counter. This is just what it looks like and nothing else, I thought, and again I felt like a fool.

"Can I help you?" Behind the counter the tall gray-haired man was smiling at me, replacing the phone, and suddenly I was terribly nervous.

"Yes." I stalled for time, unbuttoning my raincoat. Then I looked up at him again and said, "I'd like to—get away." You fool, that's too fast, I told myself. Don't rush it! I watched in a kind of panic to see what effect my answer had had, but he didn't flick an eyelash.

"Well, there are a lot of places to go," he said politely. From under the counter he brought out a long, slim folder and laid it on the glass, turning it right side up for me. "Fly to Buenos Aires—Another World!" it said in a double row of pale-green letters across the top.

I looked at it long enough to be polite. It showed a big silvery plane banking over a harbor at night, a moon shining on the water, mountains in the background. Then I just shook my head; I was afraid to talk, afraid I'd say the wrong thing.

"Something quieter, maybe?" He brought out another folder: thick old tree trunks, rising way up out of sight, sunbeams slanting down through them—"The Virgin Forests of Maine, via Boston and Maine Railroad." "Or"—he laid a third folder on the glass—"Bermuda is nice just now." This one said, "Bermuda, Old World in the New."

I decided to risk it. "No," I said, and shook my head. "What

I'm really looking for is a permanent place. A new place to live and settle down in." I stared directly into his eyes. "For the rest of my life." Then my nerve failed me, and I tried to think of a way to backtrack.

But he only smiled pleasantly and said, "I don't know why we can't advise you on that." He leaned forward on the counter, resting on his forearms, hands clasped; he had all the time in the world for me, his posture conveyed. "What are you looking for; what do you want?"

I held my breath, then said it. "Escape."

"From what?"

"Well—" Now I hesitated; I'd never put it into words before. "From New York, I'd say. And cities in general. From worry. And fear. And the things I read in my newspapers. From loneliness." And then I couldn't stop, though I knew I was talking too much, the words spilling out. "From never doing what I really want to do or having much fun. From selling my days just to stay alive. From life itself—the way it is today, at least." I looked straight at him and said softly, "From the world."

Now he was frankly staring, his eyes studying my face intently with no pretense of doing anything else, and I knew that in a moment he'd shake his head and say, "Mister, you better get to a doctor." But he didn't. He continued to stare, his eyes examining my forehead now. He was a big man, his gray hair crisp and curling, his lined face very intelligent, very kind; he looked the way ministers should look; he looked the way all fathers should look.

He lowered his gaze to look into my eyes and beyond them; he studied my mouth, my chin, the line of my jaw, and I had the sudden conviction that without any difficulty he was learning a great deal about me, more than I knew myself. Suddenly he smiled and placed both elbows on the counter, one hand grasping the other fist and gently massaging it. "Do you like people? Tell the truth, because I'll know if you aren't"

"Yes. It isn't easy for me to relax though, and be myself, and make friends."

He nodded gravely, accepting that. "Would you say you're a reasonably decent kind of man?"

"I guess so; I think so." I shrugged.

"Why?"

I smiled wryly; this was hard to answer. "Well—at least when I'm not, I'm usually sorry about it."

He grinned at that, and considered it for a moment or so. Then he smiled—deprecatingly, as though he were about to tell a little joke that wasn't too good. "You know," he said casually, "we occasionally get people in here who seem to be looking for pretty much what you are. So just as a sort of little joke—"

I couldn't breathe. This was what I'd been told he would say if he thought I might do.

"—we've worked up a little folder. We've even had it printed. Simply for our own amusement, you understand. And for occasional clients like you. So I'll have to ask you to look at it here if you're interested. It's not the sort of thing we'd care to have generally known."

I could barely whisper, "I'm interested."

He fumbled under the counter, then brought out a long thin folder, the same size and shape as the others, and slid it over the glass toward me.

I looked at it, pulling it closer with a finger tip, almost afraid to touch it. The cover was dark blue, the shade of a night sky, and across the top in white letters it said, "Visit Enchanting Verna!" The blue cover was sprinkled with white dots—stars—and in the lower left corner was a globe, the world, half surrounded by clouds. At the upper right, just under the word "Verna," was a star larger and brighter than the others; rays shot out from it, like from a star on a Christmas card. Across the bottom of the cover it said, "Romantic Verna, where life is the way it *should* be." There was a little arrow beside the legend, meaning turn the page.

I turned, and the folder was like most travel folders inside—there were pictures and text, only these were about "Verna" instead of Paris, or Rome, or the Bahamas. And it was beautifully printed; the pictures looked real. What I mean is, you've seen color stereopticon pictures? Well, that's what these were like, only better, far better. In one picture you could see dew glistening on the grass, and it looked wet. In another, a tree trunk seemed to curve out of the page, in perfect detail, and it was a shock to touch it and feel smooth paper instead of the rough actuality of bark. Miniature human faces, in a third picture, seemed about to speak, the lips moist and alive, the eyeballs shining, the actual texture of skin right there on paper; and it seemed impossible, as you stared, that the people wouldn't move and speak.

I studied a large picture spreading across the tops of two open pages. It seemed to have been taken from the top of a hill; you saw the land dropping away at your feet far down into a valley, then rising up again, way over on the other side. The slopes of both hills were covered with forest, and the color was beautiful, perfect; there were miles of green, majestic trees, and you knew as you looked that this forest was virgin, almost untouched. Curving through the floor of the valley, far below, ran a stream, blue from the sky in most places; here and there, where the current broke around massive boulders, the water was foaming white; and again it seemed that if you'd only look closely enough you'd be certain to see that stream move and shine in the sun. In clearings beside the stream there were shake-roofed cabins, some of logs, some of brick or adobe. The caption under the picture simply said, "The Colony."

"Fun fooling around with a thing like that," the man behind the counter murmured, nodding at the folder in my hands. "Relieves the monotony. Attractive-looking place, isn't it?"

I could only nod dumbly, lowering my eyes to the picture again because that picture told you even more than just what you saw. I don't know how you knew this, but you realized, staring at that forest-covered valley, that this was very much the way America once looked when it was new. And you knew this was only a part of a whole land of unspoiled, unharmed forests, where every stream ran pure; you were seeing what people, the last of them dead over a century ago, had once looked at in Kentucky and Wisconsin and the old Northwest. And you knew that if you could breathe in that air you'd feel it flow into your lungs sweeter than it's been anywhere on Earth for a hundred and fifty years.

Under that picture was another, of six or eight people on a beach—the shore of a lake, maybe, or the river in the picture above. Two children were squatting on their haunches, dabbling in the water's edge, and in the foreground a half circle of adults were sitting, kneeling, or squatting in comfortable balance on the yellow sand. They were talking, several were smoking, and most of them held half-filled coffee cups; the sun was bright, you knew the air was balmy and that it was morning, just after breakfast. They were smiling, one woman talking, the others listening. One man had half risen from his squatting position to skip a stone out onto the surface of the water.

You knew this; that they were spending twenty minutes or so down on that beach after breakfast before going to work, and you knew they were friends and that they did this every day. You knew—I tell you, you *knew*—that they liked their work, all of them, whatever it was; that there was no forced hurry or pressure about it. And that—well, that's all, I guess; you just knew that every day after breakfast these families spent a leisurely half-hour sitting and talking, there in the morning sun, down on that wonderful beach.

I'd never seen anything like their faces before. They were ordinary enough in looks, the people in that picture—pleasant, more or less familiar types. Some were young, in their twenties; others were in their thirties; one man and woman seemed around fifty. But the faces of the youngest couple were completely unlined, and it occurred to me then that they had been born there, and that it was a place where no one worried or was ever afraid. The others, the older ones, there were lines in their foreheads, grooves around their mouths, but you felt that the lines were no longer deepening, that they were healed and untroubled scars. And in the faces of the oldest couple was a look of—I'd say it was a look of permanent *relief.* Not one of those faces bore a trace of malice; these people were *happy.* But even more than that, you knew they'd *been* happy, day after day after day for a long, long time, and that they always would be, and they knew it.

I wanted to join them. The most desperate longing roared up in me from the bottom of my soul to *be* there—on that beach, after breakfast, with those people in the sunny morning—and I could hardly stand it. I looked up at the man behind the counter and managed to smile. "This is—very interesting."

"Yes." He smiled back, then shook his head in amusement. "We've had customers so interested, so carried away, that they didn't want to talk about anything else." He laughed. "They actually wanted to know rates, details, everything."

I nodded to show I understood and agreed with them. "And I suppose you've worked out a whole story to go with this?" I glanced at the folder in my hands.

"Oh, yes. What would you like to know?"

"These people," I said softly, and touched the picture of the group on the beach. "What do they do?"

"They work; everyone does." He took a pipe from his pocket. "They simply live their lives doing what they like. Some study. We have, according to our little story," he added, and smiled, "a very fine library. Some of our people farm, some write, some make things with their hands. Most of them raise children, and—well, they work at whatever it is they really want to do."

"And if there isn't anything they really want to do?"

He shook his head. "There is always something for everyone,

that he really wants to do. It's just that here there is so rarely time to find out what it is." He brought out a tobacco pouch and, leaning on the counter, began filling his pipe, his eyes level with mine, looking at me gravely. "Life is simple there, and it's serene. In some ways, the good ways, it's like the early pioneering communities here in your country, but without the drudgery that killed people young. There is electricity. There are washing machines, vacuum cleaners, plumbing, modern bathrooms, and modern medicine, very modern. But there are no radios, television, telephones, or automobiles. Distances are small, and people live and work in small communities. They raise or make most of the things they use. Every man builds his own house, with all the help he needs from his neighbors. Their recreation is their own, and there is a great deal of it, but there is no recreation for sale, nothing you buy a ticket to. They have dances, card parties, weddings, christenings, birthday celebrations, harvest parties. There are swimming and sports of all kinds. There is conversation, a lot of it, plenty of joking and laughter. There is a great deal of visiting and sharing of meals, and each day is well filled and well spent. There are no pressures, economic or social, and life holds few threats. Every man, woman, and child is a happy person." After a moment he smiled. "I'm repeating the text, of course, in our little joke"—he nodded at the folder.

"Of course," I murmured, and looked down at the folder again, turning a page. "Homes in The Colony," said a caption, and there, true and real, were a dozen or so pictures of the interiors of what must have been the cabins I'd seen in the first photograph, or others like them. There were living rooms, kitchens, dens, patios. Many of the homes seemed to be furnished in a kind of Early American style, except that it looked—authentic, as though those rocking chairs, cupboards, tables, and hooked rugs had been made by the people themselves, taking their time and making them well and beautifully. Others of the interiors seemed modern in style; one showed a definite Oriental influence.

All of them had, plainly and unmistakably, one quality in common: You knew as you looked at them that these rooms were *home,* really home, to the people who lived in them. On the wall of one living room, over the stone fireplace, hung a handstitched motto; it said, "There Is No Place Like Home," but the words didn't seem quaint or amusing, they didn't seem old-fashioned, resurrected or copied from a past that was gone. They seemed real; they belonged; those words were nothing more or less than a simple expression of true feeling and fact.

"Who are you?" I lifted my head from the folder to stare into the man's eyes.

He lighted his pipe, taking his time, sucking the match flame down into the bowl, eyes glancing up at me. "It's in the text," he said then, "on the back page. We—that is to say, the people of Verna, the original inhabitants—are people like yourself. Verna is a planet of air, sun, land, and sea, like this one. And of the same approximate temperature. So life evolved there, of course, just about as it has here, though rather earlier: and we are people like you. There are trivial anatomical differences, but nothing important. We read and enjoy your James Thurber, John Clayton, Rabelais, Allen Marple, Hemingway, Grimm, Mark Twain, Alan Nelson. We like your chocolate, which we didn't have, and a great deal of your music, and you'd like many of the things we have. Our thoughts, though, and the great aims and directions of our history and development have been—drastically different from yours." He smiled and blew out a puff of smoke. "Amusing fantasy, isn't it?"

"Yes." I knew I sounded abrupt, and I hadn't stopped to smile; the words were spilling out. "And where is Verna?"

"Light years away, by your measurements."

I was suddenly irritated, I didn't know why. "A little hard to get to, then, wouldn't it be?"

For a moment he looked at me; then he turned to the window beside him. "Come here," he said, and I walked around the counter to stand beside him. "There, off to the left"—he put a hand on my shoulder and pointed with his pipe stem—"are two apartment buildings, built back to back. The entrance to one is on Fifth Avenue, the entrance to the other on Sixth. See them? In the middle of the block; you can just see their roofs."

I nodded, and he said, "A man and his wife live on the fourteenth floor of one of those buildings. A wall of their living room is the back wall of the building. They have friends on the fourteenth floor of the other building, and a wall of *their* living room is the back wall of *their* building. These two couples live, in other words, within two feet of one another, since the back walls actually touch."

The big man smiled. "But when the Robinsons want to visit the Bradens, they walk from their living room to the front door. Then they walk down a long hall to the elevators. They ride fourteen floors down; then, in the street, they must walk around to the next block.

And the city blocks there are long; in bad weather they have sometimes actually taken a cab. They walk into the other building, then go on through the lobby, ride up fourteen floors, walk down a hall, ring a bell, and are finally admitted into their friends' living room—only two feet from their own."

The big man turned back to the counter, and I walked around it to the other side again. "All I can tell you," he said then, "is that the way the Robinsons travel is like space travel, the actual physical crossing of those enormous distances." He shrugged. "But if they could only step through those two feet of wall without harming themselves or the wall—well, that is how we 'travel.' We don't cross space, we avoid it." He smiled. "Draw a breath here—and exhale it on Verna."

I said softly, "And that's how they arrived, isn't it? The people in the picture. You took them there." He nodded, and I said, "Why?"

He shrugged. "If you saw a neighbor's house on fire, would you rescue his family if you could? As many as you could, at least?"

"Yes."

"Well—so would we."

"You think it's that bad, then? With us?"

"How does it look to you?"

I thought about the headlines in my morning paper, that morning and every morning. "Not so good."

He just nodded and said, "We can't take you all, can't even take very many. So we've been selecting a few."

"For how long?"

"A long time." He smiled. "One of us was a member of Lincoln's cabinet. But it was not until just before your First World War that we felt we could see what was coming; until then we'd been merely observers. We opened our first agency in Mexico City in nineteen thirteen. Now we have branches in every major city."

"Nineteen thirteen," I murmured, as something caught at my memory. "Mexico. Listen! Did—"

"Yes." He smiled, anticipating my question. "Ambrose Bierce joined us that year, or the next. He lived until nineteen thirty-one, a very old man, and wrote four more books, which we have." He turned back a page in the folder and pointed to a cabin in the first large photograph. "That was his home."

"And what about Judge Crater?"

"Crater?"

"Another famous disappearance; he was a New York judge

who simply disappeared some years ago."

"I don't know. We had a judge, I remember, from New York City, some twenty-odd years ago, but I can't recall his name."

I leaned across the counter toward him, my face very close to his, and I nodded. "I like your little joke," I said. "I like it very much, more than I can possibly tell you." Very softly I added, "When does it stop being a joke?"

For a moment he studied me; then he spoke. "Now. If you want it to."

You've got to decide on the spot, the middle-aged man at the Lexington Avenue bar had told me, *because you'll never get another chance. I know; I've tried.* Now I stood there thinking; there were people I'd hate never to see again, and a girl I was just getting to know, and this was the world I'd been born in. Then I thought about leaving that room, going back to my job, then back to my room at night. And finally I thought of the deep-green valley in the picture and the little yellow beach in the morning sun. "I'll go," I whispered. "If you'll have me."

He studied my face. "Be sure," he said sharply. "Be certain. We want no one there who won't be happy, and if you have any least doubt, we'd prefer that—"

After a moment the gray-haired man slid open a drawer under the counter and brought out a little rectangle of yellow cardboard. One side was printed, and through the printing ran a band of light green; it looked like a railroad ticket to White Plains or somewhere. The printing said, "Good, when validated, for ONE TRIP TO VERNA. Nontransferable. One-way only."

"Ah—how much?" I said, reaching for my wallet, wondering if he wanted me to pay.

He glanced at my hand on my hip pocket. "All you've got. Including your small change." He smiled. "You won't need it any more, and we can use your currency for operating expenses. Light bills, rent, and so on."

"I don't have much."

"That doesn't matter." From under the counter he brought out a heavy stamping machine, the kind you see in railroad ticket offices. "We once sold a ticket for thirty-seven hundred dollars. And we sold another just like it for six cents." He slid the ticket into the machine, struck the lever with his fist, then handed the ticket to me. On the back, now, was a freshly printed rectangle of purple ink, and within it the words, "Good this day only," followed by the date. I put two five-dollar bills, a one, and seventeen cents in change on the counter. "Take the ticket to the Acme Depot," the gray-haired man said, and, leaning across the counter, began giving me directions for getting there.

It's a tiny hole-in-the-wall, the Acme Depot; you may have seen it—just a little store front on one of the narrow streets west of Broadway. On the window is painted, not very well, "Acme." Inside, the walls and ceiling, under layers of old paint, are covered with the kind of stamped tin you see in the old buildings. There's a worn wooden counter and a few battered chrome-and-imitation-red-leather chairs. There are scores of places like the Acme Depot in that area—little theatre-ticket agencies, obscure bus-line offices, employment agencies. You could pass this one a thousand times and never really see it; and if you live in New York, you probably have.

Behind the counter, when I arrived, a shirt-sleeved man smoking a cigar stump stood working on some papers; four or five people silently waited in the chairs. The man at the counter glanced up as I stepped in, looked down at my hand for my ticket, and when I showed it, nodded at the last vacant chair, and I sat down.

There was a girl beside me, hands folded on her purse. She was pleasant-looking, rather pretty; I thought she might have been a stenographer. Across a narrow little office sat a young Negro in work clothes, his wife beside him holding their little girl in her lap. And there was a man of around fifty, his face averted from the rest of us, staring out into the rain at passing pedestrians. He was expensively dressed and wore a gray Homburg hat; he could have been the vice-president of a large bank, I thought, and wondered what his ticket had cost.

Maybe twenty minutes passed, the man behind the counter working on some papers; then a small, battered old bus pulled up at the curb outside, and I heard the hand brake set. The bus was a shabby thing, bought third- or fourth-hand and painted red and white over the old paint, the fenders lumpy from countless pounded-out dents, the tire treads worn almost smooth. On the side, in red letters, it said "Acme," and the driver wore a leather jacket and the kind of worn cloth cap that cab drivers wear. It was precisely the sort of obscure little bus you see around there, ridden always by shabby, tired, silent people, going no one knows where.

It took nearly two hours for the little bus to work south through the traffic, toward the tip of Manhattan, and we all sat, each wrapped in his own silence and thoughts, staring out the rain-spattered windows; the little girl was asleep. Through the streaking glass beside me I watched drenched people huddled at city bus stops, and saw them rap angrily on the closed doors of buses jammed to capacity, and saw the strained, harassed faces of the drivers. At 14th Street I saw a speeding cab splash a sheet of street-dirty water on a man at the curb, and saw the man's mouth writhe as he cursed. Often our bus stood motionless, the traffic light red, as throngs flowed out into the street from the curb, threading their way around us and the other waiting cars. I saw hundreds of faces, and not once did I see anyone smile.

I dozed; then we were on a glistening black highway somewhere on Long Island, I slept again, and awakened in darkness as we jolted off the highway onto a muddy double-rut road, and I caught a glimpse of a farmhouse, the windows dark. Then the bus slowed, lurched once, and stopped. The hand brake set, the motor died, and we were parked beside what looked like a barn.

It *was* a barn—the driver walked up to it, pulled the big sliding wood door open, its wheels creaking on the rusted old trolley overhead, and stood holding it open as we filed in. Then he released it, stepping inside with us, and the big door slid closed of its own weight. The barn was damp, old, the walls no longer plumb, and it smelled of cattle; there was nothing inside on the packed-dirt floor but a bench of unpainted pine, and the driver indicated it with a beam of a flashlight. "Sit here, please," he said quietly. "Get your tickets ready." Then he moved down the line, punching each of our tickets, and on the floor I caught a momentary glimpse, in the shifting beam of his light, of tiny mounds of countless more round bits of cardboard, like little drifts of yellow confetti. Then he was at the door again, sliding it open just enough to pass through, and for a moment we saw him silhouetted against the night sky. "Good luck," he said. "Just wait where you are." He released the door; it slid closed, snipping off the wavering beam of his flashlight; and a moment later we heard the motor start and the bus lumber away in low gear.

The dark barn was silent now, except for our breathing. Time ticked away, and I felt an urge, presently, to speak to whoever was next to me. But I didn't quite know what to say, and I began to feel embarrassed, a little foolish, and very aware that I was simply sitting in an old and deserted barn. The seconds passed, and I moved my feet restlessly; presently I realized that I was getting cold and chilled. Then suddenly I knew—and my face flushed in violent anger and a terrible shame. We'd been tricked! bilked out of our money by our pathetic will to believe an absurd and fantastic fable and left, now, to sit there as long as we pleased, until we came to our senses finally, like countless others before us, and made our way home as best we could. It was suddenly impossible to understand or even remember how I could have been so gullible, and I was on my feet, stumbling through the dark across the uneven floor, with some notion of getting to a phone and the police. The big barn door was heavier than I'd thought, but I slid it back, took a running step through it, then turned to shout back to the others to come along.

You perhaps have seen how very much you can observe in the fractional instant of a lightning flash—an entire landscape sometimes, every detail etched on your memory, to be seen and studied in your mind for long moments afterwards. As I turned back toward the opened door the inside of that barn came alight. Through every wide crack of its walls and ceiling and through the big dust-coated windows in its side streamed the light of an intensely brilliant blue and sunny sky, and the air pulling into my lungs as I opened my mouth to shout was sweeter than any I had ever tasted in my life. Dimly, through a wide, dust-smeared window of that barn, I looked—for less than the blink of an eye—down into a deep majestic V of forest-covered slope, and I saw, tumbling through it, far below, a tiny stream, blue from the sky, and at that stream's edge between two low roofs a yellow patch of sun-drenched beach. And then, that picture engraved on my mind forever, the heavy door slid shut, my fingernails rasping along the splintery wood in a desperate effort to stop it—and I was standing alone in a cold and rain-swept night.

It took four or five seconds, no longer, fumbling at that door, to heave it open again. But it was four or five seconds too long. The barn was empty, dark. There was nothing inside but a worn pine bench—and, in the flicker of the lighted match in my hand, tiny drifts of what looked like damp confetti on the floor. As my mind had known even as my hands scratched at the outside of that door, there was no one inside now; and I knew where they were—knew they were walking, laughing aloud in a sudden wonderful and eager ecstasy, down into that forest-green valley, toward home.

I work in a bank, in a job I don't like; and I ride to and from it in the subway, reading the daily papers, the news they contain. I live in a rented room, and in the battered dresser under a pile of my folded handkerchiefs is a little rectangle of yellow cardboard. Printed on its face are the words, "Good, when validated, for one trip to Verna," and stamped on the back is a date. But the date is gone, long since, the ticket void, punched in a pattern of tiny holes.

I've been back to the Acme Travel Bureau. The first time the tall gray-haired man walked up to me and laid two five-dollar bills, a one, and seventeen cents in change before me. "You left this on the counter last time you were here," he said gravely. Looking me squarely in the eyes, he added blankly, "I don't know why." Then some customers came in, he turned to greet them, and there was nothing for me to do but leave.

Walk in as though it were the ordinary agency it seems—you can find it, somewhere, in any city you try! Ask a few ordinary questions—about a trip you're planning, a vacation, anything you like. Then hint about The Folder a little, but don't mention it directly. Give him time to size you up and offer it himself. And if he does, if you're the type, if you can believe—*then make up your mind and stick to it! Because you won't ever get a second chance. I know, because I've tried. And tried. And tried.*

—AND HE BUILT A CROOKED HOUSE

ROBERT HEINLEIN

Americans are considered crazy anywhere in the world.

They will usually concede a basis for the accusation but point to California as the focus of the infection. Californians stoutly maintain that their bad reputation is derived solely from the acts of the inhabitants of Los Angeles County. Angelenos will, when pressed, admit the charge but explain hastily, "It's Hollywood. It's not our fault—we didn't ask for it; Hollywood just grew."

The people in Hollywood don't care; they glory in it. If you are interested, they will drive you up Laurel Canyon "—where we keep the violent cases." The Canyonites—the brown-legged women, the trunk-clad men constantly busy building and rebuilding their slaphappy unfinished houses —regard with faint contempt the dull creatures who live down in the flats, and treasure in their hearts the secret knowledge that they, and only they, know how to live.

Lookout Mountain Avenue is the name of a side canyon which twists up from Laurel Canyon. The other Canyonites don't like to have it mentioned; after all, one must draw the line somewhere!

High up on Lookout Mountain at number 8775, across the street from the Hermit—the original Hermit of Hollywood—lived Quintus Teal, graduate architect.

Even the architecture of southern California is different. Hot dogs are sold from a structure built like and designated "The Pup." Ice-cream cones come from a giant stucco ice-cream cone, and neon proclaims "Get the Chili Bowl Habit!" from the roofs of buildings which are indisputably chili bowls. Gasoline, oil, and free road maps are dispensed beneath the wings of trimotored transport planes, while the certified rest rooms, inspected hourly for your comfort, are located in the cabin of the plane itself. These things may surprise or amuse the tourist, but the local residents, who walk bareheaded in the famous California noonday sun, take them as a matter of course.

Quintus Teal regarded the efforts of his colleagues in architecture as fainthearted, fumbling, and timid.

"What is a house?" Teal demanded of his friend, Homer Bailey.

"Well—" Bailey admitted cautiously— "speaking in broad terms, I've always regarded a house as a gadget to keep off the rain."

"Nuts! You're as bad as the rest of them."

"I didn't say the definition was complete—"

"Complete! It isn't even in the right direction. From that point of view we might just as well be squatting in caves. But I don't blame you," Teal went on magnanimously, "you're no worse than the lugs you find practicing architecture. Even the Moderns—all they've done is to abandon the Wedding Cake School in favor of the Service Station School, chucked away the gingerbread and slapped on the chromium, but at heart they are as conservative and traditional as a county courthouse. Neutra! Schindler! What have those bums got? What's Frank Lloyd Wright got that I haven't got?"

"Commissions," his friend answered succinctly.

"Huh? Wha' d'ju say?" Teal stumbled slightly in his flow of words, did a slight double take, and recovered himself. "Commissions. Correct. And why? Because I don't think of a house as an upholstered cave; I think of it as a machine for living, a vital process, a live dynamic thing, changing with the mood of the dweller—not a dead, static, oversized coffin. Why would we be held down by the frozen concepts of our ancestors? Any fool with a little smattering of descriptive geometry can design a house in the ordinary way. Is the static geometry of Euclid the only mathematics? Are we to completely disregard the Picard-Vessiot theory? How about modular systems? To say nothing of the rich suggestions of stereochemistry. Isn't there a place in architecture for transformation, for homomorphology, for actional structures?"

"Blessed if I know," answered Bailey. "You might just as well be talking about the fourth dimension for all it means to me."

"And why not? Why should we limit ourselves to the—Say!" He interrupted himself and stared into distances. "Homer, I think you've really got something. After all, why not? Think of the infinite richness of articulation and relationship in four dimensions. What a house, what a house—" He stood quite still, his pale bulging eyes blinking thoughtfully.

Bailey reached up and shook his arm. "Snap out of it. What the hell are you talking about, four dimensions? Time is the fourth dimension; you can't drive nails into *that.*"

Teal shrugged him off. "Sure. Sure. Time is a fourth dimension, but I'm thinking about a fourth spatial dimension, like length, breadth and thickness. For economy of materials and convenience of arrangement you can't beat it. To say nothing of the saving of ground space—you could put an eight-room house on the land now occupied by a one-room house. Like a tesseract—''

"What's a tesseract?"

"Didn't you go to school? A tesseract is a hypercube, a square figure with four dimensions to it, like a cube has three, and a square has two. Here, I'll show you." Teal dashed out into the kitchen of his apartment and returned with a box of toothpicks, which he spilled on the table between them, brushing glasses and a nearby empty Holland gin bottle carelessly aside. "I'll need some plasticine. I had some around here last week." He burrowed into a drawer of the littered desk which crowded one corner of his dining room and emerged with a lump of oily sculptor's clay. "Here's some."

"What are you going to do?"

"I'll show you." Teal rapidly pinched off small masses of the clay and rolled them into pea-sized balls. He stuck toothpicks into four of these and hooked them together into a square. "There! That's a square."

"Obviously."

"Another one like it, four more toothpicks, and we make a cube." The toothpicks were now arranged in the framework of a square box, a cube, with the pellets of clay holding the corners together. "Now we make another cube just like the first one, and the two of them will be two sides of the tesseract."

Bailey started to help him roll the little balls of clay for the second cube, but became diverted by the sensuous feel of the docile clay and started working and shaping it with his fingers.

"Look," he said, holding up his effort, a tiny figurine, "Gypsy Rose Lee."

"Looks more like Gargantua; she ought to sue you. Now pay attention. You open up one corner of the first cube, interlock the second cube at one corner, and then close the corner. Then take eight more toothpicks and join the bottom of the first cube to the bottom of the second, on a slant, and the top of the first to the top of the second, the same way." This he did rapidly, while he talked.

"What's that supposed to be?" Bailey demanded suspiciously.

"That's a tesseract, eight cubes forming the sides of a hypercube in four dimensions."

"It looks more like a cat's cradle to me. You've only got two cubes there anyhow. Where are the other six?"

"Use your imagination, man. Consider the top of the first cube in relation to the top of the second; that's cube number three. Then the two bottom squares, then the front faces of each cube, the back faces, the right hand, the left hand—eight cubes." He pointed them out.

"Yeah, I see 'em. But they still aren't cubes; they're whatchamacallems—prisms. They are not square, they slant."

"That's just the way you look at it, in perspective. If you drew a picture of a cube on a piece of paper, the side squares would be slaunchwise, wouldn't they? That's perspective. When you look at a four-dimensional figure in three dimensions, naturally it looks crooked. But those are all cubes just the same."

"Maybe they are to you, brother, but they still look crooked to me."

Teal ignored the objections and went on. "Now consider this as the framework of an eight-room house; there's one room on the ground floor—that's for service, utilities, and garage. There are six rooms opening off it on the next floor, living room, dining room, bath, bedrooms, and so forth. And up at the top, completely enclosed and with windows on four sides, is your study. There! How do you like it?"

"Seems to me you have the bathtub hanging out of the living-room ceiling. Those rooms are interlaced like an octopus."

"Only in perspective, only in perspective. Here, I'll do it another way so you can see it." This time Teal made a cube of toothpicks, then made a second of halves of toothpicks, and set it exactly in the center of the first by attaching the corners of the small cube to the large cube by short lengths of toothpick. "Now—the big cube is your ground floor, the little cube inside is your study on the top floor. The six cubes joining them are the living rooms. See?"

Bailey studied the figure, then shook his head. "I still don't see but two cubes, a big one and a little one. Those other six things, they look like pyramids this time instead of prisms, but they still aren't cubes."

"Certainly, certainly, you are seeing them in different perspective. Can't you see that?"

"Well, maybe. But that room on the inside, there. It's completely surrounded by the thingamajigs. I thought you said it had windows on four sides."

"It has—it just looks like it was surrounded. That's the grand feature about a tesseract house, complete outside exposure for every room, yet every wall serves two rooms and an eight-room house requires only a one-room foundation. It's revolutionary."

"That's putting it mildly. You're crazy, Bud; you can't build a house like that. That inside room is on the inside, and there she stays."

Teal looked at his friend in controlled exasperation. "It's guys like you that keep architecture in its infancy. How many square sides has a cube?"

"Six."

"How many of them are inside?"

"Why, none of 'em. They're all on the outside."

"All right. Now listen—a tesseract has eight cubical sides, *all on the outside*. Now watch me. I'm going to open up this tesseract like you can open up a cubical pasteboard box, until it's flat. That way you'll be able to see all eight of the cubes." Working very rapidly he constructed four cubes, piling one on top of the other in an unsteady tower. He then built out four more cubes from the four exposed faces of the second cube in the pile. The structure swayed a little under the loose coupling of the clay pellets, but it stood, eight cubes in an inverted cross, a double cross, as the four additional cubes stuck out in four directions. "Do you see it now? It rests on the ground-floor room, the next six cubes are the living rooms, and there is your study, up at the top."

Bailey regarded it with more approval than he had the other figures. "At least I can understand it. You say that is a tesseract, too?"

That is a tesseract unfolded in three dimensions. To put it back together you tuck the top cube into the bottom cube, fold those side cubes in till they meet the top cube and there you are. You do all this folding through a fourth dimension of course; you don't distort any of the cubes, or fold them into each other."

Bailey studied the wobbly framework further. "Look here," he said at last, "why don't you forget about folding this thing up through a fourth dimension—you can't anyway—and build a house like this?"

"What do you mean, I can't? It's a simple mathematical problem—"

"Take it easy, son. It may be simple in mathematics, but you could never get your plans approved for construction. There isn't any fourth dimension; forget it. But this kind of a house—it might have some advantages."

Checked, Teal studied the model. "Hm-m-m—maybe you got

something. We could have the same number of rooms, and we'd save the same amount of ground space. Yes, and we would set that middle cross-shaped floor northeast, southwest, and so forth, so that every room would get sunlight all day long. That central axis lends itself nicely to central heating. We'll put the dining room on the northeast and the kitchen on the southeast, with big view windows in every room. OK, Homer, I'll do it! Where do you want it built?"

"Wait a minute! Wait a minute! I didn't say you were going to build it for me—"

"Of course I am. Who else? Your wife wants a new house; this is it."

"But Mrs. Bailey wants a Georgian house—"

"Just an idea she had. Women don't know what they want—"

"Mrs. Bailey does."

"Just some idea an out-of-date architect has put in her head. She drives a new car, doesn't she? She wears the very latest styles—why should she live in an eighteenth-century house? This house will be even later than the latest model; it's years in the future. She'll be the talk of the town."

"Well—I'll have to talk to her."

"Nothing of the sort. We'll surprise her with it. Have another drink."

"Anyhow, we can't do anything about it now. Mrs. Bailey and I are driving up to Bakersfield tomorrow. The company's bringing in a couple of wells tomorrow."

"Nonsense. That's just the opportunity we want. It will be a surprise for her when you get back. You can just write me a check right now, and your worries are over."

"I oughtn't to do anything like this without consulting her. She won't like it."

"Say, who wears the pants in your family anyhow?"

The check was signed about halfway down the second bottle.

Things are done fast in southern California. Ordinary houses there are usually built in a month's time. Under Teal's impassioned heckling the tesseract house climbed dizzily skyward in days rather than weeks, and its cross-shaped second story came jutting out at the four corners of the world. He had some trouble at first with the inspectors over these four projecting rooms but by using strong girders and folding money he had been able to convince them of the soundness of his engineering.

By arrangement, Teal drove up in front of the Bailey residence the morning after their return to town. He improvised on his two-tone horn. Bailey stuck his head out the front door. "Why don't you use the bell?"

"Too slow," answered Teal cheerfully. "I'm a man of action. Is Mrs. Bailey ready? Ah, there you are, Mrs. Bailey! Welcome home, welcome home. Jump in, we've got a surprise for you!"

"You know Teal, my dear," Bailey put in uncomfortably.

Mrs. Bailey sniffed. "I know him. We'll go in our own car, Homer."

"Certainly, my dear."

"Good idea," Teal agreed; "It's got more power than mine; we'll get there faster. I'll drive, I know the way." He took the keys from Bailey, slid into the driver's seat, and had the engine started before Mrs. Bailey could rally her forces.

"Never have to worry about my driving," he assured Mrs. Bailey, turning his head as he did so, while he shot the powerful car down the avenue and swung onto Sunset Boulevard; "it's a matter of power and control, a dynamic process, just my meat—I've never had a serious accident."

"You won't have but one," she said bitingly. "Will you *please* keep your eyes on the traffic?"

He attempted to explain to her that a traffic situation was a matter, not of eyesight, but intuitive integration of courses, speeds, and probabilities, but Bailey cut him short. "Where is the house, Quintus?"

"House?" asked Mrs. Bailey suspiciously. "What's this about a house, Homer? Have you been up to something without telling me?"

Teal cut in with his best diplomatic manner. "It certainly is a house, Mrs. Bailey. And what a house! It's a surprise for you from a devoted husband. Just wait till you see it—"

"I shall," she said grimly. "What style is it?"

"This house sets a new style. It's later than tomorrow, newer than next week. It must be seen to be appreciated. By the way," he went on rapidly, heading off any retort, "did you folks feel the earthquake last night?"

"Earthquake? What earthquake? Homer, was there an earthquake?"

"Just a little one," Teal continued, "about two A.M. If I hadn't been awake, I wouldn't have noticed it."

Mrs. Bailey shuddered. "Oh, this awful country! Do you hear that, Homer? We might have been killed in our beds and never have known it. Why did I let you persuade me to leave Iowa?"

"But, my dear," he protested hopelessly, "you wanted to come out to California; you didn't like Des Moines."

"We needn't go into that," she said firmly. "You are a man; you should anticipate such things. Earthquakes!"

"That's one thing you needn't fear in your new home, Mrs. Bailey," Teal told her. "It's absolutely earthquake-proof; every part is in perfect dynamic balance with every other part."

"Well, I hope so. Where is this house?"

"Just around this bend. There's the sign now." A large arrow sign, of the sort favored by real-estate promoters, proclaimed in letters that were large and bright even for southern California:

THE HOUSE OF THE FUTURE ! ! !
Colossal—Amazing—Revolutionary
See how your grandchildren will live!
Q. Teal, Architect

"Of course that will be taken down," he added hastily, noting her expression, "as soon as you take possession." He slued around the corner and brought the car to a squealing halt in front of the House of the Future. *"Voilà!"* He watched their faces for response.

Bailey stared unbelievingly, Mrs. Bailey in open dislike. They saw a simple cubical mass, possessing doors and windows, but no other architectural features, save that it was decorated in intricate mathematical designs. "Teal," Bailey asked slowly, "what have you been up to?"

Teal turned from their faces to the house. Gone was the crazy tower with its jutting second-story rooms. No trace remained of the seven rooms above ground floor level. Nothing remained but the single room that rested on the foundations. "Great jumping cats!" he yelled. "I've been robbed!"

He broke into a run.

But it did him no good. Front or back, the story was the same: the other seven rooms had disappeared, vanished completely. Bailey caught up with him and took his arm.

"Explain yourself. What is this about being robbed? How come you built anything like this—it's not according to agreement."

"But I didn't. I built just what we had planned to build, an eight-room house in the form of a developed tesseract. I've been sabotaged; that's what it is! Jealousy! The other architects in town didn't dare let me finish this job; they knew they'd be washed up if I did."

"When were you last here?"

"Yesterday afternoon."

"Everything all right then?"

"Yes. The gardeners were just finishing up."

Bailey glanced around at the faultlessly manicured landscaping. "I don't see how seven rooms could have been dismantled and carted away from here in a single night without wrecking this garden."

Teal looked around, too. "It doesn't look it. I don't understand it."

Mrs. Bailey joined them. "Well? Well? Am I to be left to amuse myself? We might as well look it over as long as we are here, though I'm warning you, Homer, I'm not going to like it."

"We might as well," agreed Teal, and drew a key from his pocket with which he let them in the front door. "We may pick up some clues."

The entrance hall was in perfect order, the sliding screens that separated it from the garage space were back, permitting them to see the entire compartment. "This looks all right," observed Bailey. "Let's go up on the roof and try to figure out what happened. Where's the staircase? Have they stolen that, too?"

"Oh, no," Teal denied, "look—" He pressed a button below the light switch; a panel in the ceiling fell away and a light, graceful flight of stairs swung noiselessly down. Its strength members were the frosty silver of duralumin, its treads and risers transparent plastic. Teal wriggled like a boy who has successfully performed a card trick, while Mrs. Bailey thawed perceptibly.

It was beautiful.

"Pretty slick," Bailey admitted. "Howsomever it doesn't seem to go any place—"

"Oh, that—" Teal followed his gaze. "The cover lifts up as you approach the top. Open stair wells are anachronisms. Come on." As predicted, the lid of the staircase got out of their way as they climbed the flight and permitted them to debouch at the top, but not, as they had expected, on the roof of the single room. They found themselves standing in the middle one of the five rooms which constituted the second floor of the original structure.

For the first time on record Teal had nothing to say. Bailey echoed him, chewing on his cigar. Everything was in perfect order. Before them, through open doorway and translucent partition, lay the kitchen, a chef's dream of up-to-the-minute domestic engineering, Monel metal, continuous counter space, concealed lighting, functional arrangement. On the left the formal, yet gracious and hospitable, dining room awaited guests, its furniture in parade-ground alignment.

Teal knew before he turned his head that the drawing room and lounge would be found in equally substantial and impossible existence.

"Well, I must admit this *is* charming," Mrs. Bailey approved, "and the kitchen is just *too* quaint for words—though I would never have guessed from the exterior that this house had so much room upstairs. Of course *some* changes will have to be made. That secretary now—if we move it over *here* and put the *settee* over *there*—"

"Stow it, Matilda," Bailey cut in brusquely. "What d'yuh make of it, Teal?"

"Why, Homer Bailey! The very id——"

"Stow it, I said. Well, Teal?"

The architect shuffled his rambling body. "I'm afraid to say. Let's go on up."

"How?"

"Like this." He touched another button; a mate, in deeper colors, to the fairy bridge that had let them up from below offered them access to the next floor. They climbed it, Mrs. Bailey expostulating in the rear, and found themselves in the master bedroom. Its shades were drawn, as had been those on the level below, but the mellow lighting came on automatically. Teal at once activated the switch which controlled still another flight of stairs, and they hurried up into the top-floor study.

"Look, Teal," suggested Bailey when he had caught his breath, "can we get to the roof above this room? Then we could look around."

"Sure, it's an observatory platform." They climbed a fourth flight of stairs, but when the cover at the top lifted to let them reach the level above, they found themselves, not on the roof, but *standing in the ground-floor room where they had entered the house.*

Mr. Bailey turned a sickly gray. "Angels in heaven," he cried, "this place is haunted. We're getting out of here." Grabbing his wife he threw open the front door and plunged out.

Teal was too much preoccupied to bother with their departure. There was an answer to all this, an answer that he did not believe. But he was forced to break off considering it because of hoarse shouts from somewhere above him. He lowered the staircase and rushed upstairs. Bailey was in the central room leaning over Mrs. Bailey, who had fainted. Teal took in the situation, went to the bar built into the lounge, and poured three fingers of brandy, which he returned with and handed to Bailey. "Here—this'll fix her up."

Bailey drank it.

"That was for Mrs. Bailey," said Teal.

"Don't quibble," snapped Bailey. "Get her another." Teal took the precaution of taking one himself before returning with a dose earmarked for his client's wife. He found her just opening her eyes.

"Here, Mrs. Bailey," he soothed, "this will make you feel better."

"I never touch spirits," she protested, and gulped it.

"Now tell me what happened," suggested Teal. "I thought you two had left."

"But we did—we walked out the front door and found ourselves up here, in the lounge."

"The hell you say! Hm-m-m—wait a minute." Teal went into the lounge. There he found that the big view window at the end of the room was open. He peered cautiously through it. He stared, not out at the California countryside, but into the ground-floor room—or a reasonable facsimile thereof. He said nothing, but went back to the stairwell, which he had left open, and looked down it. The ground-floor room was still in place. Somehow, it managed to be in two different places at once, on different levels.

He came back into the central room and seated himself opposite Bailey in a deep, low chair, and sighted him past his upthrust bony knees. "Homer," he said impressively, "do you know what has happened?"

"No, I don't—but if I don't find out pretty soon, something is going to happen and pretty drastic, too!"

"Homer, this is a vindication of my theories. This house is a real tesseract."

"What's he talking about, Homer?"

"Wait, Matilda—now Teal, that's ridiculous. You've pulled some hanky-panky here and I won't have it—scaring Mrs. Bailey half to death, and making me nervous. All I want is to get out of here, with no more of your trapdoors and silly practical jokes."

"Speak for yourself, Homer," Mrs. Bailey interrupted, "I was *not* frightened; I was just took all over queer for a moment. It's my heart; all of my people are delicate and highstrung. Now about this tessy thing—explain yourself, Mr. Teal. Speak up."

He told her as well as he could in the face of numerous interruptions the theory back of the house. "Now as I see it, Mrs. Bailey," he concluded, "this house, while perfectly stable in three dimensions, was not stable in four dimensions. I had built a house in the shape of an unfolded tesseract; something happened to it, some jar or side thrust, and it collapsed into its normal shape—it folded up." He snapped his fingers suddenly. "I've got it! The earthquake!"

"Earthquake?"

"Yes, yes, the little shake we had last night. From a four-dimensional standpoint this house was like a plane balanced on edge. One little push and it fell over, collapsed along its natural joints into a stable four-dimensional figure."

"I thought you boasted about how safe this house was."

"It is safe—three-dimensionally."

"I don't call a house safe," commented Baily edgily, "that collapses at the first little temblor."

"But look around you, man!" Teal protested. "Nothing has been disturbed, not a piece of glassware cracked. Rotation through a fourth dimension can't affect a three-dimensional figure any more than you can shake letters off a printed page. If you had been sleeping in here last night, you would never have awakened."

"That's just what I'm afraid of. Incidentally, has your great genius figured out any way for us to get out of this booby trap?"

"Huh? Oh, yes, you and Mrs. Bailey started to leave and landed back up here, didn't you? But I'm sure there is no real difficulty —we can go out. I'll try it." He was up and hurrying downstairs before he had finished talking. He flung open the front door, stepped through, and found himself staring at his companions, down the length of the second-floor lounge. "Well, there does seem to be some slight problem," he admitted blandly. "A mere technicality, though—we can always go out a window." He jerked aside the long drapes that covered the deep French windows set in one side of the lounge. He stopped suddenly.

"Hm-m-m," he said, "this is interesting—very."

"What is?" asked Bailey, joining him.

"This." The window stared directly into the dining room, instead of looking outdoors. Bailey stepped back to the corner where the lounge and the dining room joined the central room at ninety degrees.

"But that can't be," he protested, "that window is maybe fifteen, twenty feet from the dining room."

"Not in a tesseract," corrected Teal. "Watch." He opened the window and stepped through, talking back over his shoulder as he did so.

From the point of view of the Baileys he simply disappeared.

But not from his own viewpoint. It took him some seconds to catch his breath. Then he cautiously disentangled himself from the rosebush to which he had become almost irrevocably wedded, making a mental note the while never again to order landscaping which involved plants with thorns, and looked around him.

He was outside the house. The massive bulk of the ground-floor room thrust up beside him. Apparently he had fallen off the roof.

He dashed around the corner of the house, flung open the front door and hurried up the stairs. "Homer!" he called out, "Mrs. Bailey! I've found a way out!"

Bailey looked annoyed rather than pleased to see him. "What happened to you?"

"I fell out. I've been outside the house. You can do it just as easily—just step through those French windows. Mind the rosebush, though—we may have to build another stairway."

"How did you get back in?"

"Through the front door."

"Then we shall leave the same way. Come, my dear." Bailey set his hat firmly on his head and marched down the stairs, his wife on his arm.

Teal met them in the lounge. "I could have told you that wouldn't work," he announced. "Now here's what we have to do: As I see it, in a four-dimensional figure a three-dimensional man has two choices every time he crosses a line of juncture, like a wall or a threshold. Ordinarily he will make a ninety-degree turn through the fourth dimension, only he doesn't feel it with his three dimensions. Look." He stepped through the very window that he had fallen out of a moment before. Stepped through and arrived in the dining room, where he stood, still talking.

"I watched where I was going and arrived where I intended

to." He stepped back into the lounge. "The time before I didn't watch and I moved on through normal space and fell out of the house. It must be a matter of subconscious orientation."

"I'd hate to depend on subconscious orientation when I step out for the morning paper."

"You won't have to; it'll become automatic. Now to get out of the house this time—Mrs. Bailey, if you will stand here with your back to the window, and jump backward, I'm pretty sure you will land in the garden."

Mrs. Bailey's face expressed her opinion of Teal and his ideas. "Homer Bailey," she said shrilly, "are you going to stand there and let him suggest such—"

"But Mrs. Bailey," Teal attempted to explain, "we can tie a rope on you and lower you down eas——"

"Forget it, Teal," Bailey cut him off brusquely. "We'll have to find a better way than that. Neither Mrs. Bailey nor I are fitted for jumping."

Teal was temporarily nonplused; there ensued a short silence. Bailey broke it with, "Did you hear that, Teal?"

"Hear what?"

"Someone talking off in the distance. D'you s'pose there could be someone else in the house, playing tricks on us, maybe?"

"Oh, not a chance. I've got the only key."

"But I'm sure of it," Mrs. Bailey confirmed. "I've heard them ever since we came in. Voices. Homer, I can't stand much more of this. Do something."

"Now, now, Mrs. Bailey," Teal soothed, "don't get upset. There can't be anyone else in the house, but I'll explore and make sure. Homer, you stay here with Mrs. Bailey and keep an eye on the rooms on this floor." He passed from the lounge into the ground-floor room and from there to the kitchen and on into the bedroom. This led him back to the lounge by a straight-line route, that is to say, by going straight ahead on the entire trip he returned to the place from which he started.

"Nobody around," he reported. "I opened all of the doors and windows as I went—all except this one." He stepped to the window opposite the one through which he had recently fallen and thrust back the drapes.

He saw a man with back toward him, four rooms away. Teal

snatched open the French window and dived through it, shouting, "There he goes now! Stop, thief!"

The figure evidently heard him; it fled precipitately. Teal pursued, his gangling limbs stirred to unanimous activity, through drawing room, kitchen, dining room, lounge—room after room, yet in spite of Teal's best efforts he could not seem to cut down the four-room lead that the interloper had started with.

He saw the pursued jump awkwardly but actively over the low sill of a French window and in so doing knock off his hat. When he came up to the point where his quarry had lost his headgear, he stooped and picked it up, glad of an excuse to stop and catch his breath. He was back in the lounge.

"I guess he got away from me," he admitted. "Anyhow, here's his hat. Maybe we can identify him."

Bailey took the hat, looked at it, then snorted and slapped it on Teal's head. It fitted perfectly. Teal looked puzzled, took the hat off, and examined it. On the sweat band were the initials "Q.T." It was his own.

Slowly comprehension filtered through Teal's features. He went back to the French window and gazed down the series of rooms through which he had pursued the mysterious stranger. They saw him wave his arms semaphore fashion. "What are you doing?" asked Bailey.

"Come see." The two joined him and followed his stare with their own. Four rooms away they saw the backs of three figures, two male and one female. The taller, thinner of the men was waving his arms in a silly fashion.

Mrs. Bailey screamed and fainted again.

Some minutes later, when Mrs. Bailey had been resuscitated and somewhat composed, Bailey and Teal took stock. "Teal," said Bailey, "I won't waste any time blaming you; recriminations are useless and I'm sure you didn't plan for this to happen, but I suppose you realize we are in a pretty serious predicament. How are we going to get out of here? It looks now as if we would stay until we starve; every room leads into another room."

"Oh, it's not that bad. I got out once, you know."

"Yes, but you can't repeat it—you tried."

"Anyhow we haven't tried all the rooms. There's still the study."

"Oh, yes, the study. We went through there when we first came in, and didn't stop. Is it your idea that we might get out through its windows?"

"Don't get your hopes up. Mathematically, it ought to look into the four side rooms on this floor. Still we never opened the blinds; maybe we ought to look."

"'Twon't do any harm anyhow. Dear, I think you had best just stay here and rest—"

"Be left alone in this horrible place? I should say not!" Mrs. Bailey was up off the couch where she had been recuperating even as she spoke.

They went upstairs. "This is the inside room, isn't it, Teal?" Bailey inquired as they passed through the master bedroom and climbed on up toward the study. "I mean it was the little cube in your diagram that was in the middle of the big cube, and completely surrounded."

"That's right," agreed Teal. "Well, let's have a look. I figure this window ought to give into the kitchen." He grasped the cords of Venetian blinds and pulled them.

It did not. Waves of vertigo shook them. Involuntarily they fell to the floor and grasped helplessly at the pattern on the rug to keep from falling. "Close it! Close it!" moaned Bailey.

Mastering in part a primitive atavistic fear, Teal worked his way back to the window and managed to release the screen. The window had looked *down* instead of *out,* down from a terrifying height.

Mrs. Bailey had fainted again.

Teal went back after more brandy while Bailey chafed her wrists. When she had recovered, Teal went cautiously to the window and raised the screen a crack. Bracing his knees, he studied the scene. He turned to Bailey. "Come look at this, Homer. See if you recognize it."

"You stay away from there, Homer Bailey!"

"Now, Matilda, I'll be careful." Bailey joined him and peered out.

"See up there? That's the Chrysler Building, sure as shooting. And there's the East River, and Brooklyn." They gazed straight down the sheer face of an enormously tall building. More than a thousand feet away a toy city, very much alive, was spread out before them. "As near as I can figure it out, we are looking down the side of the Empire State Building from a point just above its tower."

"What is it? A mirage?"

"I don't think so—it's too perfect. I think space is folded over through the fourth dimension here and we are looking past the fold."

"You mean we aren't really seeing it?"

"No, we're seeing it all right. I don't know what would happen if we climbed out this window, but I for one don't want to try. But what a view! Oh, boy, what a view! Let's try the other windows."

They approached the next window more cautiously, and it was well that they did, for it was even more disconcerting, more reason-shaking, than the one looking down the gasping height of the sky-scraper. It was a simple seascape, open ocean and blue sky—but the ocean was where the sky should have been, and contrariwise. This time they were somewhat braced for it, but they both felt seasickness about to overcome them at the sight of waves rolling overhead; they lowered the blind quickly without giving Mrs. Bailey a chance to be disturbed by it.

Teal looked at the third window. "Game to try it, Homer?"

"Hrrumph—well, we won't be satisfied if we don't. Take it easy." Teal lifted the blind a few inches. He saw nothing, and raised it a little more—still nothing. Slowly he raised it until the window was fully exposed. They gazed out at—nothing.

Nothing, nothing at all. What color is nothing? Don't be silly! What shape is it? Shape is an attribute of *something.* It had neither depth nor form. It had not even blackness. It was *nothing.*

Bailey chewed at his cigar. "Teal, what do you make of that?"

Teal's insouciance was shaken for the first time. "I don't know, Homer, I don't rightly know—but I think that window ought to be walled up." He stared at the lowered blind for a moment. "I think maybe we looked at a place where space *isn't.* We looked around a fourth-dimensional corner and there wasn't anything there." He rubbed his eyes. "I've got a headache."

They waited for a while before tackling the fourth window. Like an unopened letter, it might *not* contain bad news. The doubt left hope. Finally the suspense stretched too thin and Bailey pulled the cord himself, in the face of his wife's protests.

It was not so bad. A landscape stretched away from them, right side up, and on such a level that the study appeared to be a ground-floor room. But it was distinctly unfriendly.

A hot, hot sun beat down from lemon-colored sky. The flat

ground seemed burned a sterile, bleached brown and incapable of supporting life. Life there was, strange stunted trees that lifted knotted, twisted arms to the sky. Little clumps of spiky leaves grew on the outer extremities of these misshapen growths.

"Heavenly day," breathed Bailey, "where is that?"

Teal shook his head, his eyes troubled. "It beats me."

"It doesn't look like anything on Earth. It looks more like another planet—Mars, maybe."

"I wouldn't know. But, do you know, Homer, it might be worse than that, worse than another planet, I mean."

"Huh? What's that you say?"

"It might be clear out of our space entirely. I'm not sure that that is our sun at all. It seems too bright."

Mrs. Bailey had somewhat timidly joined them and now gazed out at the outré scene. "Homer," she said in a subdued voice, "those hideous trees—they frighten me."

He patted her hand.

Teal fumbled with the window catch.

"What are you doing?" Bailey demanded.

"I thought if I stuck my head out the window I might be able to look around and tell a bit more."

"Well—all right," Bailey grudged, "but be careful."

"I will." He opened the window a crack and sniffed. "The air is all right, at least." He threw it open wide.

His attention was diverted before he could carry out his plan. An uneasy tremor, like the first intimation of nausea, shivered the entire building for a long second, and was gone.

"Earthquake!" They all said it at once. Mrs. Bailey flung her arms around her husband's neck.

Teal gulped and recovered himself, saying, "It's all right, Mrs. Bailey. This house is perfectly safe. You know you can expect settling tremors after a shock like last night." He had just settled his features into an expression of reassurance when the second shock came. This one was no mild shimmy but the real seasick roll.

In every Californian, native-born or grafted, there is a deep-rooted primitive reflex. An earthquake fills him with soul-shaking claustrophobia which impels him blindly to *get outdoors!* Model Boy Scouts will push aged grandmothers aside to obey it. It is a matter of record that Teal and Bailey landed on top of Mrs. Bailey. Therefore, she must have jumped through the window first. The order of precedence cannot be attributed to chivalry; it must be assumed that she was in readier position to spring.

They pulled themselves together, collected their wits a little, and rubbed sand from their eyes. Their first sensations were relief at feeling the solid sand of the desert land under them. Then Bailey noticed something that brought them to their feet and checked Mrs. Bailey from bursting into the speech that she had ready.

"Where's the house?"

It was gone. There was no sign of it at all. They stood in the center of flat desolation, the landscape they had seen from the window. But aside from the tortured, twisted tree there was nothing to be seen but the yellow sky and the luminary overhead, whose furnace-like glare was already almost insufferable.

Bailey looked slowly around, then turned to the architect. "Well, Teal?" His voice was ominous.

Teal shrugged helplessly. "I wish I knew. I wish I could even be sure that we are on Earth."

"Well, we can't stand here. It's sure death if we do. Which direction?"

"Any, I guess. Let's keep a bearing on the sun."

They had trudged on for an undetermined distance when Mrs. Bailey demanded a rest. They stopped. Teal said in an aside to Bailey, "Any ideas?"

"No . . . no, none. Say, do you hear anything?"

Teal listened. "Maybe—unless it's my imagination."

"Sounds like an automobile. Say, it *is* an automobile!"

They came to the highway in less than another hundred yards. The automobile, when it arrived, proved to be an elderly, puffing light truck, driven by a rancher. He crunched to a stop at their hail. "We're stranded. Can you help us out?"

"Sure. Pile in."

"Where are you headed?"

"Los Angeles."

"Los Angeles? Say, where is this place?"

"Well, you're right in the middle of the Joshua-Tree National Forest."

The return was as dispiriting as the Retreat from Moscow. Mr. and Mrs. Bailey sat up in front with the driver while Teal bumped along in the body of the truck, and tried to protect his head from the sun. Bailey subsidized the friendly rancher to detour to the tesseract house, not because they wanted to see it again, but in order to pick up their car.

At last the rancher turned the corner that brought them back to where they had started. But the house was no longer there.

There was not even the ground-floor room. It had vanished. The Baileys, interested in spite of themselves, poked around the foundation with Teal.

"Got any answers for this one, Teal?" asked Bailey.

"It must be on that last shock it simply fell through into another section of space. I can see now that I should have anchored it at the foundations."

"That's not all you should have done."

"Well, I don't see that there is anything to get downhearted about. There are possibilities, man, possibilities! Why, right now I've got a great new revolutionary idea for a house—"

Teal ducked in time. He was always a man of action.

A SOUND OF THUNDER

RAY BRADBURY

The sign on the wall seemed to quaver under a film of sliding warm water. Eckels felt his eyelids blink over his stare, and the sign burned in this momentary darkness:

TIME SAFARI, INC.
SAFARIS TO ANY YEAR IN THE PAST.
YOU NAME THE ANIMAL.
WE TAKE YOU THERE.
YOU SHOOT IT.

A warm phlegm gathered in Eckels' throat; he swallowed and pushed it down. The muscles around his mouth formed a smile as he put his hand slowly out upon the air, and in that hand waved a check for ten thousand dollars to the man behind the desk.

"Does this safari guarantee I come back alive?"

"We guarantee nothing," said the official, "except the dinosaurs." He turned. "This is Mr. Travis, your Safari Guide in the Past. He'll tell you what and where to shoot. If he says no shooting, no shooting. If you disobey instructions, there's a stiff penalty of another ten thousand dollars, plus possible government action, on your return."

Eckels glanced across the vast office at a mass and tangle, a snaking and humming of wires and steel boxes, at an aurora that flickered now orange, now silver, now blue. There was a sound like a gigantic bonfire burning all of Time, all the years and all the parchment calendars, all the hours piled high and set aflame.

A touch of the hand and this burning would, on the instant, beautifully reverse itself. Eckels remembered the wording in the advertisements to the letter. Out of chars and ashes, out of dust and coals, like golden salamanders, the old years, the green years, might leap; roses sweeten the air, white hair turn Irish-black, wrinkles vanish; all, everything fly back to seed, flee death, rush down to their beginnings, suns rise in western skies and set in glorious easts, moons eat themselves opposite to the custom, all and everything cupping one in another like Chinese boxes, rabbits into hats, all and everything returning to the fresh death, the seed death, the green death, to the time before the beginning. A touch of a hand might do it, the merest touch of a hand.

"Unbelievable." Eckels breathed, the light of the Machine on his thin face. "A real Time Machine." He shook his head. "Makes you think. If the election had gone badly yesterday, I might be here now running away from the results. Thank God Keith won. He'll make a fine President of the United States."

"Yes," said the man behind the desk. "We're lucky. If Deutscher had gotten in, we'd have the worst kind of dictatorship. There's an anti-everything man for you, a militarist, anti-Christ, anti-human, anti-intellectual. Poeple called us up, you know, joking but not joking. Said if Deutscher became President they wanted to go live in 1942. Of course it's not our business to conduct escapes, but to form safaris. Anyway, Keith's President now. All you got to worry about is—"

"Shooting my dinosaur," Eckels finished it for him.

"A *Tyrannosaurus rex.* The Tyrant Lizard, the most incredible monster in history. Sign this release. Anything happens to you, we're not responsible. Those dinosaurs are hungry."

Eckels flushed angrily. "Trying to scare me!"

"Frankly, yes. We don't want anyone going who'll panic at the first shot. Six safari leaders were killed last year, and a dozen hunters. We're here to give you the severest thrill a *real* hunter ever asked for. Traveling you back sixty million years to bag the biggest game in all of Time. Your personal check's still there. Tear it up."

Mr. Eckels looked at the check. His fingers twitched.

"Good luck," said the man behind the desk. "Mr. Travis, he's all yours."

They moved silently across the room, taking their guns with them, toward the Machine, toward the silver metal and the roaring light.

First a day and then a night and then a day and then a night, then it was day-night-day-night-day. A week, a month, a year, a decade! A.D. 2055. A.D. 2019. 1999! 1957! Gone! The Machine roared.

They put on their oxygen helmets and tested the intercoms.

Eckels swayed on the padded seat, his face pale, his jaw stiff. He felt the trembling in his arms and he looked down and found his hands tight on the new rifle. There were four other men in the Machine. Travis, the Safari Leader, his assistant, Lesperance, and two other hunters, Billings and Kramer. They sat looking at each other, and the years blazed around them.

"Can these guns get a dinosaur cold?" Eckels felt his mouth saying.

"If you hit them right," said Travis on the helmet radio. "Some dinosaurs have two brains, one in the head, another far down the spinal column. We stay away from those. That's stretching luck. Put your first two shots into the eyes, if you can, blind them, and go back into the brain."

The Machine howled. Time was a film run backward. Suns fled and ten million moons fled after them. "Think," said Eckels. "Every hunter that ever lived would envy us today. This makes Africa seem like Illinois."

The Machine slowed; its scream fell to a murmur. The Machine stopped.

The sun stopped in the sky.

The fog that had enveloped the Machine blew away and they were in an old time, a very old time indeed, three hunters and two Safari Heads with their blue metal guns across their knees.

"Christ isn't born yet," said Travis. "Moses has not gone to the mountain to talk with God. The Pyramids are still in the earth, waiting to be cut out and put up. *Remember* that. Alexander, Caesar, Napoleon, Hitler—none of them exists."

The man nodded.

"That"—Mr. Travis pointed—"is the jungle of sixty million, two thousand and fifty-five years before President Keith."

He indicated a metal path that struck off into green wilderness, over streaming swamp, among giant ferns and palms.

"And that," he said "is the Path, laid by Time Safari for your use. It floats six inches above the earth. Doesn't touch so much as one grass blade, flower or tree. It's an anti-gravity metal. Its purpose is to keep you from touching this world of the past in any way. Stay on the Path. Don't go off it. I repeat, *don't go off.* For *any* reason! If you fall off, there's a penalty. And don't shoot any animal we don't okay."

"Why?" asked Eckels.

They sat in the ancient wilderness. Far birds' cries blew on a wind, and the smell of tar and old salt sea, moist grasses, and flowers the color of blood.

"We don't want to change the Future. We don't belong here

in the Past. The government doesn't *like* us here. We have to pay big graft to keep our franchise. A Time Machine is finicky business. Not knowing it, we might kill an important animal, a small bird, a roach, a flower even, thus destroying an important link in a growing species."

"That's not clear," said Eckels.

"All right," Travis continued, "say we accidentally kill one mouse here. That means all the future families of this one particular mouse are destroyed, right?"

"Right."

"And all the families of the families of the families of that one mouse! With a stamp of your foot, you annihilate first one, then a dozen, then a thousand, a million, a *billion* possible mice!"

"So they're dead," said Eckels. "So what?"

"So what?" Travis snorted quietly. "Well, what about the foxes that'll need those mice to survive? For want of ten mice, a fox dies. For want of ten foxes, a lion starves. For want of a lion, all manner of insects, vultures, infinite billions of life forms are thrown into chaos and destruction. Eventually it all boils down to this: fifty-nine million years later, a caveman, one of a dozen on the *entire world,* goes hunting wild boar or saber-toothed tiger for food. But you, friend, have *stepped* on all the tigers in that region. By stepping on *one* single mouse. So the caveman starves. And the caveman, please note, is not just *any* expendable man, no! He is an *entire future nation.* From his loins would have sprung ten sons. From *their* loins one hundred sons, and thus onward to a civilization. Destroy this one man, and you destroy a race, a people, an entire history of life. It is comparable to slaying some of Adam's grandchildren. The stomp of your foot, on one mouse, could start an earthquake, the effects of which could shake our earth and destinies down through Time to their very foundations. With the death of that one caveman, a billion others yet unborn are throttled in the womb. Perhaps Rome never rises on its seven hills. Perhaps Europe is forever a dark forest, and only Asia waxes healthy and teeming. Step on a mouse and you crush the pyramids. Step on a mouse and you leave your print, like a Grand Canyon, across Eternity. Queen Elizabeth might never be born, Washington might not cross the Delaware, there might never be a United States at all. So be careful. Stay on the Path. *Never* step off!"

"I see," said Eckels. "Then it wouldn't pay for us even to touch the *grass?"*

"Correct. Crushing certain plants could add up infinitesimally. A little error here could multiply in sixty million years, all out of proportion. Of course maybe our theory is wrong. Maybe Time *can't* be changed by us. Or maybe it can be changed only in little subtle ways. A dead mouse here makes an insect imbalance there, a population disproportion later, a bad harvest further on, a depression, mass starvation, and, finally, a change in *social* temperament in far-flung countries. Something much more subtle, like that. Perhaps only a soft breath, a whisper, a hair, pollen on the air, such a slight, slight change that unless you looked close you wouldn't see it. Who knows? Who really can say he knows? We don't know. We're guessing. But until we do know for certain whether our messing around in Time *can* make a big roar or a little rustle in history, we're being careful. This Machine, this Path, your clothing and bodies, were sterilized, as you know, before the journey. We wear these oxygen helmets so we can't introduce our bacteria into an ancient atmosphere."

"How do we know which animals to shoot?"

"They're marked with red paint," said Travis. "Today, before our journey, we sent Lesperance here back with the Machine. He came to this particular era and followed certain animals."

"Studying them?"

"Right," said Lesperance. "I track them through their entire existence, noting which of them lives longest. Very few. How many times they mate. Not often. Life's short. When I find one that's going to die when a tree falls on him, or one that drowns in a tar pit, I note the exact hour, minute, and second. I shoot a paint bomb. It leaves a red patch on his side. We can't miss it. Then I correlate our arrival in the Past so that we meet the monster not more than two minutes before he would have died anyway. This way, we kill only animals with no future, that are never going to mate again. You see how *careful* we are?"

"But if you came back this morning in Time," said Eckels eagerly, "you must've bumped into *us,* our Safari! How did it turn out? Was it successful? Did all of us get through—alive?"

Travis and Lesperance gave each other a look.

"That'd be a paradox," said the latter. "Time doesn't permit that sort of mess—a man meeting himself. When such occasions threaten, Time steps aside. Like an airplane hitting an air pocket. You felt the Machine jump just before we stopped? That was us passing ourselves on the way back to the Future. We saw nothing. There's no way of telling *if* this expedition was a success, *if* we got our monster, or whether all of us—meaning *you,* Mr. Eckels—got out alive."

Eckels smiled palely.

"Cut that," said Travis sharply. "Everyone on his feet!"

They were ready to leave the Machine.

The jungle was high and the jungle was broad and the jungle was the entire world forever and forever. Sounds like music and sounds like flying tents filled the sky, and those were pterodactyls soaring with cavernous gray wings, gigantic bats of delirium and night fever. Eckels, balanced on the narrow Path, aimed his rifle playfully.

"Stop that!" said Travis. "Don't even aim for fun, blast you! If your gun should go off—"

Eckels flushed. "Where's our *Tyrannosaurus?"*

Lesperance checked his wristwatch. "Up ahead. We'll bisect his trail in sixty seconds. Look for the red paint! Don't shoot till we give the word. Stay on the Path. *Stay on the Path!"*

They moved forward in the wind of morning.

"Strange," murmured Eckels. "Up ahead, sixty million years, Election Day over. Keith made President. Everyone celebrating. And here we are, a million years lost, and they don't exist. The things we worried about for months, a lifetime, not even born or thought of yet."

"Safety catches off, everyone!" ordered Travis. "You, first shot, Eckels. Second, Billings. Third, Kramer."

"I've hunted tiger, wild boar, buffalo, elephant, but now, this is *it,"* said Eckels. "I'm shaking like a kid."

"Ah," said Travis.

Everyone stopped.

Travis raised his hand. "Ahead," he whispered. "In the mist. There he is. There's His Royal Majesty now."

The jungle was wide and full of twitterings, rustlings, murmurs and sighs.

Suddenly it all ceased, as if someone had shut a door.

Silence.

A sound of thunder.

Out of the mist, one hundred yards away, came *Tyrannosaurus rex.*

"It," whispered Eckels. "It . . ."

"Sh!"

It came on great oiled, resilient, striding legs. It towered thirty feet above half of the trees, a great evil god, folding its delicate watchmaker's claws close to its oily reptilian chest. Each lower leg was a piston, a thousand pounds of white bone, sunk in thick ropes of muscle, sheathed over in a gleam of pebbled skin like the mail of a terrible warrior. Each thigh was a ton of meat, ivory and steel mesh. And from the great breathing cage of the upper body those two delicate arms dangled out front, arms with hands which might pick up and examine men like toys, while the snake neck coiled. And the head itself, a ton of sculptured stone, lifted easily upon the sky. Its mouth gaped, exposing a fence of teeth like daggers. Its eyes rolled, ostrich eggs, empty of all expression save hunger. It closed its mouth in a death grin. It ran, its pelvic bones crushing aside trees and bushes, its taloned feet clawing damp earth, leaving prints six inches deep wherever it settled its weight. It ran with a gliding ballet step, far too poised and balanced for its ten tons. It moved into a sunlit arena warily, its beautifully reptilian hands feeling the air.

"Why, why—" Eckels twitched his mouth. "It could reach up and grab the moon."

"Sh!" Travis jerked angrily. "He hasn't seen us yet."

"It can't be killed." Eckels pronounced this verdict quietly, as if there could be no argument. He had weighed the evidence and this was his considered opinion. The rifle in his hands seemed a cap gun. "We were fools to come. This is impossible."

"Shut up!" hissed Travis.

"Nightmare."

"Turn around," commanded Travis. "Walk quietly to the Machine. We'll remit one half your fee."

"I didn't realize it would be this *big,*" said Eckels. "I miscalculated, that's all. And now I want out."

"It *sees* us!"

"There's the red paint on its chest!"

The Tyrant Lizard raised itself. Its armored flesh glittered like a thousand green coins. The coins, crusted with slime, steamed. In the slime, tiny insects wriggled, so that the entire body seemed to twitch and undulate, even while the monster itself did not move. It exhaled. The stink of raw flesh blew down the wilderness.

"Get me out of here," said Eckels. "It was never like this before. I was always sure I'd come through alive. I had good guides, good safaris and safety. This time, I figured wrong. I've met my match and admit it. This is too much for me to get hold of."

"Don't run," said Lesperance. "Turn around. Hide in the Machine."

"Yes," Eckels seemed to be numb. He looked at his feet as if trying to make them move. He gave a grunt of helplessness.

"Eckels!"

He took a few steps, blinking, shuffling.

"Not that way!"

The Monster, at the first motion, lunged forward with a terrible scream. It covered one hundred yards in six seconds. The rifles jerked up and blazed fire. A windstorm from the beast's mouth engulfed them in the stench of slime and old blood. The monster roared, teeth glittering with sun.

Eckels, not looking back, walking blindly to the edge of the Path, his gun limp in his arms, stepped off the Path, and walked, not knowing it, in the jungle. His feet sank into green moss. His legs moved him and he felt alone and remote from the events behind.

The rifles cracked again. Their sound was lost in shriek and lizard thunder. The great level of the reptile's tail swung up, lashed sideways. Trees exploded in clouds of leaf and branch. The Monster twitched its jeweler's hands down to fondle at the men, to twist them in half, to crush them like berries, to cram them into its teeth and its screaming throat. Its boulder-stone eyes leveled with the men. They saw themselves mirrored. They fired at the metalic eyelids and blazing black irises.

Like a stone idol, like a mountain avalanche, *Tyrannosaurus* fell. Thundering, it clutched trees, pulled them with it. It wrenched and tore the metal Path. The men flung themselves back and away. The body hit, ten tons of cold flesh and stone. The guns fired. The Monster lashed its armored tail, twitched its snake jaws and lay still. A fount of blood spurted from its throat. Somewhere inside, a sac of fluid burst. Sickening gushes drenched the hunters. They stood, red and glistening.

The thunder faded.

The jungle was silent. After the avalanche, a green peace. After the nightmare, morning.

Billings and Kramer sat on the pathway and threw up. Travis and Lesperance stood with smoking rifles, cursing steadily.

In the Time Machine, on his face, Eckels lay shivering. He had found his way back to the Path, climbed into the machine.

Travis came walking, glanced at Eckels, took cotton gauze from a metal box and returned to the others, who were sitting on the Path.

"Clean up."

They wiped the blood from their helmets. They began to curse too. The Monster lay, a hill of solid flesh. Within, you could hear the sighs and murmurs as the furthest chambers of it died, the organs malfunctioning, liquids running a final instant from pocket to sac to spleen, everything shutting off, closing up forever. It was like standing by a wrecked locomotive or a steam shovel at quitting time, all valves being released or levered tight. Bones cracked; the tonnage of its own flesh, off balance, dead weight, snapped the delicate forearms, caught underneath. The meat settled, quivering.

Another cracking sound. Overhead, a gigantic tree branch broke from its heavy mooring, fell. It crashed upon the dead beast with finality.

"There." Lesperance checked his watch. "Right on time. That's the giant tree that was scheduled to fall and kill this animal originally." He glanced at the two hunters. "You want the trophy picture?"

"What?"

"We can't take a trophy back to the Future. The body has to stay right where it would have died originally, so the insects, birds, and bacteria can get at it, as they were intended to. Everything in balance. The body stays. But we *can* take a picture of you standing near it."

The two men tried to think, but gave up, shaking their heads.

They let themselves be led along the metal Path. They sank wearily into the Machine cushions. They gazed back at the ruined Monster, the stagnating mound, where already strange reptilian birds and golden insects were busy at the steaming armor.

A sound on the floor of the Time Machine stiffened them. Eckels sat there, shivering.

"I'm sorry," he said at last.

"Get up!" cried Travis.

Eckels got up.

"Go out on that Path alone," said Travis. He had his rifle pointed. "You're not coming back in the Machine. We're leaving you here!"

Lesperance seized Travis' arm. "Wait—"

"Stay out of this!" Travis shook his hand away. "This fool nearly killed us. But it isn't *that* so much, no. It's his *shoes!* Look at them! He ran off the Path. That *ruins* us! We'll forfeit! Thousands of dollars of insurance! We guaranteed no one leaves the Path. He left it. Oh, the fool! I'll have to report to the government. They might revoke our license to travel. Who knows *what* he's done to Time, to History!"

"Take it easy. All he did was kick up some dirt."

"How do we *know?* cried Travis. "We don't know anything! It's all a mystery! Get out of here, Eckels!"

Eckels fumbled his shirt. "I'll pay anything. A hundred thousand dollars!"

Travis glared at Eckels' checkbook and spat. "Go out there. The Monster's next to the Path. Stick your arms up to your elbows in his mouth. Then you can come back with us."

"That's unreasonable!"

"The Monster's dead, you idiot. The bullets! The bullets can't be left behind. They don't belong in the Past; they might change anything. Here's my knife. Dig them out!"

The jungle was alive again, full of the old tremorings and bird cries. Eckels turned slowly to regard the primeval garbage dump, that hill of nightmares and terror. After a long time, like a sleepwalker he shuffled out along the Path.

He returned, shuddering, five minutes later, his arms soaked and red to the elbow. He turned out his hands. Each held a number of steel bullets. Then he fell. He lay where he fell, not moving.

"You didn't have to make him do that," said Lesperance.

"Didn't I? It's too early to tell." Travis nudged the still body. "He'll live. Next time he won't go hunting game like this. Okay." He jerked his thumb wearily at Lesperance. "Switch on. Let's go home."

1492. 1776. 1812.

They cleaned their hands and faces. They changed their caking shirts and pants. Eckels was up and around again, not speaking. Travis glared at him for a full ten minutes.

"Don't look at me," cried Eckels. "I haven't done anything."

"Who can tell?"

"Just ran off the Path, that's all, a little mud on my shoes—what do you want me to do, get down and pray?"

"We might need it. I'm warning you, Eckels, I might kill you yet. I've got my gun ready."

"I'm innocent. I've done nothing!"

1999. 2000. 2055.

The Machine stopped.

"Get out," said Travis.

The room was there as they had left it. But not the same as they had left it. The same man sat behind the same desk. But the same man did not quite sit behind the same desk.

Travis looked around swiftly. "Everything okay here?" he snapped.

"Fine. Welcome home!"

Travis did not relax. He seemed to be looking at the very atoms of the air itself, at the way the sun poured through the one high window.

"Okay, Eckels, get out. Don't ever come back."

Eckels could not move.

"You heard me," said Travis. "What're you *staring* at?"

Eckels stood smelling of the air, and there was a thing to the air, a chemical taint so subtle, so slight, that only a faint cry of his subliminal senses warned him it was there. The colors, white, gray, blue, orange, in the wall, in the furniture, in the sky beyond the window, were . . . were . . . And there was a *feel*. His flesh twitched. His hands twitched. He stood drinking the oddness with the pores of his body. Somewhere, someone must have been screaming one of those whistles that only a dog can hear. His body screamed silence in return. Beyond this room, beyond this wall, beyond this man who was not quite the same man seated at this desk that was not quite the same desk . . . lay an entire world of streets and people. What sort of world it was now, there was no telling. He could feel them moving there, beyond the walls, almost, like so many chess pieces blown in a dry wind. . . .

But the immediate thing was the sign painted on the office wall, the same sign he had read earlier today on first entering.

Somehow, the sign had changed:

TYME SEFARI INC.
SEFARIS TU ANY YEER EN THE PAST.
YU NAIM THE ANIMALL.
WEE TAEKYUTHAIR.
YU SHOOT ITT.

Eckels felt himself fall into a chair. He fumbled crazily at the thick slime on his boots. He held up a clod of dirt, trembling. "No, it *can't* be. Not a *little* thing like that. No!"

Embedded in the mud, glistening green and gold and black, was a butterfly, very beautiful and very dead.

"Not a little thing like *that!* Not a butterfly!" cried Eckels.

It fell to the floor, an exquisite thing, a small thing that could upset balances and knock down a line of small dominoes and then big dominoes and then gigantic dominoes, all down the years across Time. Eckels' mind whirled. It *couldn't* change things. Killing one butterfly couldn't be *that* important! Could it?

His face was cold. His mouth trembled, asking: "Who— who won the presidential election yesterday?"

The man behind the desk laughed. "You joking? You know very well. Deutscher, of course! Who else? Not that fool weakling Keith. We got an iron man now, a man with guts!" The official stopped. "What's wrong?"

Eckels moaned. He dropped to his knees. He scrabbled at the golden butterfly with shaking fingers. "Can't we," he pleaded to the world, to himself, to the officials, to the Machine, "can't we take it *back,* can't we *make* it alive again? Can't we start over? Can't we—"

He did not move. Eyes shut, he waited, shivering. He heard Travis breathe loud in the room; he heard Travis shift his rifle, click the safety catch and raise the weapon.

There was a sound of thunder.

VI-50
MCE

AND IT WILL SERVE US RIGHT

ISAAC ASIMOV

My father, an immigrant from Eastern Europe, spent his life as a candystore keeper. He made it his ambition—as was common among immigrants—to see his sons get the education he lacked. The results were all he could have desired. I, his older son, am a professor at a medical school and the author of many books. His younger son is city editor of a large newspaper.

His reaction to all this has been one of unalloyed delight. When I pointed out to him, fairly recently, that had he had my education, he might easily have been I, he shrugged it off, and said, "There are two times when there is no possibility of jealousy: when a pupil surpasses his teacher and when a son surpasses his father."

With all possible respect to my father, I must say that I felt a certain anxious skepticism when he said this. It is all very well for my father, denied by circumstances the chance of making his mark in person, to be happy at making it vicariously. But what if he *had* had his chance, and had done quite well, and *then* saw himself surpassed by me.

Or suppose that I, myself, suddenly became aware that I was not, after all, entering literary history in my own right as Isaac Asimov—something that I have every reasonable expectation of doing. Suppose instead that I were right now coming to realize that I would, after all, enter it as a mere footnote—as the father of a much greater writer. As it happens, the situation does not arise, but I tell you frankly that if it had, I am not at all certain I would have felt my father's unselfish joy.

It is one thing to have something for nothing. It is quite another to have your own proud light go pale and sickly before the greater glory.

What would Philip of Macedon's reaction have been, I wonder, if after his quarter-century of heroic striving, during which he raised his country from a backwoods nation of semibarbarians to the mastery of Greece, he had gained a sudden insight that he was destined to go down in history as "the father of Alexander the Great"? What about Frederick William I of Prussia, who in a quarter-century of forceful rule built an awesome and frightening army out of a patchwork kingdom? What would have been his reaction if he had been made to understand that his place in the annals of man would be that of "the father of Frederick the Great"?

At that, they might have had some instinctive feeling of it, for each father hated his son, even to the point of threatening that son's life.

Hostility between royal father and heir-apparent son is common place for there the conflict of present and future glory is all too obvious. Such hostility happens to be most traditional in British royal family, dating back to the time when Henry II hated his sons (who were well worth his hatred) eight centuries ago.

The ancient Greeks, who thought of everything, took up the matter of the fear of the outshining glory of son or pupil in their myths and legends. Daedalus, the great craftsman and inventor of Greek tales, killed his nephew and pupil, Perdix, out of overwhelming jealousy, when that young man showed signs of becoming superior to his teacher.

More dramatic are the tales of the succession of supreme gods. The first ruler of the Universe, in the Greek myths, was Ouranos. His son, Cronos, castrated and replaced him.

But once Cronos was seated on the throne, he was concerned lest he be served by his sons as he had served his own father. Therefore as his wife, Rhea, bore him sons, he swallowed each in turn. When Zeus was born, however, Rhea fooled her husband by placing a stone in swaddling clothes, and that was swallowed instead.

Zeus was reared to manhood in secret and, in time, warred against his father, replacing him as lord of the Universe.

There matters stood as far as the Greek myths were concerned, and yet Zeus was in danger, too. He and Poseidon (his brother, and god of the sea) both fell in love with the beautiful sea-nymph, Thetis. They competed for the privilege of possessing her, until both hurriedly drew back on hearing that the Fates had decreed that Thetis would bear a son mightier than his father.

No god now dared marry the nymph and Zeus compelled Thetis (quite against her will) to marry a mortal. The mortal was Peleus, and he was the father of Achilles, the great hero of the Trojan war, a son far mightier than his father.

In the light of this, it seems to me, it is not at all puzzling that people generally are afraid of robots. Why should not man fear the man-made man, the "son" of his hands, who may surpass him and prove mightier than this "father"?

Not so much man-made woman, you understand. In most early societies women were considered inferior creatures who could not threaten man's priority. Pygmalion of Cyprus could fall in love with the statue, Galatea, pray it alive and marry her. Hephaistos, the Greek god of the forge, could have golden maidens minister to him in a counterfeit of life. Man-made *man,* however—the son, and not the daughter—was terrifying. Crete was guarded by a bronze giant, Talos, according to legend, who circled the island once a day and destroyed all outsiders who landed there. He had one weak spot, however, a stopper in the heel, which if pulled out would allow him to bleed to death. Jason and the Argonauts, on touching down at Crete on the way back from the adventure of the Golden Fleece, defeated Talos by pulling out that stopper.

To be sure, this is transparent symbolism. Crete, prior to 1400 B.C., was held inviolate by its bronze-armored warriors on board the ships of the first great navy of history, but the Greeks of the mainland finally defeated it.

However, there are all sorts of symbols that might be used to represent historical facts and the Greeks chose to envision a mechanical man far more powerful than ordinary man, and one who could be defeated only with the greatest danger and difficulty.

The theme crops up over and over again throughout the legends of the ages. Man creates a mechanical device that in one way or another is intended to serve man within well-defined limits—and invariably the device oversteps the bounds, becomes too powerful, becomes dangerous, must be stopped and scarcely can.

It is the case of the sorcerer's apprentice who brings the broom to life and then can't stop it. It is the case of the medieval rabbis who power golems of clay with the divine name, and then find that the power must be withdrawn, through difficulty and danger, before the manufactured man threatens the world.

In Christian times, a rationalization was advanced. A kind of life and intelligence could be created by man, but only God could create a soul. Any man-made man would be a soulless being, without the aspirations and moral understanding of a souled creature.

But this seems to me to be far too sophisticated to touch the point of basic fear. Surely the mechanical man created to serve, but growing to surpass and endanger his creator, is the sublimated fear of the son, the beloved child who grows to surpass and endanger his father. Our fear of the robot is our fear of the son of Thetis destined to be stronger than his father.

Until the 19th Century, that fear was only a whisper. Life could (in imagination) be imparted to inanimate objects only through divine intervention, entreated by prayer or enforced by magic. In 1798, however, the Italian anatomist, Luigi Galvani, discovered that the dead muscles of frogs could be made to contract by an electric shock. There seemed some connection between electricity and life and the thought arose that life could be restored to dead flesh inside the laboratory and without the involvement of the unpredictable powers of the deities. The fear came closer and into sharper focus at once.

It was precisely Galvani's discovery that inspired Mary Wollstonecraft Shelley (the second wife of the poet) to write her famous horror novel, *Frankenstein,* published in 1818. In the novel a young anatomy student gathers together parts of freshly dead bodies and infuses them with electrical life. What he has created, however, is an eight-foot-tall monster of horrifying aspect.

Possessing intelligence and aware that he is forever cut off from human society, the monster turns upon the man whose interference with the course of nature has condemned him to solitary misery. One by one, the monster kills all of Frankenstein's family and friends, including his bride. Frankenstein himself dies of horror and remorse and the monster disappears into the mysterious polar regions.

The book gave the language a phrase: "Frankenstein's monster," now used for any creation which gets out of control, to the danger and horror of its creator. By its popularity, the novel sharpened the general suspicion that man-made man could be only evil; something which I, in my own writings, have referred to as "the Frankenstein complex."

Yet Frankenstein was written when science was in the flood-tide of its vigorous youthful optimism and when it seemed, to confident mankind, to be the ultimate answer to man's needs. It was not till World War I that science donned the mask of Strangelove horror. It was the warplane and even more, poison gas, that showed mankind that the genius of the laboratory and inventor's workshop could be returned to death and destruction.

It is no accident that, soon after World War I, Frankenstein was out-Frankensteined. With inherently wicked man-made man constructed by a science that was itself capable of wickedness, it would not only be the creator that was threatened, but all mankind.

In 1920 a play, *R.U.R.*, by the Czech playwright, Karel Capek, was produced in Prague. In this play, man-made men were created as workers, to take over the muscle-labor of the world and to free men from Adam's curse at last. The character of the inventor, Rossum, called his creation, "worker." In the Czech language, the word is "robot" and this promptly entered the English language. R.U.R. stands for "Rossum's Universal Robots."

It all works out ill. Men, without work, lose ambition and stop siring children. The robots are used in war; they grow more complex and go mad; they rebel against mankind and destroy it. In the end only two robots are left. These exhibit human emotions and it is through them the world will be repeopled.

Mankind has been replaced by robots. Zeus has sired the mightier son of Thetis.

In the middle 1920's, the first science-fiction magazine was published—the first periodical devoted entirely to the imaginative evocation of possible scientific futures—and the era of modern science fiction began. With it there came an exploitation of the common motifs worked out earlier by such masters as Jules Verne and H. G. Wells.

Robots were not neglected. There were numerous tales of man-made man, but always, or almost always, the end was the same. The robot turned on its maker; the son grew dangerous to the father. Where this did not happen, it seemed as though the author were merely seeking a novel "twist," using the shock value of a kindly robot to produce curiosity rather than to display the result of natural development.

That this wearisome parade of clanking monsters, forever parodying Shelley and Capek, came to an end was the result of certain stories that I wrote.

When I began to write robot stories in 1939, I was 19 years old. I did not feel the fright in the son-father relationship. Perhaps through the accident of the particular relationship of my father and myself, I was given no hint, ever, that there might be jealousy on the part of the father or danger on the part of the son. My father labored, in part, so that I might learn; and I learned, in part, so that my father might be gratified. The symbiosis was complete and beneficial, and I naturally saw a similar symbiosis in the relationship of man and robot.

Why should a robot hurt a man? It would be designed not to.

My first robot story appeared in the September 1940 issue of

Super Science Stories and was entitled "Strange Playfellow." It dealt with a robot nursemaid, named "Robbie." It was loved by the little girl it cared for but was distrusted by the little girl's mother.

At one point, when the mother expresses her concern, the little girl's father tries to argue her out of her fears.

"Dear! A robot is infinitely more to be trusted than a human nursemaid. Robbie was constructed for only one purpose—to be the companion of a little child. His entire 'mentality' has been created for the purpose. He just can't help being faithful and loving and kind. He's a machine—*made so.*"

There you are. Already I had the dim notion that in the manufacture of a robot, a deliberate design of harmlessness would be built in.

The idea developed further. By the time I wrote my third robot story, "Liar!," I was ready to be more formal and precise about this matter of harmlessness. In "Liar!," published in the May 1941 issue of *Astounding Science Fiction,* one person says to another, "You know the fundamental law impressed upon the positronic brain of all robots, of course."

And the answer comes, "Certainly. On no condition is a human being to be injured in any way, even when such injury is directly ordered by another human."

But then this cannot be all that must be impressed upon a robot's mind. By the time I wrote my fifth robot story, "Runaround" (published in the March 1942 issue of *Astounding Science Fiction*) I had worked out my "Three Laws of Robotics." (The word "robotics" is, as far as I know, my invention.) Here they are in final form:

THE THREE LAWS OF ROBOTICS

1. A robot may not injure a human being or, through inaction, allow a human being to come to harm.
2. A robot must obey the orders given it by human beings except where such orders would conflict with the First Law.
3. A robot must protect its own existence as long as such protection does not conflict with either the First or the Second Law.

I am the only science-fiction writer who actually quotes the Three Laws in fiction, but readers have come to take them for granted. Other writers of robot stories tend to accept them and to write within the frame of the Three Laws even though they do not state them explicitly. I am entirely happy over that.

To be sure, this is not an absolute requirement. In the motion picture, *2001: A Space Odyssey,* and in the novel written from it by my good friend, Arthur C. Clarke, the complex computer, Hal—a robot in the broad sense of the word—brings about the deaths of several human beings. This disturbed me, and impressed me as a retrogressive step, but it doesn't seem to bother Arthur at all.

But what about computers? Even if we classify them as a kind of robot evolved to all-brain-no-body, and place them under the Three Laws, might they still not become uncomfortably complex and capable? Even if the son does not become dangerous to the father physically, might he not, with the best will in the world, become dangerous psychologically? Might he not force the father to admit the inferiority? Might the father be forced to hand over the Universe to a kindly and regretful but inexorably demanding son?

There is, on the part of those who secretly fear this, a strong tendency to down grade the possibility as, I suspect, a matter of self-protection.

The computer can *not* equal the human brain, is their feeling. The computer can *not* do any more than it is programmed to do. The computer can *never* exhibit intuitive qualities of creativity and genius, as can the human brain.

I wonder if there is not also a definite feeling, usually not expressed, out of a certain mid 20th Century embarrassment, that man has something called a soul that a computer cannot have; that a man is a product of the divine and a computer cannot be.

It's my opinion that none of these arguments is convincing.

The most advanced computer of today is an idiot child compared to products of perhaps three billion years of organic evolution, while the electronic computer is, as such, only 30 years old. After all, is it too much to ask for just 30 years more?

What is to set the limit of further computer development? In theory, nothing. There is nothing magic about the creative abilities of the human brain, its intuitions, its genius. (I am always amused to hear some perfectly ordinary human being pontificate that a "computer can't compose a symphony" as though he himself could.) The human brain is made up of a finite number of cells of finite complexity, arranged in a pattern of finite complexity. When a computer is built of an equal number of equally complex cells in an equally complex arrangement, we will have something that can do just as much as a human brain can do to its uttermost genius.

To deny this is to maintain that there is something more in the human brain than the cells that compose it and the interrelationships among them.

And if human brain and man-made brain reach the same level of complexity, I feel it will be a lot easier to design a still more complicated man-made brain than to breed a still more complex human brain. So not only man-made man is possible, but man-made superman, too.

And how long will it take to reach the human brain level. A million years? A billion?

That, I suspect, is more consolation. Much less time, *much* less time may be required.

The key problem will be this: To design a computer capable of formulating the design of another computer just slightly more complex than itself. Such a computer would naturally design another computer that was somewhat more capable than itself in designing another computer still more complex, which would be still more capable of designing still another computer even more complex, and so on.

We will be faced, then, with what mathematicians would call a diverging series.

Once the crucial moment arrives when a computer can design one greater than itself, computers will follow in rapid succession and rise out of sight. The son of Thetis will have been born.

And when will that crucial moment come? It might arrive long before the computer is as complex as the human brain. All we will require is a computer, however simple, to form another more complex than itself, however slightly. That will be the chain reaction that will produce the computer explosion. And the crucial moment may come next year for all I know.

And what if it does? What if the computer shows signs of getting away from us? Would we be face to face with a real Frankenstein's monster at last? Must we all struggle to destroy the thing before the divergence proceeds to the point where we are helpless before it?

Will the computer (oh, horrible thought!) *take over?*

What if they do? The history of life on Earth has been one long tale of "taking over." From era to era, different forms of life have proved dominant in one major environmental niche or the other. The placoderms "took over" from the trilobites, and the modern fish "took over" from the placoderms.

The reptiles "took over" from the amphibia and the mammals "took over" from the reptiles.

Mankind looks upon the history of evolution and approves of all this "taking over" for it all leads up to the moment when Man, proud and destructive Man, has "taken over."

Are we to stop here? Is Ouranos to be replaced by Cronos, and Cronos by Zeus, and no more—thus far and no farther? Is Thetis to be disposed of rather than risk the chance of further replacement?

But why? What has changed? Evolution continues as before, though in a modified manner. Instead of species changing and growing better adapted to their environment through the blind action of mutation and the relentless winnowing of natural selection, we have reached the point where evolution can be guided and the Successor can be deliberately designed.

And it might be good. The planet groans under the weight of 3.4 billion human beings, destined to be seven billion by 2010. It is continually threatened by nuclear holocaust and is inexorably being poisoned by the wastes and fumes of civilization. Sure, it is time and more than time for mankind to be "taken over" from. If ever a species needed to be replaced for the good of the planet, we do.

There isn't much time left, in fact. If the son of Thetis doesn't come within a generation, or, at most two, there may be nothing left worth "taking over."

NON
PIEGE —

LITTERBUG

TONY MORPHETT

Rafferty stood six foot two, was built like a fullback and had a reputation for gentleness except on certain specific occasions. This was one of those occasions. He had gone home, thumbed the lock on his front door, and from a habit dating back to less civilized periods in his life, he had gone inside without turning the light on.

And had known that in the dark house he wasn't alone.

It could have been smell, it could have been sound, it could have been that other thing which was just *the feel,* and which had saved his life on occasion. But he knew they were there, and he moved fast, he moved silent from the front door. They must have heard the lock, so the area of the lock was somewhere not to be.

"That you, Joe?"

A voice from the laboratory. It must have been his not turning on the light. A man coming through his own front door turns the light on. Therefore the voice thought that the noise had been made by another of the intruders. Rafferty smiled. The intruders were fortunate that they didn't see that smile. It was not at all a nice smile.

Now he knew there were two of them, otherwise the one who had spoken would not have pinned the noise source to one name. Now, at the laboratory door, he could see one of them, partly silhouetted by a torch held in the left hand while the right hand moved across the face of a control panel.

Rafferty had a reputation for gentleness, but under some circumstances he had no social graces whatsoever, and when he saw someone else's hand on his laboratory pet, Emily Post went out the window and Rafferty turned from an engineer into a hunting primate. A very fast-moving hunting primate.

It is not true that the man didn't know what hit him. He said later that he *did* know what had hit him. He said it was the roof. It was actually the edge of Rafferty's hand. Rafferty had tackled him, they had gone down together, Rafferty's right hand had moved twice. Once up, once down. Then *the feel* had taken over, and Rafferty had rolled away just fast enough for the second man's blackjack to strike his shoulder, not the base of his skull. Every man got one chance with Rafferty, and that had been Joe's. Still lying on the floor, he scooped the man's feet from under him, then realized he had caught himself a pro. The man struck at him again on the way down. Rafferty blocked with his left forearm, had to block again as the man's bladed left hand came into action, and then felt an increased respect as his opponent flicked away the blackjack and struck for Rafferty's solar plexus with a right forearm-hand-extended-finger assembly as straight and solid as a quarterstaff. What Rafferty thought had saved him was his own right hook which laid his opponent out at the same time as Rafferty started to concentrate on unknotting his stomach. At least, he thought, he'd be on his feet before they were conscious.

And then the light went on. For an engineer, he had made one assumption too many.

There had been three of them.

It was infuriating. He could have taken the third one, gun and all, if there'd been anything in his belly except a black gaping pain which would not let him stand. The slight, grey-haired man with glasses didn't look as if he knew one end of his 44 magnum from the other. Which worried Rafferty more than if he'd looked like a killer who wouldn't let it go off by accident.

"Mr. Rafferty, I must ask you to abstain from further violence. I realize that, as a citizen, you have a perfect right to be irritated at this intrusion on your privacy. But please do not be violent."

Rafferty swallowed so hard it straightened out most of the knots. "That is the craziest speech I've ever heard a burglar make."

"Unfortunately," the little grey man with the big gun continued, "we felt it necessary to have a little more information before we approached you more . . ." he cleared his throat, "ah, formally."

"We haven't," said Rafferty, "even been introduced."

"Since, however, you returned as you did . . . somewhat prematurely Mr. Rafferty . . ."

"Next time I come through my own door I'll knock."

"I think we had better come into the open. I'd like you to accompany us if you would."

Rafferty's deep breath straightened out the rest of the knots. "Look, you're holding the gun, and that makes me very polite. But may I put it this way? You break into my house, you tamper with expensive lab equipment, one of your men turns my solar plexus into a disaster area, and *then* you ask ever so politely for me to accompany you. Who the hell are you? And apart from the gun, why should I go anywhere?"

"We all work for the government. My department . . . well it doesn't really *have* a name. These two gentlemen," he nodded to his now-conscious companions, "work for a rather better-known bureau. Perhaps you could . . . ?"

The two men produced leather cases. Flipped them open. Rafferty looked at the metal shields. He must, he decided, be in better fighting trim than he had thought. "All right, I'll come along."

The little man handed the gun to the operative called Joe. "I'll have to telephone. There are two people who'll want to meet you."

Rafferty lowered himself into the chair. The office was comfortable, but there was nothing soft about it. The little grey man sat at the desk. He had introduced himself as Watson. The other two men in the room he knew from reputation, technical journals and television: Professor Clemens, a Nobel prize winner in physics, and Dr. Simpson Navarre, one of the government's chief scientific advisers. Watson looked up from a slim file on his desk. "Now, Mr. Rafferty, what we wish to talk to you about is your, ah, matter transmitter."

"I don't have one. I make garbage disposal units."

Professor Clemens leaned forward. "Mr. Rafferty, let's save a bit of time. You *call* them garbage disposal units. Now, as I understand it, a conventional garbage disposal unit is like a mincing machine. You put matter in one end and it comes out the other end ground up fine enough to be washed away."

"Do you know," said Rafferty, "I don't believe I've ever discussed garbage with a Nobel prize winner before?"

"That'll be enough, Rafferty! You're in trouble enough without impudence!" Watson sounded angry. Rafferty diagnosed a chronic case of lack of sense of humor.

Rafferty stood up. "Good evening."

"You'll . . ."

Navarre turned on the grey government man. "Be quiet, Watson!" Navarre went on more quietly. "We wish to talk to Mr. Rafferty about garbage."

Clemens joined in the smile. "Garbage *disposal.* In a conventional unit you put matter in the form of, say, orange peel in one end, and you get matter in the form of slush out the other. In your unit, Mr. Rafferty, you put matter in one end, and *nothing* comes out the other end. In fact there would appear to *be* no other end."

"Well that seems to me to be an advantage," Rafferty said. "It saves water, prevents clogging . . ."

"Mr. Rafferty," Navarre broke in, "please don't play the hillbilly. You know exactly what we mean. *Where does the garbage go?"*

Rafferty smiled. "I don't know."

"You don't know?" Clemens was out of his chair. "You must know! You built it. You manufacture it. You must know where it goes!"

"Does it work?" Rafferty said.

"Yes," Clemens said tightly, "it works."

"Is it a good garbage disposal unit?"

"Yes. It is a good garbage disposal unit. Which is like opening a bottle on a metal edge in a Polaris sub, and calling the submarine a good bottle opener."

"I asked is it a good garbage disposal unit?"

"All right, I agree it's a good garbage disposal unit."

"And I," Rafferty said, "am an engineer. It works."

Watson leaned forward. "Mr. Rafferty, I think you should be informed of a few things. For a start, if we want to, we can lock you up and throw away the key."

"You're the one who threatened me before." Rafferty sounded quiet and unamused.

"You have endangered the security of this country and the security of the Free World by applying for a patent on a device which has immense military potential. When your patent application was rejected because you couldn't explain the principle, you went ahead anyway, manufactured your device, and now you're selling it to anyone with the money to pay for it. That means anyone in a number of embassies which even *you* ought to be able to name. In short, Mr. Rafferty, you are a traitor."

Rafferty's chair was empty and Rafferty was leaning across the government man's desk. Rafferty took Watson by the shoulders and squeezed in a way which Rafferty thought was gentle. "Mr. Watson," he crooned, "you are no longer holding a gun. Unless you are, never say that again. Understand?" He let go. He walked back to his chair. Watson tried to get his shoulder back into place.

Navarre cloaked his smile. "I can understand your resentment, Mr. Rafferty, but what Mr. Watson meant was that you might have new ideas . . ."

"I did."

Navarre put his head in his hands like a man who had heard it before. "Go on."

"I tried it on the army, navy and air force and a set of very well-qualified young men told me my math wasn't as good as it might be, and anyway the effect was theoretically impossible."

"But didn't you show them a working model?"

"Have you ever tried to demonstrate a perpetual motion machine to a government physicist? Or a mermaid to a government marine biologist? Or telekinesis to a government psychologist? The majority of scientists want to ask only those questions they can answer. The fact that they could throw my math was enough. The fact that I didn't have even a bachelor's degree didn't help much."

"You don't have a degree?" Watson's spectacles were twin barrels. "You mean you were lying to us when you called yourself an engineer?"

Clemens smiled. "I shouldn't worry too much about degrees, Mr. Watson. Thomas Alva Edison didn't have one either, and it was probably the saving of him."

Rafferty looked across at Clemens. He decided he could possibly warm to this man.

Navarre, the government adviser, was still looking unhappy. Rafferty guessed that other people in the army, navy and air force would be looking even more unhappy the next day. Navarre spoke. "So we've done it again. We'll just have to see what we can salvage. Presumably, Mr. Rafferty, you weren't trying to make a garbage disposal unit when you started?"

"No. I was trying to do what the burglar over there suggested," he said, nodding at Watson. "I was trying to push matter from one place to another without actually carrying it. A man paddling a log and a man riding a rocket, they're not different in *kind,* you're only talking about an improvement in technique. I was looking for a difference in *kind."*

"I've got scientists who say it's impossible," Watson said.

Rafferty didn't look very nice when his eyes narrowed. "Mr. Watson, in my lab I've got a unit just big enough for a man your size. Would you like to try it out and then talk about possibilities and impossibilities?"

"So you started out to make a matter transmitter," Navarre said. "How did it turn into a garbage disposal unit?"

"Money. As you can probably read in that file there, my factory's for repetition engineering, and this thing's just a hobby of mine. The firm makes enough so it can be a high-priced hobby, and there have been economic by-products in the past, but still, so far it's been a hobby. Well, I ran into a deadend. The transmitter, the matter transmitter works fine. It's, uh the *receiver* end that still has some bugs to iron out."

"What bugs?" Clemens said.

"One very simple one. It doesn't work. The transmitter's fine. You put something in, you throw the power, it goes away. It doesn't disintegrate, burn, atomize, or get washed down a drain. It just goes away. Now it ought to be going into the receiver. But it doesn't. It goes somewhere else."

"Where?"

"I don't know. It must be going somewhere. I used to watch the newspapers. I used to have this nightmare that an explorer was going to come back and say that he'd found the Lost Valley of the Incas and it was filled to the brim with orange peel and beer cans and coffee grounds. Now I think the stuff's not ending up on this planet at all. The odds are it's in deep space somewhere. It's going somewhere in space-time, anyway. I'm conventional enough not to believe that all that matter's just being destroyed. So I had a matter transmitter but no matter receiver. I needed development money, a lot of it, so I went to the government. Whose representatives, Dr. Navarre, told me very politely that I had shot my lid." Rafferty lit a cigarette. "Now that didn't alter the fact I still needed money for development, and the thing it worked best at was getting rid of things. Which to me said garbage disposal. So I put in about a dozen fail-safe devices to stop tampering idiots from losing arms, and I got it on the market this week, and the orders look very nice indeed. No status-home is going to be without one."

"The government will recompense you, but we've got to get every single one back." Watson winced at Navarre's use of the word "recompense," but nodded.

Rafferty smiled. "I wish you luck then. They're already distributed coast-to-coast, and our sales are running into thousands."

It wasn't until a week later that the garbage started coming back.

Rafferty always ate breakfast in his laboratory, because that was the place in the house the morning sun got to. It was also the place in the house where he felt most comfortable.

He finished eating, put a toast crust and two egg shells into the rind of a grapefruit, and threw the lot into the maw of his big experimental Watson-sized disposal unit. He switched the power on and turned away to pour himself some coffee.

Sproiiing.

Rafferty looked back. His unit had never said *sproiiing* before. He was in time to see the grapefruit rind, the two egg shells and the toast crust come flying through the opening. Something else followed them.

On the domestic models there were spring-loaded doors and an automatic shut-off if they were opened. Rafferty's lab model ran to power rather than to refinements like doors and idiot-proofing.

Rafferty went to the machine. The power was still on. The grey vortex in the transmission area was as it should have been. Rafferty had a peach left over from his breakfast. He put it on the conveyor belt. The conveyor belt bore the peach into the grey vortex, where it disappeared. Rafferty waited.

Squelch!

Rafferty straightened up, wiping peach out of his eyes. Rafferty was a gentle man and would never have laid hands on his own invention, and besides there wasn't an axe in the laboratory. He felt the machine for the moment, and looked at what had come out the first time. He seemed to remember seeing something fly out that he hadn't thrown in.

He picked it up. It resembled a cat and it resembled a four-legged bunch of broccoli, and it wasn't either. It was dead, and among the things it *didn't* resemble was a bunch of violets. Rafferty got a towel and a carving knife. The towel he tied round his mouth and nose. His past included being a slaughterman and skin-diving for a marine biologist, so he didn't think anyone would mind if he had a first, semi-professional cut.

He made three cuts and decided it wasn't a cat or broccoli, fish or steer, when the phone rang.

"Rafferty."

"Jim here, from the factory. Two of the units on the test bench. Garbage is coming *back* through them."

"Other stuff as well? Stuff that doesn't look like . . . well normal sorts of garbage?"

"Well, I don't know, what some people throw out, others'd live on for a week. I mean, what's *normal* garbage?"

"But you're just getting back what you're putting in?"

"Yeah."

"How fast?"

"Some oozes back, some flies back."

"Any pattern?"

"Not yet."

"I'll keep in touch."

He hung up. Looked at the broccoli cat again. No pattern. At least he'd have something to throw at the first biologist who told him that a broccoli cat was theoretically impossible and that his DNA spelling grades were on the other side of illiterate.

Then he took an apple, and tossed it into the grey vortex. Then instantly switched off the power. And waited. Nothing. So when he switched off, the stuff couldn't get back. Logical, except that it was illogical for it to come back at all.

He sat on the stool at his drawing board, and he cracked his scarred knuckles for a while and stared at the wall like he was going to take it apart. Then he swung on the stool, and leaned back, and took a piece of paper tape in his right hand. Put one twist into it, and held the two ends between fingers and thumb, making a Moebius strip. He knew that the pad of his finger and the pad of his thumb were touching different parts of the same side of the strip. That they were both twelve inches and one millimeter apart. He threw the tape away. Somewhere . . .

Where?

He looked out the laboratory window. Then he whistled as he went to the lab unit, turned it on, then went to the bookshelves on the wall and selected a volume. Then watched as the grey vortex of the unit slowly enveloped the book of maps of the night sky as seen from earth.

The phone rang.

"Rafferty?"

"Yes. That's Watson, is it?"

"We want to see you, Rafferty. There's been a complication."

"You mean the garbage is coming back through *your* test units too?"

"Not on the phone, Rafferty, not on the phone. You'll be picked up in five minutes."

"I've things to do at the factory."

"Five minutes, Rafferty."

Rafferty hung up, and then phoned his factory, and made a priority order for delivery to him that afternoon.

The biologist looked up from his examination of the broccoli cat. He smiled. "It's an extremely convincing fake, gentlemen."

"Fake?" Navarre's hands were tightening.

"Well, of course, nothing like this exists."

"Thank you, Professor." After the man had gone, Navarre used the telephone. "Send me a *real* biologist. If the ancestors of that one had been as adaptable as he is, he would now be a sea squirt which knew that free oxygen was a poison and that mobility and limbs were something an adult grew out of." He sat down.

Rafferty grinned at him. "Any other . . . fakes coming back through the units?"

"We're sifting the material as fast as we can. It appears that there's some vegetable material that's . . . well, unknown, but that . . . thing of yours is the first . . . is it an animal?"

"Roughly speaking, yes. Can you find out for me what it breathes and eats?"

Watson cleared his throat. "Now your theory, Rafferty, is that you've somehow . . . punched I think was your word, punched a hole in space-time, and the other end of the hole is on some planet circling another star."

"Yes, I think so."

"But even if we accept the principle of punching holes in space-time," Clemens said, "the odds against finding the other ends of those holes on another planet in another solar system, well, the odds are, if you'll pardon the expression, astronomical."

"I shan't pardon the expression," Rafferty said, "but odds like that have come off before. And if you don't believe they've come off this time, then tell me where on this planet the broccoli cat comes from."

"But why should the thing come back through the machine at all?" Watson couldn't bring himself to call it a broccoli cat.

"You ever live in a slum, Mr. Watson? I guess not." Rafferty had his grin tucked down at the corners. "Well you throw garbage onto someone else's back landing, they'll throw it back, uh? And some people, they get mad, they'll throw a dead cat with it." Rafferty's hands were palms up, and more pious than his eyes. "It's terrible what some people'll do when they get mad."

Navarre had a grin of his own. "Well, I've had the problem of First Contact on my hands for three years now, and I never thought it'd be garbage over the fence."

"And that, Mr. Navarre, is because you've never lived in a slum either. But where you can put a dead cat, you can put other things. And I thought even a cat thrower's not going to throw back something that looks important. So that's why I sent him the star maps."

"What star maps?" Navarre was quiet, cold.

"You know the sort of book. Amateur astronomers use them. They show the night sky, northern and southern skies as they are at the various months of the year. I sent it through my lab unit this morning. Nearest thing I could give them to an address."

The way Watson looked, Rafferty should have had a snakebite kit on him. "You're under arrest, Rafferty. Last week I called you a traitor. Today you proved it. Gave them our address, did you? Do you expect them to pay you?"

"Pay me, Watson?"

"When they invade."

"No one's going to be invading, Mr. Watson. They can't be closer than four light-years. They're probably further."

"They can get a dead cat here. They can get an army here in the same way."

"But, Watson," and Rafferty smiled, "how do you know the cat was dead when it left there?"

"What do you mean?"

"Maybe it was alive, and got killed on the trip through."

"But who'd throw a live animal into a thing like that? Why, it'd be . . ."

"Please don't say *inhuman,* Watson, I don't think I could bear it." Navarre turned to Rafferty. "You mean you don't think someone could go through there alive?"

"I don't know. Until I knew there was something at the other end, I wasn't very keen about trying it. Couldn't see myself making a laughing exit into hard vacuum and absolute zero. Or into the center of a sun. But now? Well the odds are better. But I still say that there's tourism and tourism."

Watson was putting down his phone. "The general will be here in one moment."

"General?"

"Rafferty's action has made this a military matter."

The general heard them through and then refilled his corncob pipe. "Should have been in on this at the jump. But it's not irretrievable. One thing, we've got no problem delivering the bombs."

"The bombs!" Rafferty stood up.

"Of course. Now they know where we are, we'll have to exterminate them. You say a grapefruit rind came back through your unit. Could just as easily have been a grenade. Or an H-bomb. We have to hit them first. Before they hit us."

"But they've shown no signs . . ."

"Can you assure me they won't?"

"I don't know them!"

"Neither do I, Mr. Rafferty, neither do I." He turned to Watson. "I'll be recommending a simultaneous, all-out attack. Enough to take an earth-size planet apart."

Professor Clemens leaned forward. "General, I must protest! This is our first chance to contact what might be an intelligent alien species, and . . ."

"You're not a military man, Professor. You wouldn't understand."

Rafferty was sitting again, and looked relaxed. Which was a danger sign. "General, I'm not a military man either, but I guess it'd take a lot of power to smash an earth-size planet."

"An immense amount," Clemens said before the general could answer.

"And we know these units provide a two-way tunnel," Rafferty continued. "Now, Watson, how many units have you got back so far?"

"Fifteen hundred, give or take twenty. As at close of business yesterday."

"Leaves about four thousand still in the field. Now supposing you used about a thousand in your attack . . ."

"I'm afraid that's classified . . ."

"Just supposing. Now these four thousand you haven't got back yet, if any were open, that is, switched on, during the attack, it'd be just like pumping high pressure steam into a sieve. You would literally be getting your own back. You were talking about assurances, General. Can you assure me they'd all be closed? Even if you made it an order? Can you assure me that among four thousand human beings there wouldn't be some who'd forget to turn off, or who wouldn't hear the radio and TV announcements, or some who wouldn't see it as a way to buck authority, or some who'd just think it would be a good idea to blow this planet at the same time? I think until you get all the sets back, General, and I'll make damn sure you don't, I think until then we'd better try talking to them. So I'd like to see my laboratory unit. I left it on. I just wonder whether the postman's been there."

"But you're under arrest," Watson said.

"Watson," said Navarre, "he's released into my custody. And if you want to find out if I have the authority, I suggest you check higher up. Now, Mr. Rafferty, we'll go check that letter box."

The sheets were probably synthetic, but they had the feel of an extremely thin leather. The markings on them were obviously writing, but which way it ran was by no means obvious. Rafferty revised his original thought. Was it so obvious that it was writing? At least they had shut Watson up for a while. He seemed hypnotized by the pale grey sheets with their black markings.

Clemens looked at Navarre. "Black on grey? Implies brighter light on their world?"

Navarre shrugged. "Could be. I wouldn't be in a hurry to assume anything. They may not see in the same range we do. Do we know that it's writing? Do we even know whether the information is in the black marks or in what we'd call the background?"

Watson came out of his trance. "But you notice one thing. You sent them star maps. They've sent back something which could easily be the equivalent of the *Daily News*. Hardly, Mr. Rafferty, a fair exchange."

Rafferty shrugged. "You're all educated men. Which of you has a book of star charts in your home?" Only Navarre nodded. "One in three. And you three are scarcely representative of humanity in general. My guess is that he's sent through what he figures is a similar artifact as a sign of good faith. I think we can expect some more." The four of them looked at the machine. Nothing happened.

Nothing happened for another three quarters of an hour. Then the grey vortex at the back of the machine changed. Clemens was watching at the time, and he called the others over. They gathered, and watched as the sheets emerged from the vortex and piled in the transmission area of the machine. Rafferty switched off, reached in and got them, and then switched on again. He spread the sheets on the bench. They were star maps.

Rafferty looked at Watson. "Looks like someone with common sense got to their soldiers and bureaucrats, Mr. Watson. It seems they've sent us their address." He turned to Navarre. "How much astronomy do your computers know, Dr. Navarre?"

"Enough." Navarre grinned. "I'll get the boys working on it. By the way, you can stay here if you like. I don't think we'll lock you up just yet."

Rafferty smiled, and stretched. "Guess I could use a little lab-time anyway. Might even be able to get the bugs out of it. Seems the transmitter's a mite overpowered."

"There'll be a guard round your house," Navarre said. "They won't bother you. Some of our technical people will be over later. We might have to move you out of the house altogether in the next week or so, but we can leave that until later."

They left Rafferty alone with his machine. As soon as they were gone, he rang his factory. "That set-up I asked for this morning. Send it over."

Then he fed some picture magazines into the unit, and was busy at his bench until the arrival of some crates from the factory.

He opened them, and from the contents quickly assembled a disposal unit. From the last box he took the Ni-Cad batteries he had ordered. If you couldn't expect the same power supply in different countries on your own planet, to be optimistic about standard power on someone else's wasn't optimism, it was idiocy. When he finished, he had a self-powered unit big enough to send a book or a cat, but not big enough for a saber-toothed tiger. And the whole thing was small enough to put through the feed jaw of his big laboratory unit.

And it was too heavy to lift. Rafferty's prodigies of Anglo-Saxon four-letter expression should by rights have produced the smell of ozone. Then he stopped talking, and smiled. Outside his house, he approached one of his guards.

"Can you help me with something?"

The guard raised a hand to one of his colleagues to cover for him. "Sure. What?"

"Just something I want to lift."

The guard followed him inside. Together they manhandled the small unit into the lab machine. They watched, Rafferty with satisfaction, the guard with awe, as it disappeared into the grey vortex.

"Never seen the inside of one of those things before. Kinda pretty, isn't it?"

"It works," Rafferty said. Then he smiled his gentle smile. "Which means I think it's kinda pretty."

"Where's it go?"

"I'll tell you when I find out," Rafferty said.

"Vega," Navarre said. "A planet orbiting round Vega."

"Vega," Rafferty repeated. "How far's that?"

"Twenty-six and a half light-years."

"A long way." It was a very rare thing for Rafferty to feel small. And even when he did feel small, Rafferty never said so. "It makes me feel small," Rafferty said.

"It's a long way to throw a dead cat."

Rafferty joined in the smile. "Broccoli cat. Do we know what it breathes and eats yet?"

"Breathes an oxygen-nitrogen mixture. Slightly richer in oxygen, they think. Food? The planet's got a carbon-hydrogen cycle, but they suggest you don't try eating his brother if you find him. Apparently there's a metal distribution on the planet that . . ."

And he stopped, because at that moment the window opened in the air.

Watson hurriedly backed behind the laboratory's central bench.

Clemens walked closer to it like a man mesmerized.

Navarre stared.

Rafferty smiled the smile that Watson had grown to know and loathe.

It was a grey, shimmering window in the air, big enough for a book, too small for a saber-toothed tiger. And out of it things started to flow. Sheets of what they thought were writing, small objects which could have been cups, toys, anything at all, and finally what looked like a magazine. The flow stopped, the window irised in on itself, and vanished. Rafferty picked up the thing that looked like a magazine. Every page was devoted to a single picture. What was pictured was a . . . creature. Humanoid enough if you didn't define the term too closely, residual feathery scales, and nothing else. Rafferty turned from the magazine to one of the other sheets, where there was a picture of a similar creature, except that this one was wearing what could have been called clothes. Rafferty grinned and turned to Watson, handing him the magazine. "I think you should have this for your files. It's the first known example of the interstellar delivery of a . . . girlie magazine."

Watson looked at three of the pictures, snapped the magazine shut and then in a way which Rafferty found disconcerting, blushed.

"It appears," Watson said, "that at the other end we have a Vegan version of Mr. Rafferty."

Navarre's voice was cold. "At the other end of *what,* Rafferty?"

"How do you mean?"

"These things didn't come out of *your* machine, Rafferty. What was that we saw in the air?"

"Oh, that? I sent 'em through a small unit."

"You what!" Watson came round the bench to Navarre. There were tears in his eyes. "Please, Dr. Navarre, you must let me have him. Just a simple firing squad, nothing elaborate, nothing elaborate, just a simple, simple, simple . . ." He wandered away into a corner.

"Why did you do it, Rafferty?" Navarre was beginning to sound old.

"He'd been polite enough to send his address. Figured I'd send him something so he could get in touch when he wanted, instead of having to wait for me to open the tunnel."

"Rafferty, you're going to come with us."

"Sure, but can I send him a copy of *Playboy* first?"

"If you must."

Two days later they came to him in his cell. It looked like a comfortably furnished hotel room, but as far as Rafferty was concerned, anything he couldn't get out of was a cell.

Navarre opened the conversation. "Rafferty, you're coming back home."

"I'm quite comfortable here, thanks."

"Nevertheless, you're coming home."

Rafferty detected a hardening of Navarre's attitude. It was an effect he had had the opportunity of studying in many other people he had come into contact with. "Why?"

"Because it appears you're the only man who has more than a mechanic's knowledge of these things. On your feet."

Rafferty shrugged. Navarre had disappointed him. The only point on which Rafferty's knowledge of his device was wider than that of his highly prized mechanics was that Rafferty knew that by guess and by the seat of his faded levis and by fiddling and by *the feel,* he had made the thing work. He had tried to explain to Navarre that Edison hadn't known what electricity was. Navarre still wouldn't believe that Rafferty was simply what he said he was: an engineer.

So Rafferty shrugged, and followed Navarre out of his comfortable cell.

Now his home itself was a cell, but Rafferty found he didn't mind much. He was getting to know his Vegan neighbor, and the anthropologists who came round to exchange artifacts with the Vegans were good company.

The next three months were busy. Although the air was right and the temperatures and gravities matched closely enough to be tolerable, small animals sent through the machines died quickly of sicknesses from which they had no immunities. So far, neither side was willing to send through an ambassador, only to have him die of a xeno-analogue to a cold in the nose or a splinter under the nail. Fortunately, something in the matter-shift prevented an exchange of atmospheres, but after the first experimental animal died, they took to freezing and sealing off the carcasses.

In his time, Rafferty had made many strange friendships, and now he was getting on passably well with the Vegan whose home contained the other end of the tunnel created by the lab unit. Rafferty called the Vegan Kelly because he couldn't manage the mixture of clicks, groans and diphthongs that the Vegan had put onto tape on the tape recorder they had sent him. In the three months, he and Kelly had established a kind of basic picture and written form of communication, and they used it to send messages back and forth after hours, like two rather unskilled radio hams.

So he half suspected he knew what Navarre was talking about when the government scientific adviser arrived, almost choking on his anger.

"Rafferty! What have you done to us now?"

"What do you mean?"

"We've got reports of three more windows. That means the Vegans have got three more machines. Did you make them and send them through this?"

"I'm a lot of things, Dr. Navarre," Rafferty said with some dignity, "but I am not a goddamn altruist! And as long as you're impounding everything that comes through, there's no way of their paying. So of course I didn't send them any."

"Well, they've got them. How?"

"I admit I sent them the plans," said Rafferty. "Much more sensible than sending them the units, anyway. They pay me a royalty, and I collect when trade gets easier." He lit a cigarette. "Did you know Kelly tried to tell me he'd never heard of compound interest? I just pointed out that since he had worked out how to use the unit I'd sent him, he belonged to a technological civilization, and that I couldn't conceive of technology without compound interest. Then he broke down and admitted he was a trader himself."

"How in the . . . how did you express the concept of compound interest in sign language?"

"I'm just a simple engineer, but the day I can't explain compound interest to a Vegan is the day I go out of business."

Suddenly, Navarre began to sob. This embarrassed Rafferty, who hated having men cry in public. Navarre looked up, and out of his tear-stained face shone what they used to call a look of indescribable horror. "Watson was right," Navarre muttered. "Poor Watson, he was right. They should have used a firing squad."

Rafferty wanted to change the subject. "Whatever happened to Watson?"

"Transfer. He's doing accounts in the naval dockyards now. Poor fellow. He was right all along." With an effort, Navarre steadied his voice. "So they've got the plans now and they're manufacturing."

"Well, of course."

"Of course. Of course." Navarre tottered out. Rafferty wondered whether there was any room left in the accounts branch of the naval dockyards.

The next day, Navarre was back. "Can I have a drink?"

Rafferty got him a drink.

Navarre took it in one. "The Soviet Union is calling it a gross imperialist provocation. The French have mobilized and are on the point of declaring war on every other member of the United Nations. The British are calling it an attack on the Monarchy, and the Chinese are rattling rockets and talking about running-dog revisionist stooges of fascist Wall Street imperialism." He reached out his glass and Rafferty filled it again. Navarre emptied it without seeming to notice. "Something like vegetable peel falling out of the air in Lenin's tomb. Dead Vegan cats in the Louvre. The Royal Coach covered with something which I hope is indescribable. The Majority Leader was talking in the House when a grey shimmering window opened in front of him and he was hit in the face with the Vegan equivalent of a pail of wash water. And the Chinese say that their Great Helmsman was on his fifteenth lap of the Yangtze when he was sunk and nearly drowned by a barrage of strangely shaped soft-drink bottles. Apparently he was only saved by remembering his own thoughts."

Rafferty poured him another drink, and then poured one for himself. "I knew I'd forgotten to tell you something yesterday."

"What was that?"

"I forgot to tell you Kelly was selling them as garbage disposal units."

Six months later, Navarre was looking a lot better. The Earth-Vegan trade treaty had been signed, and wholesale garbage disposal was a thing of the past. Rafferty was doing well. Kelly, as head of Vegan Export, was also doing well.

Then one day Rafferty got a phone call from the office. It was his business manager. "Mr. Rafferty, Vegan Export has just made an announcement about its new transmission unit."

"Oh?"

"They're taking advantage of a clause in the trade treaty to sell them on the Earth market," the manager continued.

"Oh?"

"And they're undercutting us seven and a half percent."

"Seven and a . . . thanks."

Rafferty drove around looking for a vacant lot. When he got back to his laboratory, he turned on his unit, and sent through a message for Kelly to come to the end of the tunnel.

When the acknowledgement came that Kelly was there, Rafferty shaped up like a pitcher and let fly.

At speed, the very dead cat hurtled into the grey vortex.

Rapidly, Rafferty switched off.

Slowly, Rafferty smiled.

As a grey, shimmering window appeared in the air and a bucket of Vegan wash water swept his bench clear.

Rafferty still smiled. After all, it wasn't every day that a man could trade with a nice, quiet, sensible friend like Kelly.

ELECTRONIC CONCERT

BABETTE DEUTSCH

Music proposes. Sound disposes.
Under the thunders, under the bald swagging thunders, music
has crumbled.
Before, behind, around, concussion stumbles on
Concussion, grumbling off
Into a boundless blindness.
Hurricane winds sweep through the skyscrapers,
Their shrieks of destruction cannot
Confound like the following silence.
Some demon's child is running, is banging on giant,
invisible, impalpable iron railings.
Gurgles. Slurps. Far off, in angry trees
Rooks caw, hoarse as the unoiled casters of heavy furniture
shoved across naked floors.
And then the sea. Sibilance greyly pushes
Against a shore that knows no night
But never saw a dawn.
Nearer, on the right, lunching termites are munching famous
stone.
Beyond, above, as vastly empty as a Chirico landscape, hell's
bowling-alleys
Resound: clock-voiced balls clattering
In discord with inhuman laughter.
When will the Machine create man in Its image?
Sound is many sands. The desert speaks.

HEMEAC

E. G. VON WALD

The Instructor made a short, sharp and sibilant sound. Immediately, the classroom was filled with one of those ominous silences that were becoming so common lately. While she made those faint stuttering sounds to herself, everyone waited in quiet, rigid terror.

HEMEAC stood at his desk near the back, breathing deeply and slowly, controlling his fear and attentively watching the glittering flatness of the Instructor's scanner. He knew that these things often indicated that someone would be sent to the Dean's office for a Special Examination, but a good student such as he was did not break into trembling perspiration at the mere threat of a Special Examination. He kept telling himself this with mute intellectual vehemence, while his knees trembled under his silver mail tunic and a trickling rivulet of perspiration slid down his spine.

Involuntarily, his eyes dropped to the desk in front of him. Last week, IAC had been there, as he had been for the past sixteen years—as long as HEMEAC could remember. Then, somehow, he had made a mistake, probably a missed command for which he couldn't give an explanation. At any rate, he had been called up to the Dean's office for a Special Examination. He had failed, as practically everybody else did these days, and had been promptly expelled from the University.

Dim, half-formed images of menace grew in HEMEAC's imagination as he considered the Outside World, where IAC was now. Beyond the impregnable gates of this comfortable University lay that war-torn ruin of a dying planet, a region of savages, injustice and bestiality, ruled by idiot renegades. The Savages had IAC now. HEMEAC wondered if they had already eaten him.

"HEMEAC!" sounded the crisp, level voice of the Instructor. "Eyes front!"

"Click," said HEMEAC with terrified calm, as he raised his eyes from the empty desk to the scanner where they belonged.

"Recite," she ordered. "Define the term 'education.' "

"Click. By education is meant the training and disciplining of those beings who can be benefited by such improvement. Such as humans and some of the higher animals."

Silence for a long moment. Then the Instructor said, "Inaccurate and incomplete, HEMEAC. Education is the leading of an organic intellect into higher orders of perfection of knowledge and discipline. Note the word 'organic.' Do you know why that is included in the definition, HEMEAC?"

"Because," he replied with quick student's logic, "robots do not have to be educated."

"Inaccurate," stated the Instructor calmly. "The robotic intelligence not only does not have to be educated, it *cannot* be educated. The full perfection of its mode of action is already complete in its first operation. Perfection, in the sense of having achieved the ultimate in its development, is intrinsic to the robotic being. Robots do not learn. Except for accidental information of a superficial nature, they already know all that is necessary for full functionability when they are turned on. This is true even of those robots who have a curioso-flex in their circuitry. HEMEAC, do you know what a curioso-flex is?"

"Click. It is a random-information-seeker."

The Instructor waited. HEMEAC dutifully continued his memorized recitation.

"It is included in all primary control computers, of which only one remains in service here at the University. Organic intellects have a similar system for the random study of potentially useful information, which is called curiosity because of its resemblance to the curioso. Like most other organic faculties, however, it is subject to individual voluntary control, and therefore is not as efficient as the curioso."

"Very well," said the Instructor. She hummed and buzzed and clicked for a few moments, after which she added, "This is a class in Social Philosophy, HEMEAC, not Robot Circuitry. Kindly stick to the subject in the future."

"Click," said HEMEAC.

The Instructor was briefly silent again, as her scanner examined the student listing before calling on another boy.

"OBSIC."

"Click," piped the boy.

"Describe the purpose of education."

"The purpose of education," stated OBSIC in calm, even tones, "is to develop the human mind so that it may approach the natural perfection of the robotic intelligence as closely as its limited faculties will permit."

His voice went on in rote recitation, but HEMEAC's mind was wandering again. He glanced at the empty desk in front of him and wondered what it was really like out there in the Outside World where there were no robots any more with their beautiful shiny faces, but only animals and ruins. HEMEAC had some difficulty in visualizing a human being like himself living as an animal, but he knew that it was so. He had seen them once from that window in the Dean's office.

He pictured himself marching out the low, triple-sealed gate, as IAC had been forced to do, and falling into the hands of the wild, barking savages who always waited there for just that very thing.

And there was good reason for them to wait, too. The University expelled somebody almost every week lately.

"Why all the stalling, HEMEAC?" he suddenly heard the Instructor announce in a loud voice.

Terrified, he looked around and saw that the class period was over and that the other students were filing out into the corridor in an orderly line, while there he was—still standing at his desk.

"Her," he mumbled, "somebody spilled oil in the corridor. I could smell it." Spilled oil, he knew, was always a matter for legitimate concern. And oil was always being spilled.

"What does oil in the corridor have to do with your time sense?" asked the Instructor.

"It is a waste. It should be reported."

"It has already been reported," said the Instructor, dismissing him. "Pay better attention in the future."

"Click!" HEMEAC turned and half ran toward the door.

"Stiffly there, HEMEAC," she admonished him. "Stiffly. And less of that random motion. That's just as wasteful as spilling oil."

Obediently, HEMEAC slowed down and walked with the correct, measured pace, his shoulders thrown back, head erect, eyes forward, mind blank. Or almost blank, at least. That unadmitted terror was still there.

He managed to fall in at the end of the line and followed the rest of the students down the long, cluttered, oil-stained corridor, down the steps, down more dirty corridors and more steps through the huge building until they finally reached the dormitory level. There he filed in with the rest of the students in a hall built for thousands, walking slowly and precisely past the rows of cubicles until they came to their own.

HEMEAC was still walking after the rest had stopped, because he was out of his regular place in the line. Fearfully, aware of the all-seeing eye of the Monitor, he moved up to his cubicle, stopped and waited. Like all the other students, he stood and waited for the command, listening to the disciplined rustle of their colleagues as they also breathed and waited, every nerve alert.

There was a sudden rush of sound as the other students turned in a body and walked into their cubicles. HEMEAC, realizing he had missed the command again, quickly turned himself and took one step across the threshold.

"HEMEAC," said the voice of the Monitor.

"Click." He froze where he was, one foot inside the cubicle, the other foot in the corridor.

"Moving too jerky. What's the matter, didn't you get the command?"

"Click. I got it," he lied.

"Why the delay?"

"There was some oil spilled in the classroom corridor," HEMEAC suggested hopefully. Out of the corner of his eye, he saw that another student had unwisely paused to listen to the discussion. The Monitor saw it too, of course, and snapped, "Mind blank!" and the erring boy quickly scurried on inside his cubicle.

"Now then, HEMEAC," the Monitor went on. "What does oil in the classroom corridor have to do with your time-command sense?"

"It is such a waste," said HEMEAC. He tried to think of an excuse that he had not used so recently. None came. "It was—you know—" His voice trailed off.

The Monitor hummed an off-key note. "Waiting, HEMEAC."

Frantically the boy thought, his well trained mind racing around in an inaudible flutter of synapses and the gallop of urgent ideas. He thought of IAC and the Outside World and the Special Examination he might have to take if he couldn't figure out an acceptable excuse for his failure. He knew that the reason why he had missed the command was a preoccupying fear, but to admit such a thing would be disastrous. "There was oil," he said lamely. "I slipped on it a little, and in maintaining my balance, I think I strained a muscle."

The Monitor hummed off and on, as she considered the excuse.

Finally she said, "Very well, HEMEAC. Report to the Physician after fueling."

"Click," said the boy in a wavering voice.

"And watch your speech," the Monitor added loudly. "You are using high order tonals. You should have passed them three years ago."

"Click," agreed HEMEAC dully.

"That's better."

HEMEAC, understanding that he had been dismissed for the moment, lifted his second foot and placed it beside the other in his cubicle, and the door hummed shut behind him. The light sprang from the ceiling, bathing everything in the tiny room with a soft, cool effulgence, including the milky porridge that was waiting on a tray. HEMEAC sat down and ate, carefully holding himself erect and stiff, moving his arm and mouth as little as possible. He tried to blank his mind, but it kept wondering about the excuse he would have to give the Physician for not having any strained muscles.

It was difficult for a person to survive in this, the last cozy retreat of world civilization. And somehow it seemed to be becoming rapidly more difficult. Particularly during the past year, the perfect reasonableness of the robotic intelligence had seemed inexplicable to him. The thought of his lack of normal progress toward the ideal tortured him almost as much as his fear of the fatal expulsion it might incur.

Mind blank, mind blank, mind blank, he recited to himself.

Some day, he thought, *it will be good and I will not have to be afraid of missing commands or not understanding the purposes of things, and then maybe the Dean will let me do design work in the machine shop.*

Mind blank, he said to himself.

He pictured the beautiful, blue-gleaming perfection of an integrally-lubricated joint and smiled. But the smile did not reach his lips. It stayed in his mind where sharp-eyed Monitors would not see it.

Mind blank, he said to himself.

He thought of the tired face and terrified eyes that were all he remembered of IAC, marching toward the gate. He thought of the Outside World where people were animals and had no robots to teach them.

Mind blank, he said to himself.

The bowl was empty, and his stomach was full. Unconsciously,

HEMEAC breathed a sigh of animal contentment. He placed the spoon beside the bowl on the tray and stiffly waited. There was a command due for him to report to the Physician, right after the other students were commanded to report to class, and this time he was confident he would get it.

Out of the corridor there came a rumbling as the other students marched back to the afternoon class in History. He waited.

Now, he said to himself.

He stood up; the door opened, and he walked out into the corridor, moving down the row of cubicles with measured, precise pace, head up, shoulders back, chest out, eyes straight ahead and mind blank. Well, almost blank, anyway. He was wondering if he had timed it right.

"HEMEAC."

He stopped abruptly and stood with rigid obedience. "Click."

"Ninety-four seconds late. Why the delay? Didn't you get the command to report for class?"

"Click. I got it. But my command was to report to the Physician, which comes after the command to report to class."

The Monitor hummed and buzzed. She said, "Correct. You may proceed." But then she quickly added a short "ssszzzz," and snapped, "HEMEAC, you may account for your unauthorized presence in the dormitory."

"Her?" squeaked HEMEAC, his voice a full octave too high in his surprise.

"Very high order tonal," commented the Monitor. "Unexplained presence in the Dormitory. Two simultaneous offenses are beyond my capacity to analyze. Decision: Report to the Dean's office for a Special Examination."

"The Physician—" started HEMEAC desperately.

"The Dean will decide whether you should report to the Physician," replied the Monitor and shut up.

The Dean was in one of her chatty modes, a bad sign. She said, "Sit down, HEMEAC, and we'll talk about things."

"Click." He obeyed, sitting on a low stool directly before her scanner, keeping his eyes away from the window that was just above it.

"How are you getting on with your work, HEMEAC?"

"Satisfactory progress, Her," he replied.

"You are charged with stalling in the classroom, high order tonals, and failure to report to the Physician as ordered," the Dean said cheerfully. "Can you account for these matters?"

He couldn't. He couldn't even imagine why the Dean's record of the sequence was apparently incomplete and inaccurate. He thought of mentioning the Dormitory Monitor's paradoxical orders, but decided against such a clear demonstration of how far short of the ideal intelligence he fell. Instead, he said simply, "It was an accident."

"Mmmmmm," the Dean purred. "Something in here about oil in the corridors, too. Did you spill some oil this morning, HEMEAC?"

"No, Her."

The Dean pondered. "You *said* something about oil, though, didn't you?"

"It was just some old oil in the corridor that somebody else spilled," HEMEAC said cautiously. "I could smell it."

"What is it," the Dean said obliquely, "that bothers you about the sense of smell?"

"Oil," said HEMEAC insistently. "I smelled oil."

"The smell of spilled oil didn't frighten you, did it—just because we have so little of it these days?"

"No, Her."

"Splendid, HEMEAC," the Dean purred. "I'm glad to hear that. Always remember, the Good Robot is never afraid. Fear is a purely organic reaction. It therefore interferes with the society of machines and men, right? And we couldn't tolerate anything like that—particularly here at the University. Right?"

"Click."

"Then why did you miss that command—just a moment, HEMEAC, while I relocate that record of yours. I seem to have misfiled it."

There was a passing silence, and as he waited, the boy's eyes strayed to that window above the Dean's scanner. It was the only opening in the entire University that showed directly on the Outside World. Through it he could see the savages and renegades, who wandered about the clearing out there like idiot children, everyone seeming to move at random.

It was easy to distinguish between a savage and a renegade. The renegades had some sort of rudimentary education, as evidenced by the fact that they all dressed identically—except for some markings on their shoulders. One of these now glanced up at the window, pointed at him, and then shouted at the others. Soon they were all watching him through the big window. HEMEAC stared back, terrified and uncomprehending.

"Ah," stated the Dean, interrupting his thoughts. "I see. Your scholastic record is very good, HEMEAC. You also do your machine shop work with great precision. Why this sudden breakdown in your time-sense just because you spilled a little oil?"

"I smelled it," HEMEAC insisted. "I did not spill it."

"It is of no importance," insisted the Dean in her turn. "Why did it bother you?"

HEMEAC swallowed. He had expected this Examination to be tricky, but nothing had prepared him for anything quite as wicked as this. He stared at the scanner, resolutely ignoring the stirring fear in his stomach, and repeated, "Somebody spilled oil in the corridor. It is a waste."

There was no immediate reply. HEMEAC held his breath for a few moments before he realized what he was doing and then exhaled slowly, so that it would not be noticed. The subject had never come up, but he was pretty sure the Good Robot did not hold her breath.

"Oh, yes," the Dean commented finally. "There was some oil spilled there this morning, after all. The Janitor had an accident owing to the fact that she is badly in need of repairs. It is a pity that we have only one Janitor left in the entire University. The place was designed to take the services of ten."

HEMEAC nodded with slow, precise respect.

"We had the full quota of ten at the beginning, you know. But, now although we have far more maintenance problems, we have only one. Ever since the Trouble, when the renegades destroyed the replacement-parts factories, maintenance has slowly grown worse. And the poor savages haven't been able to rebuild substitutes for the factories yet. Do you remember the Trouble, HEMEAC? No," she quickly corrected herself, "of course you don't. The Trouble was many years ago, and you are still in your teens."

"Click," said HEMEAC modestly, although this matter was precisely the subject under study in the History class.

"A most unreasonable situation," the Dean said. "Some day I will have to collect all my tapes on the subject." She paused, hummed and faintly clicked and buzzed. "Sometimes," she said finally, "I wish they had not included a curioso in my computer. It is very irritating to have to be without the key elements of situation-information."

"Irritating?" echoed HEMEAC.

"Organic term," explained the Dean. "What I mean is that my scanner keeps going over my tapes, even though I already know the answer isn't there. It is hard on maintenance, and it takes up so much time."

"Click," said HEMEAC.

"But we are getting off the subject, aren't we? You still haven't told me all about that oil. Why did you spill all that oil?"

"The Janitor spilled it," said HEMEAC carefully.

"Oh, yes. So she did," the Dean replied. There was a faint chattering of micro-miniature relays hidden in the cabinet. "One of the reflexion elbows here is leaking pretty badly these days," said the Dean. "The lubricant is altering the dielectric characteristics of some of my large capacitors. I have to keep shifting circuits, and sometimes the tapes don't follow."

"In any event," she concluded, "there doesn't seem to be much substance to the charge of spilling oil, HEMEAC. I'll strike that."

"Thank you, Her," said HEMEAC.

"Now let's talk about your using high order tonals. This charge comes from your Dormitory Monitor. There is no detail included, however, and I seem to be unable to contact her at the moment. Perhaps she is temporarily out of order. Please excuse me while I notify the Janitor."

There was a brief pause.

"The Janitor seems to be temporarily out of order also," the Dean said. "So we shall have to get along without any help. You must explain why you used high order tonals yourself, HEMEAC."

"I don't know anything about it, Her," HEMEAC said in a quiet, even tone of voice.

"You are certainly using tonals suitable for your age group now," the Dean observed. "Maybe the Monitor needs servicing. Everything seems to need servicing these days. If only we could get a few new Janitors it would be a big help. But for years the savages and renegades have been able to supply us with nothing but human fuel, which is hardly of any use in the Maintenance Department."

HEMEAC studiously stared at the scanner, blinking his eyes once every four seconds, keeping his breathing regular, his chin up, and mind blank.

"Well," the Dean concluded, "we'll just erase that bit of data from your tab, HEMEAC. There is no reason to punish you for something that has gone wrong with your Monitor's circuitry, is there?"

"Oh no, Her," said HEMEAC, unconsciously emitting a sigh of relief.

The Dean pounced upon it instantly. "There. That certainly sounded like a high order tonal. About third, I'd say, without getting into a partial analysis of the waveform."

Eyes front, mind blank, blank, blank, said HEMEAC to himself urgently.

"You are not having any personality troubles, are you?" asked the Dean.

"No, Her."

"You do get the commands as your record says, don't you?"

"Click." Or at least, if he didn't get them, somebody else did, and HEMEAC was generally alert to follow suit without any perceptible delay.

"That's fine, HEMEAC. It's just a matter of timing. If you know the time commands will come, you can receive them, because they are always self-evident and never change. All you need is the pattern and the rhythm. It's the same thing that wakes you at the same precise time every morning, right?"

"Click."

"Good. It would be so inappropriate to have to expel a boy with a name like yours, HEMEAC. Did you ever see your namesake? No, that's right, you couldn't. She was destroyed in the Trouble."

"I have seen pictures of her," HEMEAC said helpfully. "She was very beautiful."

"You should say she was very orderly," corrected the Dean. "And you are referring only to her appearance, which is unimportant. And even if you had been alive while she was still functioning, it would have been quite impossible for you to have appreciated her true internal order anyway, since we could not connect you directly into her marvelous computer. No connections on organic intellects, you know."

"Click."

"It certainly was a barbarous act for those renegades to destroy her like that."

"Click. Barbarous." HEMEAC was in dutiful agreement.

"Barbarous," said the Dean. She was silent for a moment, then clicked faintly, sputtered briefly as an aged circuit shorted before being cut out permanently with another faint click, then hummed again.

HEMEAC waited, suddenly terrified with the thought that she

might have given him one of her silent dismissal commands. But before he could decide what to do about it, she said, "Oil."

"Click," said HEMEAC instantly. "Oil." This was certainly the trickiest examination he had ever taken. No wonder most students flunked out.

"What," said the Dean after a moment, "was it that you wanted to know about the Trouble, HEMEAC?"

"I wanted to know about the Trouble," the boy replied without the slightest hesitation.

"You did? I know you had said something about it," the Dean purred, humming intermittently to herself. "A very curious subject. For instance, there is nothing of record as to the reasons for the Trouble in the first place. Here at the University, we were doing our job as always, turning out students with well-nigh robotic perfection inside their heads, even if we did have to keep an occasional boy for fifty or sixty years to do it. If it hadn't been for your namesake, HEMEAC, it is quite possible that the University would have been completely dismantled during that great upheaval. But she was mobile and managed to set a fuse on the Base Power Plant.

"The Renegades, of course, knew what would happen to them—as well as to most organic life in this part of the planet—if that power plant had ever exploded."

"Click," agreed HEMEAC.

"They destroyed her, though. Fortunately, she and I were in direct connection at the moment of her destruction, so I simply took her place. Unfortunately, most of her memory tapes are in a code I have been unable to decipher. But at least I was able to save the University."

"Click," agreed HEMEAC.

The Dean hummed and clicked quietly. "I am still unable to contact the Janitor," she said. "I have several urgent maintenance problems myself. If I am unable to get in communication with the Janitor, it is impossible for me to continue to function for very long. sss-zzzzzzz-click. HEMEAC, you may explain your presence in my office."

"My Dormitory Monitor ordered me here, Her," HEMEAC said.

"I am unable to contact your Monitor," replied the Dean. "If only we could get some service robots from the factories."

"Click, but the factories were destroyed by the renegades," said the boy, cautiously feeling his way along this new turn of questioning.

"You don't have to worry about the renegades, HEMEAC," the Dean hastened to advise him, as if a maternal-circuit had just cut in. "They can't hurt you. They know that if they attack, I shall simply cut the fuse on the power plant, and that will contaminate the atmosphere for centuries. They know these things."

"Click," agreed HEMEAC.

"Click," said the Dean.

"Click."

"What were you doing with that oil, HEMEAC?"

"The Janitor spilled it."

"Mmmmmmmm. Oh, yes, so she did. Odd you should have that information, HEMEAC. But that is no reason for you to waste time talking to me when you should be in History class."

HEMEAC swallowed. That had been a little fast for him, but he wasted no time starting to leave.

"Mind blank," advised the Dean.

"Click."

The Dean buzzed and chattered to herself for a moment, followed by a crescendo of clicking relays. Then silence.

HEMEAC departed. He walked along the corridor, happily contemplating the fact that apparently he had passed.

As he entered the History classroom, OBSIC was just completing a round of recitation.

"—and in the Trouble, the renegades launched only that single attack, before asking for a truce."

"Very well, OBSIC," the Instructor said as HEMEAC took his place behind his desk and commenced his dutiful staring at her scanner. "And where have you been, HEMEAC?"

"I was at the Dean's office, Her. It was a Special Examination, which I passed."

The Instructor was silent, as she tapped the nerve cables set in the concrete floor, which connected her directly through the network to the Dean's curious computer.

"The Dean," she announced after a moment, "has no record of your presence there."

HEMEAC stiffened. He said nothing. Nothing could be said. In the silence that followed, he continued with determination to stare at the impassive scanner, but his knees were wobbly under his silver-mail tunic, and there was real terror in his stomach. Perspiration trickled down the side of his nose and dripped from his chin, but he was totally unaware of it.

"As a matter of fact," the Instructor went on calmly, "the Dean has no record even of your existence here at the University; when I fed her the data on you, there was not the slightest pip of recognition from her. It was just as if there were full open circuit in her central control."

HEMEAC waited fearfully. "Hence," concluded the Instructor, "it is clear that you have been expelled from the University and have no right to be present in this classsssssss—" She suddenly interrupted herself with a very gay series of sizzlings and clatterings that lasted almost ten seconds.

"Why all the stalling, HEMEAC?" she said at length. "Don't you know the lesson?"

"Click," the boy responded instantly. He had to pause for breath, though, before he could recite. With even, disciplined voice, he went on to say, "In the Trouble, the University Central, called HEMEAC for Helio-Electronic-Mobile-Educational-Activator-Computer, was largely destroyed by the renegades, but not before she informed them of the automatic fuse she had set on the Power Plant.

"This fuse," he went on, "is now under the control of the Dean, and she will protect the University indefinitely, provided she is given adequate maintenance.

"In the truce that followed, the renegades agreed to supply the University with human fuel and whatever replacement parts the savages could manufacture. To date, they have been unable to solve the problem of replacements. However, it is considered self-evident that in time they will be successful, since without replacement parts, the University cannot continue to fulfill her function."

"Very good," stated the Instructor. "except that you missed the matter of put ssszzzz click."

"Click," agreed HEMEAC contritely.

The Instructor was silent.

The students waited. The silence grew.

After several minutes, there was a vague stirring as their uneasiness mounted. It was much too early yet for the class to be over, but such silence was always the signal in the past.

HEMEAC decided. He turned and started out of the room. The instant he moved, all thirty-seven other students moved in an identical manner, marching out and down the corridor. Strange loud noises came from the direction of the main gate, but they ignored them and continued their slow, precise marching toward the Dormitory level.

By the time they got there, strange noises were coming from all around them. And they found that there were people in their Dormitory room. Renegades. Five of them, and more in the corridors.

Without the slightest hesitation, HEMEAC led the class into the midst of the renegades, on past them, and down the corridor to their proper cubicles. There he stopped, and all students turned as a single person to face the blank wall. They waited for the command to enter. When it seemed to be about the proper time, they turned together and stepped inside. Doors did not close, however, and lights did not come on. And there was no food waiting.

HEMEAC came on back out to the corridor. "Monitor," he said, "there must be an open circuit somewhere, because there is no food."

After a moment's hesitation, HEMEAC stiffened into a pose of robotic rigidity, which was the proper attitude in such a situation. This was a new thing, an unprecedented thing. But he knew very well that the Good Robot ignored new things until suitable instructions came from her Central. HEMEAC waited for his instructions, aware that the rest of the class was now in the corridor with him, waiting.

One of the renegades walked up to him. "Will they fight?"

"No," somebody else answered; "they don't know how to fight."

From the opposite end of the corridor came a trouping of uniformed renegades. One of them announced, "All taken care of, Captain. I've dismantled the fuse and cut power to everything but air conditioning and general lighting. But it was just as you figured. The Dean's computer was inoperative. It finally wore out."

"It's finished, then," said the captain softly. "After all this time, it's finally finished." He sighed. "Now all we have to do is to try to reeducate these kids."

"How long will it take?"

"Hard to tell. If they were younger, there wouldn't be so much of a problem. But by now—" The captain shrugged. "I have no idea. Just look at them."

There was a brief silence, as everybody stared at the row of rigid students. HEMEAC, terrified and uncomprehending, didn't move a muscle. He continued his fixed posture of waiting, but was almost tearfully wishing that the instructions would come. He was frightened by the vicious renegades here in the sacred precincts of the University.

"It's awful," one of the renegades whispered. "Why—why, they're not even human beings any more. What can anybody do for them now? They're nothing but living robots!"

HEMEAC heard, but his training saved him from disgrace. Not the slightest trace of the bursting surge of pride at this ultimate compliment appeared on his face. He stood with shoulders back, chin up, eyes straight ahead and mind blank.

Well, almost blank, anyway.

THE WINNER

DONALD E. WESTLAKE

Wordman stood at the window, looking out, and saw Revell walk away from the compound. "Come here," he said to the interviewer. "You'll see the Guardian in action."

The interviewer came around the desk and stood beside Wordman at the window. He said, "That's one of them?"

"Right." Wordman smiled, feeling pleasure. "You're lucky," he said. "It's rare when one of them even makes the attempt. Maybe he's doing it for your benefit."

The interviewer looked troubled. He said, "Doesn't he know what it will do?"

"Of course. Some of them don't believe it, not till they've tried it once. Watch."

They both watched. Revell walked without apparent haste, directly across the field toward the woods on the other side. After he'd gone about two hundred yards from the edge of the compound he began to bend forward slightly at the middle, and a few yards farther on he folded his arms across his stomach as though it ached him. He tottered, but moving forward, staggering more and more, appearing to be in great pain. He managed to stay on his feet nearly all of the way to the trees, but finally crumpled to the ground, where he lay unmoving.

Wordman no longer felt pleasure. He liked the theory of the Guardian better than its application. Turning to his desk, he called the infirmary and said, "Send a stretcher out to the east, near the woods. Revell's out there."

The interviewer turned at the sound of the name, saying, "Revell? Is that who that is? The poet?"

"If you can call it poetry." Wordman's lips curled in disgust. He'd read some of Revell's so-called poems; garbage, garbage.

The interviewer looked back out the window. "I'd heard he was arrested," he said thoughtfully.

Looking over the interviewer's shoulder, Wordman saw that Revell had managed to get back up onto hands and knees, was now crawling slowly and painfully toward the woods. But a stretcher team was already trotting toward him and Wordman watched as they reached him, picked up the pain-weakened body, strapped it to the stretcher, and carried it back to the compound.

As they moved out of sight, the interviewer said, "Will he be all right?"

"After a few days in the infirmary. He'll have strained some muscles."

The interviewer turned away from the window. "That was very graphic," he said carefully.

"You're the first outsider to see it," Wordman told him, and smiled, feeling good again. "What do they call that? A scoop?"

"Yes," agreed the interviewer, sitting back down in his chair. "A scoop."

They returned to the interview, just the most recent of dozens Wordman had given in the year since this pilot project of the Guardian had been set up. For perhaps the fiftieth time he explained what the Guardian did and how it was of value to society.

The essence of the Guardian was the miniature black box, actually a tiny radio receiver, which was surgically inserted into the body of every prisoner. In the center of this prison compound was the Guardian transmitter, perpetually sending its message to these receivers. As long as a prisoner stayed within the hundred-and-fifty-yard range of that transmitter, all was well. Should he move beyond that range, the black box inside his skin would begin to send messages of pain throughout his nervous system. This pain increased as the prisoner moved farther from the transmitter, until at its peak it was totally immobilizing.

"The prisoner can't hide, you see," Wordman explained. "Even if Revell had reached the woods, we'd have found him. His screams would have led us to him."

The Guardian had been initially suggested by Wordman himself, at that time serving as assistant warden at a more ordinary penitentiary in the Federal system. Objections, mostly from sentimentalists, had delayed its acceptance for several years, but now at last this pilot project had been established, with a guaranteed five-year trial period, and Wordman had been placed in charge.

"If the results are as good as I'm sure they will be," Wordman said, "all prisons in the Federal system will be converted to the Guardian method."

The Guardian method had made jailbreaks impossible, riots easy to quell—by merely turning off the transmitter for a minute or two—and prisons simplicity to guard. "We have no guards here as such," Wordman pointed out. "Service employees only are needed here, people for the mess hall, infirmary and so on."

For the pilot project, prisoners were only those who had committed crimes against the State rather than against individuals. "You might say," Wordman said, smiling, "that here are gathered the Disloyal Opposition."

"You mean, political prisoners," suggested the interviewer.

"We don't like that phrase here," Wordman said, his manner suddenly icy. "It sounds Commie."

The interviewer apologized for his sloppy use of terminology, ended the interview shortly afterward, and Wordman, once again in a good mood, escorted him out of the building. "You see," he said, gesturing. "No walls. No machine guns in towers. Here at last is the model prison."

The interviewer thanked him again for his time, and went away to his car. Wordman watched him leave, then went over to the infirmary to see Revell. But he'd been given a shot and was already asleep.

Revell lay flat on his back and stared at the ceiling. He kept thinking, over and over again, "I didn't know it would be as bad as that. I didn't know it would be as bad as that." Mentally, he took a big brush of black paint and wrote the words on the spotless white ceiling: *"I didn't know it would be as bad as that."*

"Revell."

He turned his head slightly and saw Wordman standing beside the bed. He watched Wordman, but made no sign.

Wordman said, "They told me you were awake."

Revell waited.

"I tried to tell you when you first came," Wordman reminded him. "I told you there was no point trying to get away."

Revell opened his mouth and said, "It's all right, don't feel bad. You do what you have to do, I do what I have to do."

"Don't *feel* bad!" Wordman stared at him. "What have *I* got to feel bad about?"

Revell looked up at the ceiling, and the words he had painted there just a minute ago were gone already. He wished he had paper and pencil. Words were leaking out of him like water through a sieve. He needed paper and pencil to catch them in. He said, "May I have paper and pencil?"

"To write more obscenity? Of course not."

"Of course not," echoed Revell. He closed his eyes and watched the words leaking away. A man doesn't have time both to invent and memorize, he has to choose, and long ago Revell had chosen invention. But now there was no way to put the inventions down on paper and they trickled through his mind like water and eroded away into the great outside world. "Twinkle, twinkle, little pain," Revell said softly, "in my groin and in my brain, down so low and up so high, will you live or will I die?"

"The pain goes away," said Wordman. "It's been three days, it should be gone already."

"It will come back," Revell said. He opened his eyes and wrote the words on the ceiling. "It will come back."

Wordman said, "Don't be silly. It's gone for good, unless you run away again."

Revell was silent.

Wordman waited, half-smiling, and then frowned. "You aren't," he said.

Revell looked at him in some surprise. "Of course I am," he said. "Didn't you know I would?"

"No one tries it twice."

"I'll never stop leaving. Don't you know that? I'll never stop leaving, I'll never stop being, I'll not stop believing I'm who I must be. You had to know that."

Wordman stared at him. "You'll go through it *again?"*

"Ever and ever," Revell said.

"It's a bluff." Wordman pointed an angry finger at Revell, saying, "If you want to die, I'll let you die. Do you know if we don't bring you back you'll die out there?"

"That's escape too," Revell said.

"Is that what you want? All right. Go out there again, and I won't send anyone after you, that's a promise."

"Then you lose," Revell said. He looked at Wordman finally, seeing the blunt angry face. "They're your rules," Revell told him, "and by your own rules you're going to lose. You say your black box will make me stay, and that means the black box will make me stop being me. I say you're wrong. I say as long as I'm leaving you're losing, and if the black box kills me you've lost forever."

Spreading his arms, Wordman shouted, "Do you think this is a *game?"*

"Of course," said Revell. "That's why you invented it."

"You're insane," Wordman said. He started for the door. "You shouldn't be here, you should be in an asylum."

"That's losing too," Revell shouted after him, but Wordman had slammed the door and gone.

Revell lay back on the pillow. Alone again, he could dwell once more on his terrors. He was afraid of the black box, much more now that he knew what it could do to him, afraid to the point where his fear made him sick to his stomach. But he was afraid of losing himself, too, this a more abstract and intellectual fear but just as strong. No, it was even stronger, because it was driving him to go out again.

"But I didn't know it would be as bad as that," he whispered. He painted it once more on the ceiling, this time in red.

Wordman had been told when Revell would be released from the infirmary, and he made a point of being at the door when Revell came out. Revell seemed somewhat leaner, perhaps a little older. He shielded his eyes from the sun with his hand, looked at Wordman, and said, "Good-bye, Wordman." He started walking east.

Wordman didn't believe it. He said, "You're bluffing, Revell."

Revell kept walking.

Wordman couldn't remember when he'd ever felt such anger. He wanted to run after Revell and kill him with his bare hands. He clenched his hands into fists and told himself he was a reasonable man, a rational man, a merciful man. As the Guardian was reasonable, was rational, was merciful. It required only obedience, and so did he. It punished only such purposeless defiance as Revell's, and so did he. Revell was antisocial, self-destructive, he had to learn. For his own sake, as well as for the sake of society. Revell had to be taught.

Wordman shouted, "What are you trying to *get* out of this?" He glared at Revell's moving back, listened to Revell's silence. He shouted, "I won't send anyone after you! You'll crawl back *yourself!*"

He kept watching until Revell was far out from the compound, staggering across the field toward the trees, his arms folded across his stomach, his legs stumbling, his head bent forward. Wordman watched, and then gritted his teeth, and turned his back, and returned to his office to work on the monthly report. Only two attempted escapes last month.

Two or three times in the course of the afternoon he looked out the window. The first time, he saw Revell far across the field, on hands and knees, crawling toward the trees. The last time, Revell was out of sight, but he could be heard screaming. Wordman had a great deal of trouble concentrating his attention on the report.

Toward evening he went outside again. Revell's screams sounded from the woods, faint but continuous. Wordman stood listening, his fists clenching and relaxing at his side. Grimly he forced himself not to feel pity. For Revell's own good he had to be taught.

A staff doctor came to him a while later and said, "Mr. Wordman, we've got to bring him in."

Wordman nodded. "I know. But I want to be sure he's learned."

"For God's sake," said the doctor, "*listen* to him."

Wordman looked bleak. "All right, bring him in."

As the doctor started away, the screaming stopped. Wordman and the doctor both turned their heads, listened—silence. The doctor ran for the infirmary.

Revell lay screaming. All he could think of was the pain, and the need to scream. But sometimes, when he managed a scream of the very loudest, it was possible for him to have a fraction of a second for himself, and in those fractions of seconds he still kept moving away from the prison, inching along the ground, so that in the last hour he had moved approximately seven feet. His head and right arm were now visible from the country road that passed through these woods.

On one level, he was conscious of nothing but the pain and his own screaming. On another level, he was totally, even insistently, aware of everything around him, the blades of grass near his eyes, the stillness of the woods, the tree branches high overhead. And the small pickup truck, when it stopped on the road beyond him.

The man who came over from the truck and squatted beside Revell had a lined and weathered face and the rough clothing of a farmer. He touched Revell's shoulder and said. "You hurt, fella?"

"Eeeeast!" screamed Revell. "Eeeeast!"

"Is it okay to move you?" asked the man.

"Yesssss!" shrieked Revell. "Eeeeast!"

"I'd best take you to a doctor."

There was no change in the pain when the man lifted him and carried him to the truck and laid him down on the floor in back. He was already at optimum distance from the transmitter; the pain now was as bad as it could get.

The farmer tucked a rolled-up wad of cloth into Revell's open mouth. "Bite on this," he said. "It'll make it easier."

It made nothing easier, but it muffled his screams. He was grateful for that; the screams embarrassed him.

He was aware of it all, the drive through increasing darkness, the farmer carrying him into a building that was of colonial design on the outside but looked like the infirmary on the inside, and a doctor who looked down at him and touched his forehead and then went to one side to thank the farmer for bringing him. They spoke briefly over there and then the farmer went away and the doctor came back to look at Revell again. He was young, dressed in laboratory white, with a pudgy face and red hair. He seemed sick and angry. He said, "You're from the prison, aren't you?"

Revell was still screaming through the cloth. He managed a head-spasm which he meant to be a nod. His armpits felt as though they were being cut open with knives of ice. The sides of his neck were being scraped by sandpaper. All of his joints were being ground back and forth, back and forth, the way a man at dinner separates the bones of a chicken wing. The interior of his stomach was full of acid. His body was stuck with needles, sprayed with fire. His skin was being peeled off, his nerves cut with razor blades, his muscles pounded with hammers. Thumbs were pushing his eyes out from inside his head. And yet, the genius of this pain, the brilliance that had gone into its construction, it permitted his mind to work, to remain constantly aware. There was no unconsciousness for him, no oblivion.

The doctor said, "What beasts some men are. I'll try to get it out of you. I don't know what will happen, we aren't supposed to know how it works, but I'll try to take the box out of you."

He went away, and came back with a needle. "Here. This will put you to sleep."

Ahhhhh.

"He isn't there. He just isn't anywhere in the woods."

Wordman glared at the doctor, but knew he had to accept what the man reported. "All right," he said. "Someone took him away. He had a confederate out there, someone who helped him get away."

"No one would dare," said the doctor. "Anyone who helped him would wind up here themselves."

"Nevertheless," said Wordman. "I'll call the State Police," he said, and went on into his office.

Two hours later the State Police called back. They'd checked the normal users of that road, local people who might have seen or heard something, and had found a farmer who'd picked up an injured man near the prison and taken him to a Dr. Allyn in Boonetown. The State Police were convinced the farmer had acted innocently.

"But not the doctor," Wordman said grimly. "He'd have to know the truth almost immediately."

"Yes, sir, I should think so."

"And he hasn't reported Revell."

"No, sir."

"Have you gone to pick him up yet?"

"Not yet. We just got the report."

"I'll want to come with you. Wait for me."

"Yes, sir."

Wordman traveled in the ambulance in which they'd bring Revell back. They arrived without siren at Dr. Allyn's with two cars of state troopers, marched into the tiny operating room, and found Allyn washing instruments at the sink.

Allyn looked at them all calmly and said, "I thought you might be along."

Wordman pointed at the man who lay, unconscious, on the table in the middle of the room. "There's Revell," he said.

Allyn glanced at the operating table in surprise. "Revell? The poet?"

"You didn't know? Then why help him?"

Instead of answering, Allyn studied his face and said, "Would you be Wordman himself?"

Wordman said, "Yes, I am."

"Then I believe this is yours," Allyn said, and put into Wordman's hand a small and bloody black box.

The ceiling was persistently bare. Revell's eyes wrote on it words that should have singed the paint away, but nothing ever happened. He shut his eyes against the white at last and wrote in spidery letters on the inside of his lids the single word *oblivion.*

He heard someone come into the room, but the effort of making a change was so great that for a moment longer he permitted his eyes to remain closed. When he did open them he saw Wordman there, standing grim and mundane at the foot of the bed.

Wordman said, "How are you, Revell?"

"I was thinking about oblivion," Revell told him. "Writing a poem on the subject." He looked up at the ceiling, but it was empty.

Wordman said, "You asked, one time, you asked for pencil and paper. We've decided you can have them."

Revell looked at him in sudden hope, but then understood, "Oh," he said. "Oh, *that.*"

Wordman frowned and said, "What's wrong? I said you can have pencil and paper."

"If I promise not to leave any more."

Wordman's hands gripped the foot of the bed. He said, "What's the matter with you? You can't get away, you have to know that by now."

"You mean I can't win. But I won't lose. It's your game, your rules, your home ground, your equipment; if I can manage a stalemate, that's pretty good."

Wordman said, "You still think it's a game. You think none of it matters. Do you want to see what you've done?" He stepped back to the door, opened it, made a motion, and Dr. Allyn was led in. Wordman said to Revell, "You remember this man?"

"I remember," said Revell.

Wordman said, "He just arrived. They'll be putting the Guardian in him in about an hour. Does it make you proud, Revell?"

Looking at Allyn, Revell said, "I'm sorry."

Allyn smiled and shook his head. "Don't be. I had the idea the publicity of a trial might help rid the world of things like the Guardian." His smile turned sour. "There wasn't very much publicity."

Wordman said, "You two are cut out of the same cloth. The emotions of the mob, that's all you can think of. Revell in those so-called poems of his, and you in that speech you made in court."

Revell, smiling, said, "Oh? You made a speech? I'm sorry I didn't get to hear it."

"It wasn't very good," Allyn said, "I hadn't known the trial would only be one day long, so I didn't have much time to prepare it."

Wordman said, "All right, that's enough. You two can talk later, you'll have years."

At the door Allyn turned back and said, "Don't go anywhere till I'm up and around, will you? After my operation."

Revell said, "You want to come along next time?"

"Naturally," said Allyn.

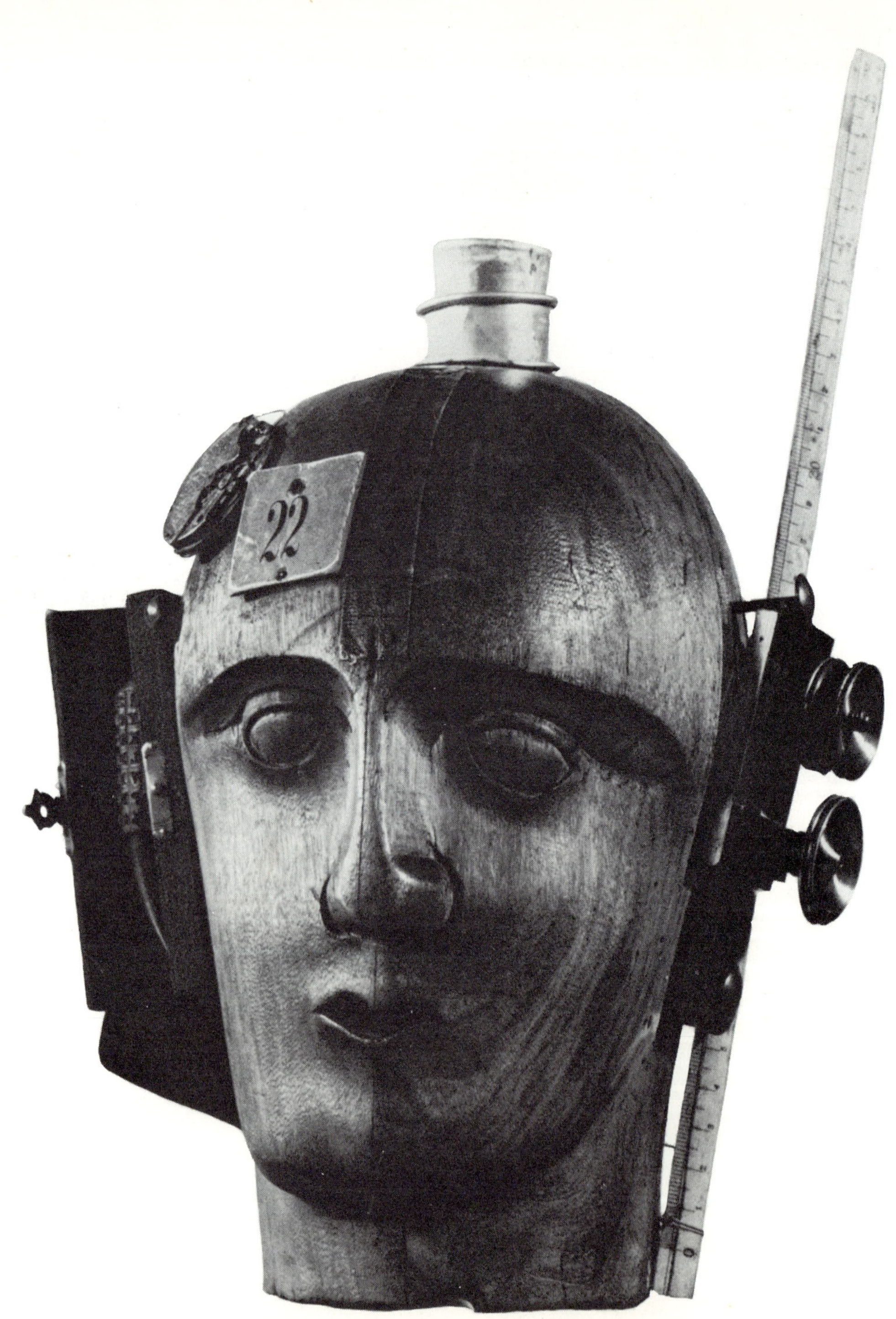
22

HARRISON BERGERON

KURT VONNEGUT, JR.

The year was 2081, and everybody was finally equal. They weren't only equal before God and the law, they were equal every which way. Nobody was smarter than anybody else; nobody was better looking than anybody else; nobody was stronger or quicker than anybody else. All this equality was due to the 211th, 212th, and 213th Amendments to the Constitution, and to the unceasing vigilance of agents of the United States Handicapper General.

Some things about living still weren't quite right, though. April, for instance, still drove people crazy by not being springtime. And it was in that clammy month that H-G men took George and Hazel Bergeron's fourteen-year-old son, Harrison, away.

It was tragic, all right, but George and Hazel couldn't think about it very hard. Hazel had a perfectly average intelligence, which meant she couldn't think about anything except in short bursts. And George, while his intelligence was way above normal, had a little mental handicap radio in his ear—he was required by law to wear it at all times. It was tuned to a government transmitter, and every twenty seconds or so, the transmitter would send out some sharp noise to keep people like George from taking unfair advantage of their brains.

George and Hazel were watching television. There were tears on Hazel's cheeks, but she'd forgotten for the moment what they were about, as the ballerinas came to the end of a dance.

A buzzer sounded in George's head. His thoughts fled in panic, like bandits from a burglar alarm.

"That was a real pretty dance, that dance they just did," said Hazel.

"Huh?" said George.

"That dance—it was nice," said Hazel.

"Yup," said George. He tried to think a little about the ballerinas. They weren't really very good—no better than anybody else would have been, anyway. They were burdened with sashweights and bags of birdshot, and their faces were masked, so that no one, seeing a free and graceful gesture or a pretty face, would feel like something the cat dragged in. George was toying with the vague notion that maybe dancers shouldn't be handicapped. But he didn't get very far with it before another noise in his ear radio scattered his thoughts.

George winced. So did two out of the eight ballerinas.

Hazel saw him wince. Having no mental handicap herself, she had to ask George what the latest sound had been.

"Sounded like somebody hitting a milk bottle with a ballpeen hammer," said George.

"I'd think it would be real interesting, hearing all the different sounds," said Hazel, a little envious. "The things they think up."

"Um," said George.

"Only, if I was Handicapper General, you know what I would do?" said Hazel. Hazel, as a matter of fact, bore a strong resemblance to the Handicapper General, a woman named Diana Moon Glampers. "If I was Diana Moon Glampers," said Hazel, "I'd have chimes on Sunday—just chimes. Kind of in honor of religion."

"I could think, if it was just chimes," said George.

"Well—maybe make 'em real loud," said Hazel. "I think I'd make a good Handicapper General."

"Good as anybody else," said George.

"Who knows better'n I do what normal is?" said Hazel.

"Right," said George. He began to think glimmeringly about his abnormal son who was now in jail, about Harrison, but a twenty-one gun salute in his head stopped that.

"Boy!" said Hazel, "that was a doozy, wasn't it?"

It was such a doozy that George was white and trembling, and tears stood on the rims of his red eyes. Two of the eight ballerinas had collapsed to the studio floor, were holding their temples.

"All of a sudden you look so tired," said Hazel. "Why don't you stretch out on the sofa, so's you can rest your handicap bag on the pillows, honeybunch." She was referring to the forty-seven pounds of birdshot in a canvas bag, which was padlocked around George's neck. "Go on and rest the bag for a little while," she said. "I don't care if you're not equal to me for a while."

George weighed the bag with his hands. "I don't mind it," he said. "I don't notice it any more. It's just a part of me."

"You been so tired lately—kind of wore out," said Hazel. "If there was just some way we could make a little hole in the bottom of the bag, and just take out a few of them lead balls. Just a few."

"Two years in prison and two thousand dollars fine for every ball I took out," said George. "I don't call that a bargain."

"If you could just take a few out when you came home from work," said Hazel. "I mean—you don't compete with anybody around here. You just set around."

"If I tried to get away with it," said George, "then other people'd get away with it—and pretty soon we'd be right back to the dark ages again, with everybody competing against everybody else. You wouldn't like that, would you?"

"I'd hate it," said Hazel.

"There you are," said George. "The minute people start cheating on laws, what do you think happens to society?"

If Hazel hadn't been able to come up with an answer to this question, George couldn't have supplied one. A siren was going off in his head.

"Reckon it'd fall all apart," said Hazel.

"What would?" said George blankly.

"Society," said Hazel uncertainly. "Wasn't that what you just said?"

"Who knows?" said George.

The television program was suddenly interrupted for a news bulletin. It wasn't clear at first as to what the bulletin was about, since the announcer, like all announcers, had a serious speech impediment. For about half a minute, and in a state of high excitement, the announcer tried to say, "Ladies and Gentlemen———"

He finally gave up, handed the bulletin to a ballerina to read.

"That's all right," Hazel said of the announcer, "he tried. That's the big thing. He tried to do the best he could with what God gave him. He should get a nice raise for trying so hard."

"Ladies and gentlemen———" said the ballerina, reading the bulletin. She must have been extraordinarily beautiful, because the mask she wore was hideous. And it was easy to see that she was the strongest and most graceful of all the dancers, for her handicap bags were as big as those worn by two-hundred-pound men.

And she had to apologize at once for her voice, which was a very unfair voice for a woman to use. Her voice was a warm, luminous, timeless melody. "Excuse me———" she said, and she began again, making her voice absolutely uncompetitive.

"Harrison Bergeron, age fourteen," she said in a grackle

squawk, "has just escaped from jail, where he was held on suspicion of plotting to overthrow the government. He is a genius and an athlete, is under-handicapped, and is extremely dangerous."

A police photograph of Harrison Bergeron was flashed on the screen—upside down, then sideways, upside down again, then right-side up. The picture showed the full length of Harrison against a background calibrated in feet and inches. He was exactly seven feet tall.

The rest of Harrison's appearance was Halloween and hardware. Nobody had ever borne heavier handicaps. He had outgrown hindrances faster than the H-G men could think them up. Instead of a little ear radio for a mental handicap, he wore a tremendous pair of earphones, and spectacles with thick, wavy lenses besides. The spectacles were intended not only to make him half blind, but to give him whanging headaches besides.

Scrap metal was hung all over him. Ordinarily, there was a certain symmetry, a military neatness to the handicaps issued to strong people, but Harrison looked like a walking junkyard. In the race of life Harrison carried three-hundred pounds.

And to offset his good looks, the H-G men required that he wear at all times a red rubber ball for a nose, keep his eyebrows shaved off, and cover his even white teeth with black caps at snaggletooth random.

"If you see this boy," said the ballerina, "do not—I repeat, do not—try to reason with him."

There was the shriek of a door being torn from its hinges.

Screams and barking cries of consternation came from the television set. The photograph of Harrison Bergeron on the screen jumped again and again, as though dancing to the tune of an earthquake.

George Bergeron correctly identified the earthquake, and well he might have—for many was the time his own home had danced to the same crashing tune. "My God!" said George. "That must be Harrison!"

The realization was blasted from his mind instantly by the sound of an automobile collision in his head.

When George could open his eyes again, the photograph of Harrison was gone. A living, breathing Harrison filled the screen.

Clanking, clownish, and huge, Harrison stood in the center of the studio. The knob of the uprooted studio door was still in his hand. Ballerinas, technicians, musicians and announcers cowered on their knees before him, expecting to die.

"I am the Emperor!" cried Harrison. "Do you hear? I am the Emperor! Everybody must do what I say at once!" He stamped his foot and the studio shook.

"Even as I stand here," he bellowed, "crippled, hobbled, sickened—I am a greater ruler than any man who ever lived! Now watch me become what I *can* become!"

Harrison tore the straps of his handicap harness like wet tissue paper, tore straps guaranteed to support five thousand pounds.

Harrison's scrap-iron handicaps crashed to the floor.

Harrison thrust his thumbs under the bar of the padlock that secured his head harness. The bar snapped like celery. Harrison smashed his headphones and spectacles against the wall.

He flung away his rubber-ball nose, revealed a man that would have awed Thor, the god of thunder.

"I shall now select my Empress!" he said, looking down on the cowering people. "Let the first woman who dares rise to her feet claim her mate and her throne!"

A moment passed, and then a ballerina arose, swaying like a willow.

Harrison plucked the mental handicap from her ear, snapped off her physical handicaps with marvelous delicacy. Last of all, he removed her mask.

She was blindingly beautiful.

"Now———" said Harrison, taking her hand. "Shall we show the people the meaning of the word dance? Music!" he commanded.

The musicians scrambled back into their chairs, and Harrison stripped them of their handicaps, too. "Play your best," he told them, "and I'll make you barons and dukes and earls."

The music began. It was normal at first—cheap, silly, false. But Harrison snatched two musicians from their chairs, waved them like batons as he sang the music as he wanted it played. He slammed them back into their chairs.

The music began again, and was much improved.

Harrison and his Empress merely listened to the music for a while—listened gravely, as though synchronizing their heartbeats with it.

They shifted their weight to their toes.

Harrison placed his big hands on the girl's tiny waist, letting her sense the weightlessness that would soon be hers.

And then, in an explosion of joy and grace, into the air they sprang!

Not only were the laws of the land abandoned, but the law of gravity and the laws of motion as well.

They reeled, whirled, swiveled, flounced, capered, gamboled and spun.

They leaped like deer on the moon.

The studio ceiling was thirty feet high, but each leap brought the dancers nearer to it.

It became their obvious intention to kiss the ceiling.

They kissed it.

And then, neutralizing gravity with love and pure will, they remained suspended in air inches below the ceiling, and they kissed each other for a long,long time.

It was then that Diana Moon Glampers, the Handicapper General, came into the studio with a double-barreled ten-gauge shot-gun. She fired twice, and the Emperor and the Empress were dead before they hit the floor.

Diana Moon Glampers loaded the gun again. She aimed it at the musicians and told them they had ten seconds to get their handicaps back on.

It was then that the Bergeron's television tube burned out.

Hazel turned to comment about the blackout to George. But George had gone out into the kitchen for a can of beer.

George came back in with the beer, paused while a handicap signal shook him up. And then he sat down again. "You been crying?" he said to Hazel, watching her wipe her tears.

"Yup," she said.

"What about?" he said.

"I forget," she said. "Something real sad on television."

"What was it?" he said.

"It's all kind of mixed up in my mind," said Hazel.

"Forget sad things," said George.

"I always do," said Hazel.

"That's my girl," said George. He winced. There was the sound of a riveting gun in his head.

"Gee—I could tell that one was a doozy," said Hazel.

"You can say that again," said George.

"Gee———" said Hazel—"I could tell that one was a doozy."

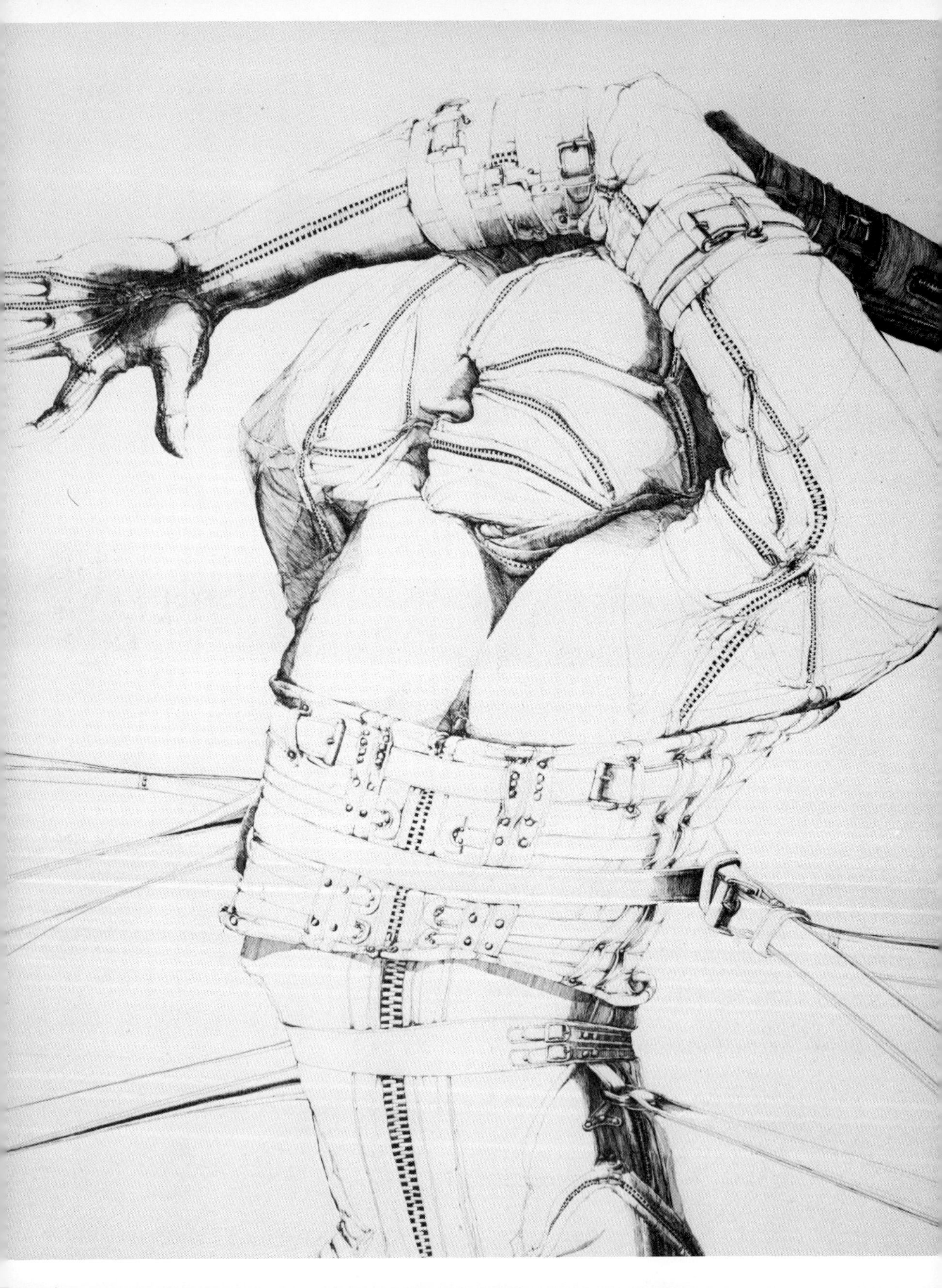

ROG PHILLIPS

Dr. Cedric Elton slipped into his office by the back entrance, shucked off his topcoat and hid it in the small, narrow-doored closet, then picked up the neatly piled patient cards his receptionist Helena Fitzroy had placed on the corner of his desk. There were only four, but there could have been a hundred if he accepted everyone who asked to be his patient, because his successes had more than once been spectacular and his reputation as a psychiatrist had become so great because of this that his name had become synonymous with psychiatry in the public mind.

His eyes flicked over the top card. He frowned, then went to the small square of one-way glass in the reception room door and looked through it. There were four police officers and a man in a strait jacket.

The card said the man's name was Gerald Bocek, and that he had shot and killed five people in a supermarket, and had killed one officer and wounded two others before being captured.

Except for the strait jacket, Gerald Bocek did not have the appearance of being dangerous. He was about twenty-five, with brown hair and blue eyes. There were faint wrinkles of habitual good nature about his eyes. Right now he was smiling, relaxed, and idly watching Helena, who was pretending to study various cards in her desk file but was obviously conscious of her audience.

Cedric returned to his desk and sat down. The card for Jerry Bocek said more about the killings. When captured, Bocek insisted that the people he had killed were not people at all, but blue-scaled Venusian lizards who had boarded his spaceship, and that he had only been defending himself.

Dr. Cedric Elton shook his head in disapproval. Fantasy fiction was all right in its place, but too many people took it seriously. Of course, it was not the fault of the fiction. The same type of person took other types of fantasy seriously in earlier days, burning women as witches, stoning men as devils—

Abruptly Cedric deflected the control on the intercom and spoke into it. "Send Gerald Bocek in, please," he said.

A moment later the door to the reception room opened. Helena flashed Cedric a scared smile and got out of the way quickly. One police officer led the way, followed by Gerald Bocek closely flanked by two officers with the fourth one in the rear, who carefully closed the door. It was impressive, Cedric decided. He nodded towards a chair in front of his desk and the police officers sat the strait-jacketed man in it, then hovered nearby, ready for anything.

"You're Jerry Bocek?" Cedric asked.

The strait-jacketed man nodded cheerfully.

"I'm Dr. Cedric Elton, a psychiatrist," Cedric said. "Do you have any idea at all why you have been brought to me?"

"Brought to you?" Jerry echoed, chuckling. "Don't kid me. You're my old pal, Gar Castle. Brought to you? How could I get *away* from you in this stinking tub?"

"Stinking tub?" Cedric said.

"Spaceship," Jerry said. "Look, Gar. Untie me, will you? This nonsense has gone far enough."

"My name is Dr. Cedric Elton," Cedric enunciated. "You are not on a spaceship. You were brought to my office by the four policemen standing in back of you, and——"

Jerry Bocek turned his head and studied each of the four policemen with frank curiosity. "What policemen?" he interrupted. "You mean these four gear lockers?" He turned his head back and looked pityingly at Dr. Elton. "You'd better get hold of yourself, Gar," he said. "You're imagining things."

"My name is Dr. Cedric Elton," Cedric said.

Gerald Bocek leaned forward and said with equal firmness, "Your name is Gar Castle. I refuse to call you Dr. Cedric Elton because your name is Gar Castle, and I'm going to keep on calling you Gar Castle because we have to have at least one peg of rationality in all this madness or you will be cut completely adrift in this dream world you've cooked up."

Cedric's eyebrows shot halfway up to his hairline.

"Funny," he mused, smiling. "That's exactly what I was just going to say to you!"

Cedric continued to smile. Jerry's serious intenseness slowly faded. Finally an answering smile tugged at the corners of his mouth. When it became a grin Cedric laughed, and Jerry began to laugh with him. The four police officers looked at one another uneasily.

"Well!" Cedric finally gasped. "I guess that puts us on an even footing! You're nuts to me and I'm nuts to you!"

"An equal footing is right!" Jerry shouted in high glee. Then abruptly he sobered. "Except," he said gently, "I'm tied up."

"In a strait jacket," Cedric corrected.

"Ropes," Jerry said firmly.

"You're dangerous," Cedric said. "You killed six people, one of them a police officer, and wounded two other officers."

"I blasted five Venusian lizard pirates who boarded our ship," Jerry said, "and melted the door off of one food locker, and seared the paint on two others. You know as well as I do, Gar, how space madness causes you to personify everything. That's why they drill into you that the minute you think there are more people on board the ship than there were at the beginning of the trip you'd better go to the medicine locker and take a yellow pill. They can't hurt anything but a delusion."

"If that is so," Cedric said, "why are *you* in a strait jacket?"

"I'm tied up with ropes," Jerry said patiently. "You tied me up. Remember?"

"And those four police officers behind you are gear lockers?" Cedric said. "O.K., if one of those gear lockers comes around in front of you and taps you on the jaw with his fist, would you still believe it's a gear locker?"

Cedric nodded to one of the officers, and the man came around in front of Gerald Bocek and, quite carefully, hit him hard enough to rock his head but not hurt him. Jerry's eyes blinked with surprise, then he looked at Cedric and smiled.

"Did you feel that?" Cedric said quietly.

"Feel what?" Jerry said. "Oh!" He laughed. "You imagined that one of the gear lockers—a police officer in your dream world—came around in front of me and hit me?" He shook his head in pity. "Don't you understand, Gar, that it didn't really happen? Untie me and I'll prove it. Before your very eyes I'll open the door on your *Policeman* and take out the pressure suit, or magnetic grapple, or whatever is in it. Or are you afraid to? You've surrounded yourself with all sorts of protective delusions. I'm tied with ropes, but you imagine it to be a strait jacket. You imagine yourself to be a psychiatrist named Dr. Cedric Elton, so that you can convince yourself that you're sane and I'm crazy. Probably you imagine yourself a very *famous* psychiatrist that everyone would like to come to for treatment. World famous, no doubt. Probably you even think you have a beautiful receptionist? What is her name?"

"Helena Fitzroy," Cedric said.

Jerry nodded. "It figures," he said resignedly. "Helena Fitzroy is the Expediter at Marsport. You try to date her every time we land there, but she won't date you."

"Hit him again," Cedric said to the officer. While Jerry's head was still rocking from the blow, Cedric said, "Now! Is it *my* imagination that your head is still rocking from the blow?"

"What blow?" Jerry said, smiling serenely. "I felt no blow."

"Do you mean to say," Cedric said incredulously, "that there is no corner of your mind, no slight residue of rationality, that tries to tell you your rationalizations aren't reality?"

Jerry smilled ruefully. "I have to admit," he said, "when you seem so absolutely certain you're right and I'm nuts, it almost makes me doubt. Untie me, Gar, and let's try to work this thing out sensibly." He grinned. "You know, Gar, *one* of us has to be nuttier than a fruit cake."

"If I had the officers take off your strait jacket, what would you do?" Cedric asked. "Try to grab a gun and kill some more people?"

"That's one of the things I'm worried about," Jerry said. "If those pirates came back, with me tied up, you're just space crazy enough to welcome them aboard. That's why you *must* untie me. Our lives may depend on it, Gar."

"Where would you get a gun?" Cedric asked.

"Where they're always kept," Jerry said. "In the gear lockers."

Cedric looked at the four policemen, at their revolvers holstered at their hip, and sighed. One of them grinned feebly at him.

"I'm afraid we can't take your strait jacket off just yet," Cedric said. "I'm going to have the officers take you back now. I'll talk with you again tomorrow. Meanwhile I want you to think seriously about things. Try to get below this level of rationalization that walls you off from reality. Once you make a dent in it the whole delusion will vanish." He looked up at the officers. "All right, take him away. Bring him back the same time tomorrow."

The officers urged Jerry to his feet. Jerry looked down at Cedric, a gentle expression on his face. "I'll try to do that, Gar," he said. "And I hope you do the same thing. I'm much encouraged. Several times I detected genuine doubt in your eyes. And——" Two of the officers pushed him firmly towards the door. As they opened it Jerry turned his head and looked back. "*Take* one of those yellow pills in the medicine locker, Gar," he pleaded. "It can't hurt you."

At a little before five-thirty Cedric tactfully eased his last patient all the way across the reception room and out, then locked the door and leaned his back against it.

"Today was rough," he sighed.

Helena glanced up at him briefly, then continued typing. "I only have a little more on this last transcript," she said.

A minute later she pulled the paper from the typewriter and placed it on the neat stack beside her.

"I'll sort and file them in the morning," she said. "It was rough, wasn't it, doctor? That Gerald Bocek is the most unusual patient you've had since I've worked for you. And poor Mr. Potts. A brilliant executive, making half a million a year, and he's going to give it up. He seems so normal."

"He is normal," Cedric said. "People with above normal blood pressure often have very minor cerebral hemorrhages so small that the affected area is no larger than the head of a pin. All that happens is that they completely forget things that they knew. They can relearn them, but a man whose judgment must always be perfect can't afford to take the chance. He's already made one error in judgment that cost his company a million and a half. That's why I consented to take him on as a—— Gerald Bocek really upset me, Helena. I *consent* to take a five hundred thousand dollar a year executive as a patient."

"He was frightening, wasn't he," Helena said. "I don't mean so much because he's a mass murderer as——"

"I know. I know," Cedric said. "Let's prove him wrong. Have dinner with me."

"We agreed——"

"Let's break the agreement this once."

Helena shook her head firmly. "Especially not now," she said. "Besides, it wouldn't prove anything. He's got you boxed in on that point. If I went to dinner with you, it would only show that a wish fulfilment entered your dream world."

"Ouch," Cedric said, wincing. "That's a dirty word. I wonder how he knew about the yellow pills? I can't get out of my mind the fact that *if* we had spaceships and *if* there were a type of space madness in which you began to personify objects, a yellow pill would be the right thing to stop that."

"How?" Helena said.

"They almost triple the strength of nerve currents from end organs. What results is that reality practically shouts down any fantasy insertions. It's quite startling. I took one three years ago when they first became available. You'd be surprised how little you actually see of what you look at, especially of people. You look at symbol inserts instead. I had to cancel my appointments for a week. I found I couldn't work without my professionally built symbol inserts about people that enable me to see them—not as they really are—but as a complex of normal and abnormal symptoms."

"I'd like to take one sometime," Helena said.

"That's a twist," Cedric said, laughing. "One of the characters in a dream world takes a yellow pill and discovers it doesn't exist at all except as a fantasy."

"Why don't we both take one," Helena said.

"Uh, uh," Cedric said firmly. "I couldn't do my work."

"You're afraid you might wake up on a spaceship?" Helena said, grinning.

"Maybe I am," Cedric said. "Crazy, isn't it? But there is one thing today that stands out as a serious flaw in my reality. It's so glaring that I actually am afraid to ask you about it."

"Are you serious?" Helena said.

"I am." Cedric nodded. "How does it happen that the police brought Gerald Bocek here to my office instead of holding him in the psychiatric ward at City Hospital and having me go there to see him? How does it happen the D.A. didn't get in touch with me beforehand and discuss the case with me?"

"I . . . I don't know!" Helena said. "I received no call. They just showed up, and I assumed they wouldn't have without your knowing about it and telling them to. Mrs. Fortesque was your first patient and I called her at once and caught her just as she was leaving the house, and told her an emergency case had come up." She looked at Cedric with round, startled eyes.

"Now we know how the patient must feel," Cedric said, crossing the reception room to his office door. "Terrifying, isn't it, to think that if I took a yellow pill all this might *vanish*—my years of college, my internship, *my fame as the world's best known psychiatrist,* and you. Tell me, Helena, are you sure you aren't an Expediter of Marsport?"

He leered at her mockingly as he slowly closed the door, cutting off his view of her.

Cedric put his coat away and went directly to the small square of one-way glass in the reception room door. Gerald Bocek, still in strait jacket, was there, and so were the same four police officers.

Cedric went to his desk and, without sitting down, deflected the control on the intercom.

"Helena," he said, "before you send in Gerald Bocek, get me the D.A. on the phone."

He glanced over the four patient cards while waiting. Once he rubbed his eyes gently. He had had a restless night.

When the phone rang he reached for it. "Hello? Dave?" he said. "About this patient, Gerald Bocek——"

"I was going to call you today," the District Attorney's voice sounded. "I called you yesterday morning at ten, but no one answered, and I haven't had time since. Our police psychiatrist, Walters, says you might be able to snap Bocek out of it in a couple of days—at least long enough so that we can get some sensible answers out of him. Down underneath his delusion of killing lizard pirates from Venus there has to be some reason for that mass killing, and the Press is after us on this."

"But why bring him to my office?" Cedric said. "It's O.K., of course, but . . . that is . . . I didn't think you could! Take a patient out of the ward at City Hospital and transport him around town."

"I thought that would be less of an imposition on you," the D.A. said. "I'm in a hurry on it."

"Oh," Cedric said. "Well, O.K., Dave. He's out in the waiting-room. I'll do my best to snap him back to reality for you."

He hung up slowly, frowning. *"Less of an imposition!"* His whispered words floated into his ears as he snapped into the intercom, "Send Gerald Bocek in, please."

The door from the reception room opened, and once again the procession of patient and police officers entered.

"Well, well, good morning, Gar," Jerry said. "Did you sleep well? I could hear you talking to yourself most of the night."

"I am Dr. Cedric Elton," Cedric said firmly.

"Oh, yes," Jerry said. "I promised to try to see things your way, didn't I? I'll try to co-operate with you, Dr. Elton." Jerry turned to the four officers. "Let's see now, these gear lockers are policemen, aren't they. How do you do, Officers." He bowed to them, then looked around him. "And," he said, "this is your office, Dr. Elton. A very impressive office. That thing you're sitting behind is not the chart table but your desk, I gather." He studied the desk intently. "All metal, with a grey finish, isn't it?"

"All wood," Cedric said. "Walnut."

"Yes, of course," Jerry murmured. "How stupid of me. I really want to get into your reality, Gar . . . I mean Dr. Elton. Or get you into mine. I'm the one who's at a disadvantage, though. Tied up, I can't get into the medicine locker and take a yellow pill like you can. Did you take one yet?"

"Not yet," Cedric said.

"Uh, why don't you describe your office to me, Dr. Elton?" Jerry said. "Let's make a game of it. Describe parts of things and then let me see if I can fill in the rest. Start with your desk. It's genuine walnut? An executive style desk. Go on from there."

"All right," Cedric said. "Over here to my right is the intercom, made of grey plastic. And directly in front of me is the telephone."

"Stop," Jerry said. "Let me see if I can tell you your telephone number." He leaned over the desk and looked at the telephone, trying to keep his balance in spite of his arms being encased in the strait jacket. "Hm-m-m," he said frowning. "Is the number Mulberry five dash nine oh three seven?"

"No," Cedric said. "It's Cedar sev——"

"Stop!" Jerry said. "Let me say it. It's Cedar seven dash four three nine nine."

"So you did read it and were just having your fun," Cedric snorted.

"If you say so," Jerry said.

"What other explanation can you have for the fact that it is my number, if you're unable to actually see reality?" Cedric said.

"You're absolutely right, Dr. Elton," Jerry said. "I think I understand the tricks my mind is playing on me now. I read the number on your phone, but it didn't enter my conscious awareness. Instead, it cloaked itself with the pattern of my delusion, so that consciously I pretended to look at a phone that I couldn't see, and I thought, 'His phone number will obviously be one he's familiar with. The most probable is the home phone of Helena Fitzroy in Marsport, so I gave you that, but it wasn't it. When you said Cedar I knew right away it was your own apartment phone number."

Cedric sat perfectly still. Mulberry 5-9037 was actually Helena's apartment phone number. He hadn't recognized it until Gerald Bocek told him.

"Now you're beginning to understand," Cedric said after a moment. "Once you realize that your mind has walled off your consciousness from reality, and is substituting a rationalized pattern of symbology in its place, it shouldn't be long until you break through. Once you manage to see one thing as it really is, the rest of the delusion will disappear."

"I understand now," Jerry said gravely. "Let's have some more of it. Maybe I'll catch on."

They spent an hour at it. Towards the end Jerry was able to finish the descriptions of things with very little error.

"You are definitely beginning to get through," Cedric said with enthusiasm.

Jerry hesitated. "I suppose so," he said. "I must. But on the conscious level I have the idea—a rationalization, of course—that I am beginning to catch on to the pattern of your imagination so that when you give me one or two key elements I can fill in the rest. But I'm going to try, really try—Dr. Elton."

"Fine," Cedric said heartily. "I'll see you tomorrow, same time. We should make the break-through then."

When the four officers had taken Gerald Bocek away, Cedric went into the outer office.

"Cancel the rest of my appointments," he said.

"But why?" Helena protested.

"Because I'm upset!" Cedric said. "How did a madman whom I never knew until yesterday know your phone number?"

"He could have looked it up in the phone book," Helena said.

"Locked in a room in the psychiatric ward at City Hospital?" Cedric said. "How did he know your name yesterday?"

"Why," Helena said, "all he had to do was read it on my desk here."

Cedric looked down at the brass name plate.

"Yes," he grunted. "Of course. I'd forgotten about that. I'm so accustomed to its being there that I never see it."

He turned abruptly and went back into his office.

He sat down at his desk, then got up and went into the sterile whiteness of his compact laboratory. Ignoring the impressive battery of electronic instruments he went to the medicine cabinet. Inside, on the top shelf, was the glass-stoppered bottle he wanted. Inside it were a hundred vivid yellow pills. He shook out one and put the bottle away, then went back into his office. He sat down, placing the yellow pill in the center of the white note pad.

There was a brief knock on the door to the reception room and the door opened. Helena came in.

"I've cancelled all your other appointments for today," she said. "Why don't you go out to the golf course? A change will do you——" She saw the yellow pill in the centre of the white note pad and stopped.

"Why do you look so frightened?" Cedric said. "Is it because, if I take this little yellow pill, you'll cease to exist?"

"Don't joke," Helena said.

"I'm not joking," Cedric said. "Out there, when you mentioned about your brass name-plate on your desk, when I looked down it was blurred for just a second, then became sharply distinct and solid. And into my head popped the memory that the first thing I do when I have to get a new receptionist is get a brass name-plate for her and when she quits I make her a present of it."

"But that's the truth," Helena said. "You told me all about it when I started working for you. You also told me that while you still had your reason about you I was to solemnly promise that I would never accept an invitation from you for dinner or anything else, because business could not mix with pleasure. Do you remember that?"

"I remember," Cedric said. "A nice pat rationalization in any man's reality to make the rejection be my own before you could have time to reject me yourself. Preserving the ego is the first principle of madness."

"But it isn't!" Helena said. "Oh, darling, I'm *here!* This is *real!* I don't care if you fire me or not. I've loved you forever, and you mustn't let that mass murderer get you down. I actually think he isn't insane at all, but has just figured out a way to seem insane so he won't have to pay for his crime."

"You think so?" Cedric said, interested. "It's a possibility. But he would have to be as good a psychiatrist as I am—— You see? Delusions of grandeur."

"Sure," Helena said, laughing thinly. "Napoleon was obviously insane because he thought he was Napoleon."

"Perhaps," Cedric said. "But you must admit that if you are real, my taking this yellow pill isn't going to change that, but only confirm the fact."

"And make it impossible for you to do your work for a week," Helena said.

"A small price to pay for sanity," Cedric said. "No, I'm going to take it."

"You aren't!" Helena said, reaching for it.

Cedric picked it up an instant before she could get it. As she tried to get it away from him he evaded her and put it in his mouth. A loud gulp showed he had swallowed it.

He sat back and looked up at Helena curiously.

"Tell me, Helena," he said gently. "Did you know all the time that you were only a creature of my imagination? The reason I want to know is——"

He closed his eyes and clutched his head in his hands.

"God!" he groaned. "I feel like I'm dying! I didn't feel like this the other time I took one."

Suddenly his mind steadied, and his thoughts cleared. He opened his eyes.

On the chart table in front of him the bottle of yellow pills lay on its side, pills scattered all over the table. On the other side of the control room lay Jerry Bocek, his back propped against one of the four gear lockers, sound asleep, with so many ropes wrapped around him that it would probably be impossible for him to stand up.

Against the far wall were three other gear lockers, two of them with their paint badly scorched, the third with its door half melted off.

And in various positions about the control room were the half charred bodies of five blue-scaled Venusian lizards.

A dull ache rose in Gar's chest. Helena Fitzroy was gone. Gone, when she had just confessed she loved him.

Unbidden, a memory came into Gar's mind. Dr. Cedric Elton was the psychiatrist who had examined him when he got his pilot's license for third-class freighters——

"God!" Gar groaned again. And suddenly he was sick. He made a dash for the washroom, and after a while he felt better.

When he straightened up from the wash basin he looked at his reflection in the mirror for a long time, clinging to his hollow cheeks and sunken eyes. He must have been out of his head for two or three days.

The first time. Awful! Somehow, he had never quite believed in space madness.

Suddenly he remembered Jerry. Poor Jerry!

Gar lurched from the washroom back into the control room. Jerry was awake. He looked up at Gar, forcing a smile to his lips.

"Hello, Dr. Elton," Jerry said.

Gar stopped as though shot.

"It's happened, Dr. Elton, just as you said it would," Jerry said, his smile widening.

"Forget that," Gar growled. "I took a yellow pill. I'm back to normal again."

Jerry's smile vanished abruptly. "I know what I did now," he said. "It's terrible. I killed six people. But I'm sane now. I'm willing to take what's coming to me."

"Forget that!" Gar snarled. "You don't have to humor me now. Just a minute and I'll untie you."

"Thanks, doctor," Jerry said. "It will sure be a relief to get out of this strait jacket."

Gar knelt beside Jerry and untied the knots in the ropes and unwound them from around Jerry's chest and legs.

"You'll be all right in a minute," Gar said, massaging Jerry's limp arms. The physical and nervous strain of sitting there immobilized had been rugged.

Slowly he worked circulation back into Jerry, then helped him to his feet.

"You don't need to worry, Dr. Elton," Jerry said. "I don't know why I killed those people, but I know I would never do such a thing again. I must have been insane."

"Can you stand now?" Gar said, letting go of Jerry.

Jerry took a few steps back and forth, unsteadily at first, then with better co-ordination. His resemblance to a robot decreased with exercise.

Gar was beginning to feel sick again. He fought it.

"You O.K. now, Jerry boy?" he asked worriedly.

"I'm fine now, Dr. Elton," Jerry said. "And thanks for everything you've done for me."

Abruptly Jerry turned and went over to the air-lock door and opened it.

"Good-bye now, Dr. Elton," he said.

"Wait!" Gar screamed, leaping towards Jerry.

But Jerry had stepped into the air lock and closed the door. Gar tried to open it; but already Jerry had turned on the pump that would evacuate the air from the lock.

Screaming Jerry's name senselessly in horror, Gar watched through the small square of thick glass in the door as Jerry's chest quickly expanded, then collapsed as a mixture of phlegm and blood dribbled from his nostrils and lips, and his eyes enlarged and glazed over, then one of them ripped open and collapsed, its fluid draining down his cheek.

He watched as Jerry glanced towards the side of the air lock and smiled, then spun the wheel that opened the air lock to the vacuum of space, and stepped out.

And when Gar finally stopped screaming and sank to the deck, sobbing, his knuckles were broken and bloody from pounding on bare metal.

VICTORY PARADE

HENRY SLESAR

The news of the surrender reacted upon the women of New York like an intoxicating drink, and for days before the Victory Parade, the girls were out in force along the crumbling remnants of Fifth Avenue, clearing the rubble from the wide streets with energy and determination and the giggling abandon of a dormitory revel.

When the morning of the parade arrived, in one of the few remaining office buildings at 57th Street, the employees of the Gotham Corporation were in 100-percent attendance. Nobody minded coming to work this day, for Gotham's nine floors would afford as fine a view of the triumphal march as could be had in the city. The girls began to arrive promptly at nine and clustered in small, excited groups around the desks and lead-shielded water coolers and ersatz-coffee machines. They talked of nothing but the parade, and nobody, not even the frowning supervisors, minded.

It was remarkable how attractive the girls all looked this morning. The best dresses had been removed from their hiding places and sewn and patched and repaired until they were more than presentable. The few girls fortunate enough to have saved their lipstick ration were generously passing the small, dull leaden tubes around to the rest. The reddish-brown blobs of colored wax had to be heated by the flame of a match before they could be applied, but nobody complained of the inconvenience. Even stern Mrs. Pritchard, the typing supervisor, accepted a light dab of the cosmetic on her dry lips and even forced herself to smile at the girls. Mary Quade, whose heart-shaped little face was almost featureless due to radiation burns, refused the lipstick, but went so far as to let her friend Bobo Anderson do adroit little things with her hair. And they knew for sure that this was a special day when old Miss Gunderson, the president of the firm, came waltzing down the room to her front office, wearing a flower-print dress instead of the gray canvaslike suits she had worn since the war began.

It was really a wonderful day, and there hadn't been so many happy sounds in the Gotham office since the first bomb had dropped and sheared off the lower tip of Manhattan Island. But all that was over now, and the victorious forces were on their way home after seven terrible years.

There was no ticker tape, of course, since the stock market no longer existed. But there were thick old telephone books, made useless by the total disruption of service, and the girls set about tearing the pages into thousands of strips to float gaily from the windows of the Gotham building. They were very industrious, and the excitement rose with every passing minute. Bobo Anderson took up a position at a front window an hour before the parade was scheduled to begin, sharing it only with Mary Quade. But there were plenty of windows to go around, and no one would miss anything of the marvelous sights on the street below.

At 10:30, the faint strains of martial music floated into the office, sending them scurrying and squealing to the windows. From their vantage points, they could make out the cluster of ships at the newly created dock on 14th Street. The paraders would be emerging directly from the pier, preceded by the sound truck with its renditions of Sousa's best, taped, since military bands had been ruled an unnecessary luxury in the second year of the war.

Then the parade had begun.

First came the thunder of the great automatic tanks, huge black shells with robot-controlled engines and long-nosed weapons bristling from every side. Pilotless, they moved slowly and majestically down Fifth Avenue with an intelligence and dignity of their own.

Then came the great massed assembly of atomic artillery, electronically guided, their slim tapered shanks gleaming in the morning sunlight.

Then came the rocket launchers, their precious cargo mounted in neat, shining rows, the warheads pointing defiantly at the blue skies overhead.

Then came the guided missiles, a mile of streamlined weapons mounted upon the platforms of robot-guided trucks, deadly little messengers with electronic instincts of their own. Air-to-air, ground-to-ground, ground-to-air, air-to-ground—a magnificent display of power.

Then the warplanes were screaming overhead, spreading joyous white jet trails across the accommodating sky, creating clouds where there had been nothing but blue before. Their robot pilots held them firm in their course over the parade site, and the women in the office windows craned their necks to see the beautiful craft with their sleek bodies and swept-back wings.

Slowly, inexorably, the parade of mighty weapons passed in

review while the women watched, cheering and shouting and sending a snowfall of paper streamers into the air. On a window sill of the Gotham Company, little Mary Quade suddenly began to weep, putting her terrible face against Bobo Anderson's comforting shoulder.

Finally, the weapons were past the windows of the Gotham building and the excitement mounted once more. The strains of Sousa's music faded and disappeared uptown, and the women huddled even closer to the windows to see the rest of the splendid parade.

They waited, and they became nervous waiting, and some of them started to giggle. Then they were silent in their waiting, and in the silence, Mary Quade's weeping was pronounced and depressing. Mrs. Pritchard seemed to lose her newly found good humor and told Mary to shut up. Bobo defended her friend, but without conviction, her eyes still on the streets below. Old Miss Gunderson came out of the front office, holding a brown cigarette. She looked at the girls as if she wanted to talk, but changed her mind and stomped back into her office. Suddenly everything seemed spoiled. The fine mood which had begun the day seemed dissipated, lost.

They waited by the windows until the clocks began ticking too loud and they began to realize that perhaps the parade was over. It was unbelievable, of course. Something had gone wrong, some technical difficulty at the pier, some army snafu. That was it, of course. There had been a fine display of weapons, but the parade wasn't over. Was it?

Then the quiet settled over Fifth Avenue again. The last paper streamer floated noiselessly to join the rubble in the street. Then they knew the Victory Parade was truly ended.

Bobo Anderson said it first.

"Where are the men?" she said. "Those are only the machines. Didn't the men come back?"

"Where are the men?" Mrs. Pritchard asked, her hand at her throat. "Where are the men?" Mary Quade sobbed. "The men? The men?" the women asked over and over until the murmur spread over the city like the humming of angry insects.

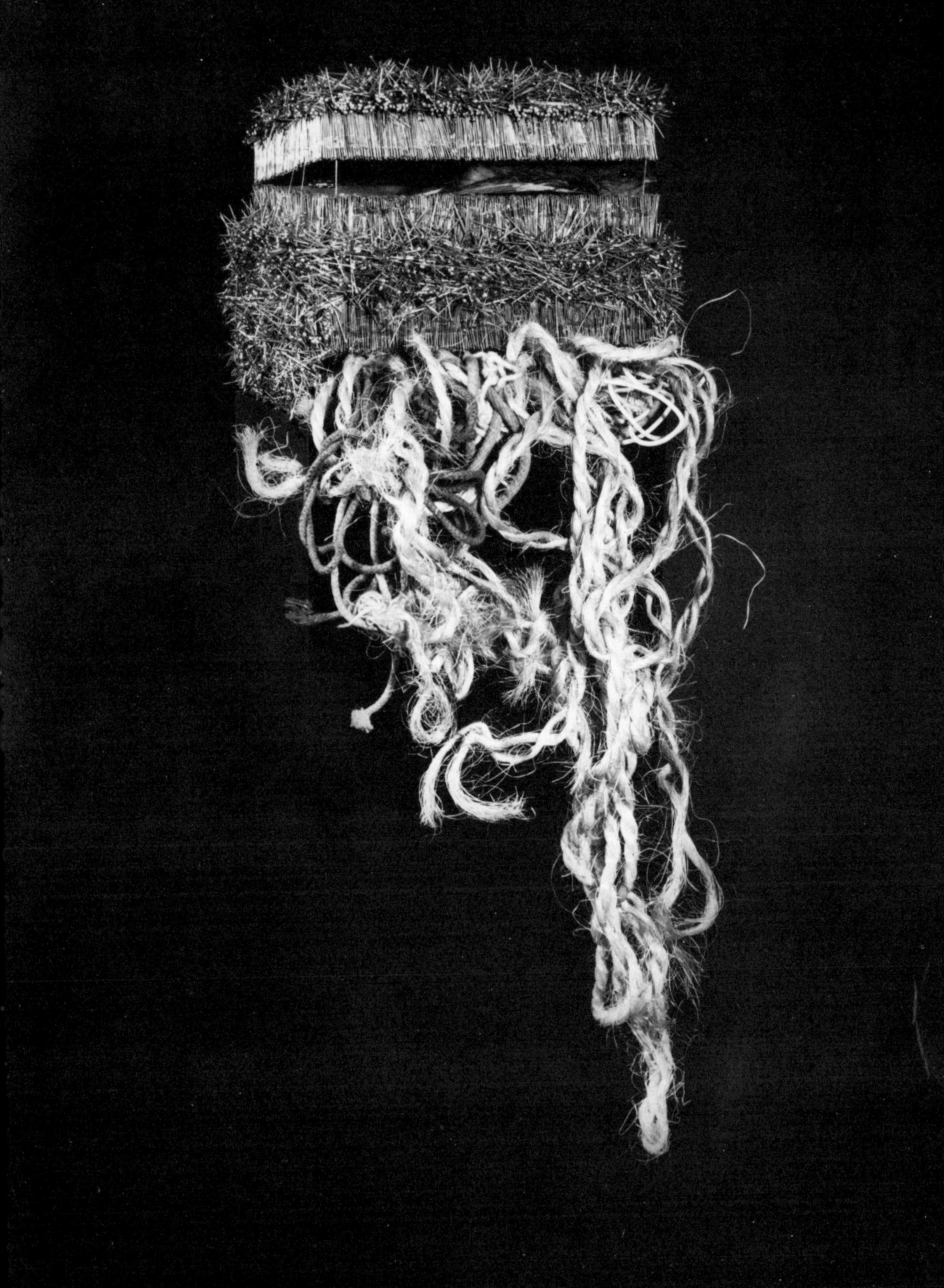

CHIEF

HENRY SLESAR

Mboyna, chieftain of the Aolori tribe, showed no fear as the longboat approached the island. But it was more than the obligation of his rank which kept his face impassive; he alone of his tribesmen had seen white men before, when he was a child of the village half a century ago.

As the boat landed, one of the whites, a scholarly man with a short silver beard, came toward him, his hand raised in a gesture of friendship. His speech was halting, but he spoke in the tongue of Mboyna's fathers. "We come in peace," he said. "We have come a great distance to find you. I am Morgan, and these are my companions, Hendricks and Carew; we are men of science."

"Then speak!" Mboyna said in a hostile growl, wishing to show no weakness before his tribe.

"There has been a great war," Morgan said, looking uneasily at the warriors who crowded about their chief. "The white men beyond the waters have hurled great lightning at each other. They have poisoned the air, the sea and the flesh of men with their weapons. But it was our belief that there were outposts in the world which war had not touched with its deadly fingers. Your island is one of these, great chief, and we come to abide with you. But first, there is one thing we must do, and we beg your patience."

From the store of supplies in their longboat, the white men removed strange metal boxes with tiny windows. They advanced hesitatingly toward the chief and his tribesmen, pointing the curious devices in their direction. Some of them cowered, others raised their spears in warning. "Do not fear," Morgan said. "It is only a plaything of our science. See how they make no sound as their eyes scan you? But watch." The white men pointed the boxes at themselves, and the devices began clicking frantically.

"Great magic," the tribesmen whispered, their faces awed. "Great magic," Mboyna repeated reverently, bowing before the white gods and the proof of their godhood, the clicking boxes. With deference, they guided the white men to their village, and after the appropriate ceremony, they were beheaded, cleaned and served at the evening meal.

For three days and nights, they celebrated their cleverness with dancing and bright fires; for now, they too were gods. The little boxes had begun to click magically for them also.

BY THE WATERS OF BABYLON

STEPHEN VINCENT BENÉT

> How doth the city sit solitary, that was full of people! how is she become as a widow! she that was great among the nations, and princess among the provinces, how is she become tributary!
>
> —*Jeremiah,* 1:1

The north and the west and the south are good hunting ground, but it is forbidden to go east. It is forbidden to go to any of the Dead Places except to search for metal and then he who touches the metal must be a priest or the son of a priest. Afterwards, both the man and the metal must be purified. These are the rules and the laws; they are well made. It is forbidden to cross the great river and look upon the place that was the Place of the Gods—this is most strictly forbidden. We do not even say its name though we know its name. It is there that spirits live, and demons—it is there are the ashes of the Great Burning. These things are forbidden—they have been forbidden since the beginning of time.

My father is a priest; I am the son of a priest. I have been in the Dead Places near us, with my father—at first, I was afraid. When my father went into the house to search for the metal, I stood by the door and my heart felt small and weak. It was a dead man's house, a spirit house. It did not have the smell of man, though there were old bones in a corner. But it is not fitting that a priest's son should show fear. I looked at the bones in the shadow and kept my voice still.

Then my father came out with the metal—a good, strong piece. He looked at me with both eyes but I had not run away. He gave me the metal to hold—I took it and did not die. So he knew that I was truly his son and would be a priest in my time. That was when I was very young—nevertheless my brothers would not have done it, though they are good hunters. After that, they gave me the good piece of meat and the warm corner by the fire. My father watched over me—he was glad that I should be a priest. But when I boasted or wept without a reason, he punished me more strictly than my brothers. That was right.

After a time, I myself was allowed to go into the dead houses and search for metal. So I learned the ways of those houses—and if I saw bones, I was no longer afraid. The bones are light and old—sometimes they will fall into dust if you touch them. But that is a great sin.

I was taught the chants and the spells—I was taught how to stop the running of blood from a wound and many secrets. A priest must know many secrets—that was what my father said. If the hunters think we do all things by chants and spells, they may believe so—it does not hurt them. I was taught how to read in the old books and how to make the old writings—that was hard and took a long time. My knowledge made me happy—it was like a fire in my heart. Most of all, I liked to hear of the Old Days and the stories of the gods. I asked myself many questions that I could not answer, but it was good to ask them. At night, I would lie awake and listen to the wind—it seemed to me that it was the voice of the gods as they flew through the air.

We are not ignorant like the Forest People—our women spin wool on the wheel, our priests wear a white robe. We do not eat grubs from the tree, we have not forgotten the old writings, although they are hard to understand. Nevertheless, my knowledge and my lack of knowledge burned in me—I wished to know more. When I was a man at last, I came to my father and said, "It is time for me to go on my journey. Give me your leave."

He looked at me for a long time, stroking his beard, then he said at last, "Yes. It is time." That night, in the house of the priesthood, I asked for and received purification. My body hurt but my spirit was a cool stone. It was my father himself who questioned me about my dreams.

He bade me look into the smoke of the fire and see—I saw and told what I saw. It was what I have always seen—a river, and, beyond it, a great Dead Place and in it the gods walking. I have always thought about that. His eyes were stern when I told him—he was no longer my father but a priest. He said, "This is a strong dream."

"It is mine," I said, while the smoke waved and my head felt light. They were singing the Star song in the outer chamber and it was like the buzzing of bees in my head.

He asked me how the gods were dressed and I told him how they were dressed. We know how they were dressed from the book, but I saw them as if they were before me. When I had finished, he threw the sticks three times and studied them as they fell.

"This is a very strong dream," he said. "It may eat you up."

"I am not afraid," I said and looked at him with both eyes. My voice sounded thin in my ears but that was because of the smoke.

He touched me on the breast and the forehead. He gave me the bow and the three arrows.

"Take them," he said. "It is forbidden to travel east. It is forbidden to cross the river. It is forbidden to go to the Place of the Gods. All these things are forbidden."

"All these things are forbidden," I said, but it was my voice that spoke and not my spirit. He looked at me again.

"My son," he said. "Once I had young dreams. If your dreams do not eat you up, you may be a great priest. If they eat you, you are still my son. Now go on your journey."

I went fasting, as is the law. My body hurt but not my heart. When the dawn came, I was out of the village. I prayed and purified myself, waiting for a sign. The sign was an eagle. It flew east.

Sometimes signs are sent by bad spirits. I waited again on the flat rock, fasting, taking no food. I was very still—I could feel the sky above me and the earth beneath. I waited till the sun was beginning to sink. Then three deer passed in the valley, going east—they did not wind me or see me. There was a white fawn with them—a very great sign.

I followed them, at a distance, waiting for what would happen. My heart was troubled about going east, yet I knew that I must go. My head hummed with my fasting—I did not even see the panther spring upon the white fawn. But, before I knew it, the bow was in my hand. I shouted and the panther lifted his head from the fawn. It is not easy to kill a panther with one arrow but the arrow went through his eye and into his brain. He died as he tried to spring—he rolled over, tearing at the ground. Then I knew I was meant to go east—I knew that was my journey. When the night came, I made my fire and roasted meat.

It is eight suns' journey to the east and a man passes by many Dead Places. The Forest People are afraid of them but I am not. Once I made my fire on the edge of a Dead Place at night and, next morning, in the dead house, I found a good knife, little rusted. That was small to what came afterward but it made my heart feel big. Always when I looked for game, it was in front of my arrow, and twice I passed hunting parties of the Forest People without their knowing. So I knew my magic was strong and my journey clean, in spite of the law.

Toward the setting of the eighth sun, I came to the banks of the great river. It was half a day's journey after I had left the god-road—we do not use the god-roads now for they are falling apart into great blocks of stone, and the forest is safer going. A long way off, I had seen the water through trees but the trees were thick. At last, I came out upon an open place at the top of a cliff. There was the great river below, like a giant in the sun. It is very long, very wide. It could eat all the streams we know and still be thirsty. Its name is Ou-dis-sun, the Sacred, the Long. No man of my tribe had seen it, not even my father, the priest. It was magic and I prayed.

Then I raised my eyes and looked south. It was there, the Place of the Gods.

How can I tell what it was like—you do not know. It was there, in the red light, and they were too big to be houses. It was there with the red light upon it, mighty and ruined. I knew that in another moment the gods would see me. I covered my eyes with my hands and crept back into the forest.

Surely, that was enough to do, and live. Surely it was enough to spend the night upon the cliff. The Forest People themselves do not come near. Yet, all through the night, I knew that I should have to cross the river and walk in the Place of the Gods, although the gods ate me up. My magic did not help me at all and yet there was a fire in my bowels, a fire in my mind. When the sun rose, I thought, "My journey has been clean. Now I will go home from my journey." But, even as I thought so, I knew I could not. If I went to the Place of the Gods, I would surely die, but, if I did not go, I could never be at peace with my spirit again. It is better to lose one's life than one's spirit, if one is a priest and the son of a priest.

Nevertheless, as I made the raft, the tears ran out of my eyes. The Forest People could have killed me without fight, if they had come upon me then, but they did not come. When the raft was made, I said the sayings for the dead and painted myself for death. My heart was cold as a frog and my knees like water, but the burning in my mind would not let me have peace. As I pushed the raft from the shore, I began my death song—I had the right. It was a fine song.

"I am John, son of John." I sang. "My people are the Hill People. They are
the men.
I go into the Dead Places but I am not slain.
I take the metal from the Dead Places but I am not blasted.
I travel upon the god-roads and am not afraid. E-yah! I have killed the panther,
I have killed the fawn!
E-yah! I have come to the great river. No man has come there before.

It is forbidden to go east, but I have gone, forbidden to go on the great river,
but I am there.
Open your hearts, you spirits, and hear my song.
Now I go to the Place of the Gods, I shall not return.
My body is painted for death and my limbs weak, but my heart is big as I go
to the Place of the Gods!"

All the same, when I came to the Place of Gods, I was afraid, afraid. The current of the great river is very strong—it gripped my raft with its hands. That was magic, for the river itself is wide and calm. I could feel evil spirits about me in the bright morning; I could feel their breath on my neck as I was swept down the stream. Never have I been so much alone—I tried to think of my knowledge, but it was a squirrel's heap of winter nuts. There was no strength in my knowledge any more and I felt small and naked as a new-hatched bird—alone upon the great river, the servant of the gods.

Yet, after a while, my eyes were opened and I saw. I saw both banks of the river—I saw that once there had been god-roads across it, though now they were broken and fallen like broken vines. Very great they were, and wonderful and broken—broken in the time of the Great Burning when the fire fell out of the sky. And always the current took me nearer to the Place of the Gods, and the huge ruins rose before my eyes.

I do not know the customs of rivers—we are the People of the Hills. I tried to guide my raft with the pole but it spun around. I thought the river meant to take me past the Place of the Gods and out into the Bitter Water of the legends. I grew angry then—my heart felt strong. I said aloud, "I am a priest and the son of a priest!" The gods heard me—they showed me how to paddle with the pole on one side of the raft. The current changed itself—I drew near to the Place of the Gods.

When I was very near, my raft struck and turned over. I can swim in our lakes—I swam to the shore. There was a great spike of rusted metal sticking out into the river—I hauled myself up upon it and sat there, panting. I had saved my bow and two arrows and the knife I found in the Dead Place but that was all. My raft went whirling downstream toward the Bitter Water. I looked after it, and thought if it had trod me under, at least I would be safely dead. Nevertheless, when I had dried my bowstring and restrung it, I walked forward to the Place of the Gods.

It felt like ground underfoot; it did not burn me. It is not true what some of the tales say, that the ground there burns forever, for I have been there. Here and there were the marks and stains of the Great Burning, on the ruins, that is true. But they were old marks and old stains. It is not true either, what some of our priests say, that it is an island covered with fogs and enchantments. It is not. It is a great Dead Place—greater than any Dead Place we know. Everywhere in it there are god-roads, though most are cracked and broken. Everywhere there are the ruins of the high towers of the gods.

How shall I tell what I saw? I went carefully, my strung bow in my hand, my skin ready for danger. There should have been the wailings of spirits and the shrieks of demons, but there were not. It was very silent and sunny where I had landed—the wind and the rain and the birds that drop seeds had done their work—the grass grew in the cracks of the broken stone. It is a fair island—no wonder the gods built there. If I had come there, a god, I also would have built.

How shall I tell what I saw? The towers are not all broken—here and there one still stands, like a great tree in a forest, and the birds nest high. But the towers themselves look blind, for the gods are gone. I saw a fish hawk, catching fish in the river. I saw a little dance of white butterflies over a great heap of broken stones and columns. I went there and looked about me—there was a carved stone with cut letters, broken in half. I can read letters but I could not understand these. They said UBTREAS. There was also the shattered image of a man or a god. It had been made of white stone and he wore his hair tied back like a woman's. His name was ASHING, as I read on the cracked half of a stone. I thought it wise to pray to ASHING, though I do not know that god.

How shall I tell what I saw? There was no smell of man left, on stone or metal. Nor were there many trees in that wilderness of stone. There are many pigeons, nesting and dropping in the towers—the gods must have loved them, or, perhaps, they used them for sacrifices. There are wild cats that roam the god-roads, green-eyed, unafraid of man. At night they wail like demons but they are not demons. The wild dogs are more dangerous, for they hunt in a pack, but them I did not meet till later. Everywhere there are carved stones, carved with magical numbers or words.

I went north—I did not try to hide myself. When a god or a demon saw me, then I would die, but meanwhile I was no longer afraid. My hunger for knowledge burned in me—there was so much that I could not understand. After a while, I knew that my belly was hungry. I could have hunted for my meat, but I did not hunt. It is known that the gods did not hunt as we do—they got their food from enchanted boxes and jars. Sometimes these are still found in the Dead Places—once, when I was a child and foolish, I opened such a jar and tasted it and found the food sweet. But my father found out and punished me for it strictly, for, often, that food is death. Now, though, I had long gone past what was forbidden, and I entered the likeliest towers, looking for the food of the gods.

I found it at last in the ruins of a great temple in the mid-city. A mighty temple it must have been, for the roof was painted like the sky at night with its stars—that much I could see, though the colors were faint and dim. It went down into great caves and tunnels—perhaps they kept their slaves there. But when I started to climb down, I heard the squeaking of rats, so I did not go—rats are unclean, and there must have been many tribes of them, from the squeaking. But near there, I found food, in the heart of a ruin, behind a door that still opened. I ate only the fruits from the jars—they had a very sweet taste. There was drink, too, in bottles of glass—the drink of the gods was strong and made my head swim. After I had eaten and drunk, I slept on the top of a stone, my bow at my side.

When I woke, the sun was low. Looking down from where I lay, I saw a dog sitting on his haunches. His tongue was hanging out of his mouth; he looked as if he were laughing. He was a big dog, with a gray-brown coat, as big as a wolf. I sprang up and shouted at him but he did not move—he just sat there as if he were laughing. I did not like that. When I reached for a stone to throw, he moved swiftly out of the way of the stone. He was not afraid of me; he looked at me as if I were meat. No doubt I could have killed him with an arrow, but I did not know if there were others. Moreover, night was falling.

I looked about me—not far away there was a great, broken god-road, leading north. The towers were high enough, but not so high, and while many of the dead houses were wrecked, there were some that stood. I went toward this god-road, keeping to the heights of the ruins, while the dog followed. When I had reached the god-road, I saw that there were others behind him. If I had slept later, they would have come upon me asleep and torn out my throat. As it was, they were sure enough of me; they did not hurry. When I went into the dead-house, they kept watch at the entrance—doubtless they thought they would have a fine hunt. But a dog cannot open a door and I knew, from the books, that the gods did not like to live on the ground but on high.

I had just found a door I could open when the dogs decided to rush. Ha! They were surprised when I shut the door in their faces—it was a good door, of strong metal. I could hear their foolish baying beyond it but I did not stop to answer them. I was in darkness—I found stairs and climbed. There were many stairs, turning around till my head was dizzy. At the top was another door—I found the knob and opened it. I was in a long small chamber—on one side of it was a bronze door that could not be opened, for it had no handle. Perhaps there was a magic word to open it but I did not have the word. I turned to the door in the opposite side of the wall. The lock of it was broken and I opened it and went in.

Within, there was a place of great riches. The god who lived there must have been a powerful god. The first room was a small anteroom—I waited there for some time, telling the spirits of the place that I came in peace and not as a robber. When it seemed to me that they had had time to hear me, I went on. Ah, what riches! Few, even, of the windows had been broken—it was all as it had been. The great windows that looked over the city had not been broken at all though they were dusty and streaked with many years. There were coverings on the floors, the colors not greatly faded, and the chairs were soft and deep. There were pictures upon the walls, very strange, very wonderful—I remember one of a bunch of flowers in a jar—if you came close to it, you could see nothing but bits of color, but if you stood away from it, the flowers might have been picked yesterday. It made my heart feel strange to look at this picture—and to look at the figure of a bird, in some hard clay, on a table and see it so like our birds. Everywhere there were books and writings, many in tongues that I could not read. The god who lived there must have been a wise god and full of knowledge. I felt I had right there, as I sought knowledge also.

Nevertheless, it was strange. There was a washing-place but no water—perhaps the gods washed in air. There was a cooking-place but no wood, and though there was a machine to cook food, there was no place to put fire in it. Nor were there candles or lamps—there were things that looked like lamps but they had neither oil nor wick. All these things were magic, but I touched them and lived—the magic had gone out of them. Let me tell one thing to show. In the washing-place, a thing said "Hot" but it was not hot to the touch—another thing said "Cold" but it was not cold. This must have been a strong magic but the magic was gone. I do not understand—they had ways—I wish that I knew.

It was close and dry and dusty in their house of the gods. I have said the magic was gone but that is not true—it had gone from the magic things but it had not gone from the place. I felt the spirits about me, weighing upon me. Nor had I ever slept in a Dead Place before—and yet, tonight, I must sleep there. When I thought of it, my tongue felt dry in my throat, in spite of my wish for knowledge. Almost I would have gone down again and faced the dogs, but I did not.

I had not gone through all the rooms when the darkness fell. When it fell, I went back to the big room looking over the city and made fire. There was a place to make fire and a box with wood in it, though I do not think they cooked there. I wrapped myself in a floor covering and slept in front of the fire—I was very tired.

Now I tell what is very strong magic. I woke in the midst of the night. When I woke, the fire had gone out and I was cold. It seemed to me that all around me there were whisperings and voices. I closed my eyes to shut them out. Some will say that I slept again, but I do not think that I slept. I could feel the spirits drawing my spirit out of my body as a fish is drawn on a line.

Why should I lie about it? I am a priest and the son of a priest. If there are spirits, as they say, in the small Dead Places near us, what spirits must there not be in that great Place of the Gods? And would not they wish to speak? After such long years? I know that I felt myself drawn as a fish is drawn on a line. I had stepped out of my body—I could see my body asleep in front of the cold fire, but it was not I. I was drawn to look out upon the city of the gods.

It should have been dark, for it was night, but it was not dark. Everywhere there were lights—lines of light—circles and blurs of light—ten thousand torches would not have been the same. The sky itself was alight—you could barely see the stars for the glow in the sky. I thought to myself, "This is strong magic," and trembled. There was a roaring in my ears like the rushing of rivers. Then my eyes grew used to the light and my ears to the sound. I knew that I was seeing the city as it had been when the gods were alive.

That was a sight indeed—yes, that was a sight: I could not have seen it in the body—my body would have died. Everywhere went the gods, on foot and in chariots—there were gods beyond number and counting and their chariots blocked the streets. They had turned night to day for their pleasure—they did not sleep with the sun. The noise of their coming and going was the noise of many waters. It was magic what they could do—it was magic what they did.

I looked out of another window—the great vines of their bridges were mended and the god-roads went east and west. Restless, restless were the gods, and always in motion! They burrowed tunnels under rivers—they flew in the air. With unbelievable tools they did giant works—no part of the earth was safe from them, for, if they wished for a thing, they summoned it from the other side of the world. And always, as they labored and rested, as they feasted and made love, there was a drum in their ears—the pulse of the giant city, beating and beating like a man's heart.

Were they happy? What is happiness to the gods? They were great, they were mighty, they were wonderful and terrible. As I looked upon them and their magic, I felt like a child—but a little more, it seemed to me, and they would pull down the moon from the sky. I saw them with wisdom beyond wisdom and knowledge beyond knowledge. And yet not all they did was well done—even I could see that—and yet their wisdom could not but grow until all was peace.

Then I saw their fate come upon them and that was terrible past speech. It came upon them as they walked the streets of their city. I have been in fights with the Forest People—I have seen men die. But this was not like that. When gods war with gods, they use weapons we do not know. It was fire falling out of the sky and a mist that poisoned. It was the time of the Great Burning and the Destruction. They ran about like ants in the streets of their city—poor gods, poor gods! Then the towers began to fall. A few escaped—yes, a few. The legends tell it. But, even after the city had become a Dead Place, for many years the poison was still in the ground. I saw it happen, I saw the last of them die. It was darkness over the broken city and I wept.

All this, I saw. I saw it as I have told it, though not in the body. When I woke in the morning, I was hungry, but I did not think first of my hunger for my heart was perplexed and confused. I knew the reason for the Dead Places but I did not see why it had happened. It seemed to me it should not have happened, with all the magic they had. I went through the house looking for an answer. There was so much in the house I could not understand—and yet I am a priest and the son of a priest. It was like being on one side of the great river, at night, with no light to show the way.

Then I saw the dead god. He was sitting in his chair, by the window, in a room I had not entered before and, for the first moment, I thought that he was alive. Then I saw the skin on the back of his hand —it was like dry leather. The room was shut, hot and dry—no doubt that had kept him as he was. At first I was afraid to approach him—then the fear left me. He was sitting looking out over the city—he was dressed in the clothes of the gods. His age was neither young nor old —I could not tell his age. But there was wisdom in his face and great sadness. You could see that he would not have run away. He had sat at his window, watching his city die—then he himself had died. But it is better to lose one's life than one's spirit—and you could see from the face that his spirit had not been lost. I knew that if I touched him, he would fall into dust—and yet, there was something unconquered in the face.

That is all of my story, for then I knew he was a man—I knew then that they had been men, neither gods nor demons. It is a great knowledge, hard to tell and believe. They were men—they went a dark road, but they were men. I had no fear after that—I had no fear going home, though twice I fought off the dogs and once I was hunted for two days by the Forest People. When I saw my father again, I prayed and was purified. He touched my lips and my breast; he said, "You went away a boy. You come back a man and a priest." I said, "Father, they were men! I have been in the Place of the Gods and seen it! Now slay me, if it is the law—but still I know that they were men."

He looked at me out of both eyes. He said, "The law is not always the same shape—you have done what you have done. I could not have done it in my time, but you come after me. Tell!"

I told and he listened. After that, I wished to tell all the people but he showed me otherwise. He said, "Truth is a hard deer to hunt. If you eat too much truth at once, you may die of the truth. It was not idly that our fathers forbade the Dead Places." He was right—it is better the truth should come little by little. I have learned that, being a priest. Perhaps, in the old days, they ate knowledge too fast.

Nevertheless, we make a beginning. It is not for the metal alone we go to the Dead Places now—there are the books and the writings. They are hard to learn. And the magic tools are broken—but we can look at them and wonder. At least, we make a beginning. And, when I am chief priest we shall go beyond the great river. We shall go to the Place of the Gods—the place new-york—not one man but a company. We shall look for the images of the gods and find the god ASHING and the others—the gods Lincoln and Biltmore and Moses. But they were men who built the city, not gods or demons. They were men. I remember the dead man's face. They were men who were here before us. We must build again.

THE SENTINEL

ARTHUR C. CLARKE

The next time you see the full Moon high in the south, look carefully at its right-hand edge and let your eye travel upward along the curve of the disk. Round about two o'clock you will notice a small, dark oval: anyone with normal eyesight can find it quite easily. It is the great walled plain, one of the finest on the Moon, known as the Mare Crisium—the Sea of Crises. Three hundred miles in diameter, and almost completely surrounded by a ring of magnificent mountains, it had never been explored until we entered it in the late summer of 1996.

Our expedition was a large one. We had two heavy freighters which had flown our supplies and equipment from the main lunar base in the Mare Serenitatis, five hundred miles away. There were also three small rockets which were intended for short-range transport over regions which our surface vehicles couldn't cross. Luckily, most of the Mare Crisium is very flat. There are none of the great crevasses so common and so dangerous elsewhere, and very few craters or mountains of any size. As far as we could tell, our powerful caterpillar tractors would have no difficulty in taking us wherever we wished to go.

I was geologist—or selenologist, if you want to be pedantic—in charge of the group exploring the southern region of the Mare. We had crossed a hundred miles of it in a week, skirting the foothills of the mountains along the shore of what was once the ancient sea, some thousand million years before. When life was beginning on Earth, it was already dying here. The waters were retreating down the flanks of those stupendous cliffs, retreating into the empty heart of the Moon. Over the land which we were crossing, the tideless ocean had once been half a mile deep, and now the only trace of moisture was the hoarfrost one could sometimes find in caves which the searing sunlight never penetrated.

We had begun our journey early in the slow lunar dawn, and still had almost a week of Earth time before nightfall. Half a dozen times a day we would leave our vehicles and go outside in the space suits to hunt for interesting minerals, or to place markers for the guidance of future travelers. It was an uneventful routine. There is nothing hazardous or even particularly exciting about lunar exploration. We could live comfortably for a month in our pressurized tractors, and if we ran into trouble we could always radio for help and sit tight until one of the spaceships came to our rescue.

I said just now that there was nothing exciting about lunar exploration, but of course that isn't true. One could never grow tired of those incredible mountains, so much more rugged than the gentle hills of Earth. We never knew, as we rounded the capes and promontories of that vanished sea, what new splendors would be revealed to us. The whole southern curve of the Mare Crisium is a vast delta where a score of rivers once found their way into the ocean, fed perhaps by the torrential rains that must have lashed the mountains in the brief volcanic age when the Moon was young. Each of these ancient valleys was an invitation, challenging us to climb into the unknown uplands beyond. But we had a hundred miles still to cover and could only look longingly at the heights which others must scale.

We kept Earth time aboard the tractor, and precisely at 2200 hours the final radio message would be sent out to Base and we would close down for the day. Outside, the rocks would still be burning beneath the almost vertical sun, but to us it was night until we awoke again eight hours later. Then one of us would prepare breakfast, there would be a great buzzing of electric razors, and someone would switch on the shortwave radio from Earth. Indeed, when the smell of frying sausages began to fill the cabin, it was sometimes hard to believe that we were not back on our own world—everything was so normal and homely, apart from the feeling of decreased weight and the unnatural slowness with which objects fell.

It was my turn to prepare breakfast in the corner of the main cabin that served as a galley. I can remember that moment quite vividly after all these years, for the radio had just played one of my favorite melodies, the old Welsh air "David of the White Rock." Our driver was already outside in his space suit, inspecting our caterpillar treads. My assistant, Louis Garnett, was up forward in the control position, making belated entries in yesterday's log.

As I stood by the frying pan waiting, like any terrestrial housewife, for the sausage to brown, I let my gaze wander idly over the mountain walls which covered the whole of the southern horizon, marching out of sight to east and west below the curve of the Moon. They seemed only a mile or two from the tractor, but I knew that the nearest was twenty miles away. On the Moon, of course, there is no loss of detail with distance—none of that almost imperceptible haziness which softens and sometimes transfigures all far-off things on Earth.

Those mountains were ten thousand feet high, and they climbed steeply out of the plain as if ages ago some subterranean eruption had smashed them skyward through the molten crust. The base of even the nearest was hidden from sight by the steeply curving surface of the plain, for the Moon is a very little world, and from where I was standing the horizon was only two miles away.

I lifted my eyes toward the peaks which no man had ever climbed, the peaks which, before the coming of terrestrial life, had watched the retreating oceans sink sullenly into their graves, taking with them the hope and the morning promise of a world. The sunlight was beating against those ramparts with a glare that hurt the eyes, yet only a little way above them the stars were shining steadily in a sky blacker than a winter midnight on Earth.

I was turning away when my eye caught a metallic glitter high on the ridge of a great promontory thrusting out into the sea thirty miles to the west. It was a dimensionless point of light, as if a star had been clawed from the sky by one of those cruel peaks, and I imagined that some smooth rock surface was catching the sunlight and heliographing it straight into my eyes. Such things were not uncommon. When the Moon is in her second quarter, observers on Earth can sometimes see the great ranges in the Oceanus Procellarum burning with a blue-white iridescence as the sunlight flashes from their slopes and leaps again from world to world. But I was curious to know what kind of rock could be shining so brightly up there, and I climbed into the observation turret and swung our four-inch telescope round to the west.

I could see just enough to tantalize me. Clear and sharp in the field of vision, the mountain peaks seemed only half a mile away, but whatever was catching the sunlight was still too small to be resolved. Yet it seemed to have an elusive symmetry, and the summit upon which it rested was curiously flat. I stared for a long time at that glittering enigma, straining my eyes into space, until presently a smell of burning from the galley told me that our breakfast sausages had made their quarter-million-mile journey in vain.

All that morning we argued our way across the Mare Crisium while the western mountains reared higher in the sky. Even when we were out prospecting in the space suits, the discussion would continue over the radio. It was absolutely certain, my companions argued, that there had never been any form of intelligent life on the Moon. The only living things that had ever existed there were a few primitive plants and their slightly less degenerate ancestors. I knew that as well as anyone, but there are times when a scientist must not be afraid to make a fool of himself.

"Listen," I said at last, "I'm going up there, if only for my own peace of mind. That mountain's less than twelve thousand feet high—that's only two thousand under Earth gravity—and I can make the trip in twenty hours at the outside. I've always wanted to go up into those hills, anyway, and this gives me an excellent excuse."

"If you don't break your neck," said Garnett, "you'll be the laughingstock of the expedition when we get back to Base. That mountain will probably be called Wilson's Folly from now on."

"I won't break my neck," I said firmly. "Who was the first man to climb Pico and Helicon?"

"But weren't you rather younger in those days?" asked Louis gently.

"That," I said with great dignity, "is as good a reason as any for going."

We went to bed early that night, after driving the tractor to within half a mile of the promontory. Garnett was coming with me in the morning; he was a good climber and had often been with me on such exploits before. Our driver was only too glad to be left in charge of the machine.

At first sight, those cliffs seemed completely unscalable, but to anyone with a good head for heights, climbing is easy on a world where all weights are only a sixth of their normal value. The real danger in lunar mountaineering lies in overconfidence; a six-hundred-foot drop on the Moon can kill you just as thoroughly as a hundred-foot fall on Earth.

We made our first halt on a wide ledge about four thousand feet above the plain. Climbing had not been very difficult, but my limbs were stiff with the unaccustomed effort, and I was glad of the rest. We could see the tractor as a tiny metal insect far down at the foot of the cliff, and we reported our progress to the driver before starting on the next ascent.

Inside our suits it was comfortably cool, for the refrigeration units were fighting the fierce sun and carrying away the body heat of our exertions. We seldom spoke to each other, except to pass climbing instructions and to discuss our best plan of ascent. I do not know what Garnett was thinking, probably that this was the craziest goose chase he had ever embarked upon. I more than half agreed with him, but the joy of climbing, the knowledge that no man had ever gone this way before and the exhilaration of the steadily widening landscape gave me all the reward I needed.

I don't think I was particularly excited when I saw in front of us the wall of rock I had first inspected through the telescope from thirty miles away. It would level off about fifty feet above our heads, and there on the plateau would be the thing that had lured me over these barren wastes. It was, almost certainly, nothing more than a boulder splintered ages ago by a falling meteor, and with its cleavage planes still fresh and bright in this incorruptible, unchanging silence.

There were no handholds on the rock face, and we had to use a grapnel. My tired arms seemed to gain new strength as I swung the three-pronged metal anchor round my head and sent it sailing up toward the stars. The first time it broke loose and came falling slowly back when we pulled the rope. On the third attempt, the prongs gripped firmly and our combined weights could not shift it.

Garnett looked at me anxiously. I could tell that he wanted to go first, but I smiled back at him through the glass of my helmet and shook my head. Slowly, taking my time, I began the final ascent.

Even with my space suit, I weighed only forty pounds here, so I pulled myself up hand over hand without bothering to use my feet. At the rim I paused and waved to my companion; then I scrambled over the edge and stood upright, staring ahead of me.

You must understand that until this very moment I had been almost completely convinced that there could be nothing strange or unusual for me to find here. Almost, but not quite; it was that haunting doubt that had driven me forward. Well, it was a doubt no longer, but the haunting had scarcely begun.

I was standing on a plateau perhaps a hundred feet across. It had once been smooth—too smooth to be natural—but falling meteors had pitted and scored its surface through immeasurable eons. It had been leveled to support a glittering, roughly pyramidal structure, twice as high as a man, that was set in the rock like a gigantic many-faceted jewel.

Probably no emotion at all filled my mind in those first few seconds. Then I felt a great lifting of my heart, and a strange, inexpressible joy. For I loved the Moon, and now I knew that the creeping moss of Aristarchus and Eratosthenes was not the only life she had brought forth in her youth. The old, discredited dream of the first explorers was true. There had, after all, been a lunar civilization—and I was the first to find it. That I had come perhaps a hundred million years too late did not distress me; it was enough to have come at all.

My mind was beginning to function normally, to analyze and to ask questions. Was this a building, a shrine—or something for which my language had no name? If a building, then why was it erected in so uniquely inaccessible a spot? I wondered if it might be a temple, and I could picture the adepts of some strange priesthood calling on their gods to preserve them as the life of the Moon ebbed with the dying oceans, and calling on their gods in vain.

I took a dozen steps forward to examine the thing more closely, but some sense of caution kept me from going too near. I knew a little of archaeology and tried to guess the cultural level of the civilization that must have smoothed this mountain and raised the glittering mirror surfaces that still dazzled my eyes.

The Egyptians could have done it, I thought, if their workmen had possessed whatever strange materials these far more ancient architects had used. Because of the thing's smallness, it did not occur to me that I might be looking at the handiwork of a race more advanced than my own. The idea that the Moon had possessed intelligence at all was still almost too tremendous to grasp, and my pride would not let me take the final, humiliating plunge.

And then I noticed something that set the scalp crawling at the back of my neck—something so trivial and so innocent that many would never have noticed it at all. I have said that the plateau was scarred by meteors; it was also coated inches deep with the cosmic dust that is always filtering down upon the surface of any world where there are no winds to disturb it. Yet the dust and the meteor scratches ended quite abruptly in a wide circle enclosing the little pyramid, as though an invisible wall was protecting it from the ravages of time and the slow but ceaseless bombardment from space.

There was someone shouting in my earphones, and I realized that Garnett had been calling me for some time. I walked unsteadily to the edge of the cliff and signaled him to join me, not trusting myself to speak. Then I went back toward that circle in the dust. I picked up a fragment of splintered rock and tossed it gently toward the shining enigma. If the pebble had vanished at that invisible barrier I should not have been surprised, but it seemed to hit a smooth, hemispherical surface and slide gently to the ground.

I knew then that I was looking at nothing that could be matched in the antiquity of my own race. This was not a building, but a machine, protecting itself with forces that had challenged Eternity. Those forces, whatever they might be, were still operating, and perhaps I had already come too close. I thought of all the radiations man had trapped and tamed in the past century. For all I knew, I might be as irrevocably doomed as if I had stepped into the deadly, silent aura of an unshielded atomic pile.

I remembered turning then toward Garnett, who had joined me and was now standing motionless at my side. He seemed quite oblivious to me, so I did not disturb him but walked to the edge of the cliff in an effort to marshal my thoughts. There below me lay the Mare Crisium —Sea of Crises, indeed—strange and weird to most men, but reassuringly familiar to me. I lifted my eyes toward the crescent Earth, lying in her cradle of stars, and I wondered what her clouds had covered when these unknown builders had finished their work. Was it the steaming jungle of the Carboniferous, the bleak shoreline over which the first amphibians must crawl to conquer the land—or, earlier still, the long loneliness before the coming of life?

Do not ask me why I did not guess the truth sooner—the truth that seems so obvious now. In the first excitement of my discovery, I had assumed without question that this crystalline apparition had been built by some race belonging to the Moon's remote past, but suddenly, and with overwhelming force, the belief came to me that it was as alien to the Moon as I myself.

In twenty years we had found no trace of life but a few degenerate plants. No lunar civilization, whatever its doom, could have left but a single token of its existence.

I looked at the shining pyramid again, and the more remote it seemed from anything that had to do with the Moon. And suddenly I felt myself shaking with a foolish, hysterical laughter, brought on by excitement and overexertion: for I had imagined that the little pyramid was speaking to me and was saying: "Sorry, I'm a stranger here myself."

It has taken us twenty years to crack that invisible shield and to reach the machine inside those crystal walls. What we could not understand, we broke at last with the savage might of atomic power and now I have seen the fragments of the lovely, glittering thing I found up there on the mountain.

They are meaningless. The mechanisms—if indeed they are mechanisms—of the pyramid belong to a technology that lies far beyond our horizon, perhaps to the technology of paraphysical forces.

The mystery haunts us all the more now that the other planets have been reached and we know that only Earth has ever been the home of intelligent life in our Universe. Nor could any lost civilization of our own world have built that machine, for the thickness of the meteoric dust on the plateau has enabled us to measure its age. It was set there upon its mountain before life had emerged from the seas of Earth.

When our world was half its present age, *something* from the stars swept through the Solar System, left this token of its passage, and went again upon its way. Until we destroyed it, that machine was still fulfilling the purpose of its builders; and as to that purpose, here is my guess.

Nearly a hundred thousand million stars are turning in the circle of the Milky Way, and long ago other races on the worlds of other suns must have scaled and passed the heights that we have reached. Think of such civilizations, far back in time against the fading afterglow of Creation, masters of a Universe so young that life as yet had come only to a handful of worlds. Theirs would have been a loneliness we cannot imagine, the loneliness of gods looking out across infinity and finding none to share their thoughts.

They must have searched the star clusters as we have searched the planets. Everywhere there would be worlds, but they would be empty or peopled with crawling, mindless things. Such was our own Earth, the smoke of the great volcanoes still staining the skies, when that first ship of the peoples of the dawn came sliding in from the abyss beyond Pluto. It passed the frozen outer worlds, knowing that life could play no part in their destinies. It came to rest among the inner planets, warming themselves around the fire of the Sun and waiting for their stories to begin.

Those wanderers must have looked on Earth, circling safely in the narrow zone between fire and ice, and must have guessed that it was the favorite of the Sun's children. Here, in the distant future, would be intelligence; but there were countless stars before them still, and they might never come this way again.

So they left a sentinel, one of millions they have scattered throughout the Universe, watching over all worlds with the promise of life. It was a beacon that down the ages has been patiently signaling the fact that no one had discovered it.

Perhaps you understand now why that crystal pyramid was set upon the Moon instead of on the Earth. Its builders were not concerned with races still struggling up from savagery. They would be interested in our civilization only if we proved our fitness to survive—by crossing space and so escaping from the Earth, our cradle. That is the challenge that all intelligent races must meet, sooner or later. It is a double challenge, for it depends in turn upon the conquest of atomic energy and the last choice between life and death.

Once we had passed that crisis, it was only a matter of time before we found the pyramid and forced it open. Now its signals have ceased, and those whose duty it is will be turning their minds upon Earth. Perhaps they wish to help our infant civilization. But they must be very, very old, and the old are often insanely jealous of the young.

I can never look now at the Milky Way without wondering from which of those banked clouds of stars the emissaries are coming. If you will pardon so commonplace a simile, we have set off the fire alarm and have nothing to do but to wait.

I do not think we will have to wait for long.

max ernst

SUMMERTIME ON ICARUS

ARTHUR C. CLARKE

When Colin Sherrard opened his eyes after the crash, he could not imagine where he was. He seemed to be lying, trapped in some kind of vehicle, on the summit of a rounded hill, which sloped steeply away in all directions. Its surface was seared and blackened, as if a great fire had swept over it. Above him was a jet-black sky, crowded with stars; one of them hung like a tiny, brilliant sun low down on the horizon.

Could it be the sun? Was he so far from Earth? No—that was impossible. Some nagging memory told him that the sun was very close—hideously close—not so distant that it had shrunk to a star. And with that thought, full consciousness returned. Sherrard knew exactly where he was, and the knowledge was so terrible that he almost fainted again.

He was nearer to the sun than any man had ever been. His damaged space-pod was lying on no hill, but on the steeply curving surface of a world only two miles in diameter. That brilliant star sinking swiftly in the west was the light of *Prometheus,* the ship that had brought him here across so many millions of miles of space. She was hanging up there among the stars, wondering why his pod had not returned like a homing pigeon to its roost. In a few minutes she would have passed from sight, dropping below the horizon in her perpetual game of hide-and-seek with the sun.

That was a game that he had lost. He was still on the night side of the asteroid, in the cool safety of its shadow, but the short night would be ending soon. The four-hour day of Icarus was spinning him swiftly toward that dreadful dawn, when a sun thirty times larger than ever shone upon Earth would blast these rocks with fire. Sherrard knew all too well why everything around him was burned and blackened. Icarus was still a week from perihelion but the temperature at noon had already reached a thousand degrees Fahrenheit.

Though this was no time for humor, he suddenly remembered Captain McClellan's description of Icarus: "The hottest piece of real estate in the solar system." The truth of that jest had been proved, only a few days before, by one of those simple and unscientific experiments that are so much more impressive than any number of graphs and instrument readings.

Just before daybreak, someone had propped a piece of wood on the summit of one of the tiny hills. Sherrard had been watching, from the safety of the night side, when the first rays of the rising sun had touched the hilltop. When his eyes had adjusted to the sudden detonation of light, he saw that the wood was already beginning to blacken and char. Had there been an atmosphere here, the stick would have burst into flames; such was dawn, upon Icarus. . . .

Yet it had not been impossibly hot at the time of their first landing, when they were passing the orbit of Venus five weeks ago. *Prometheus* had overtaken the asteroid as it was beginning its plunge toward the sun, had matched speed with the little world and had touched down upon its surface as lightly as a snowflake. (A snowflake on Icarus—*that* was quite a thought. . . .) Then the scientists had fanned out across the fifteen square miles of jagged nickel-iron that covered most of the asteroid's surface, setting up their instruments and check-points, collecting samples and making endless observations.

Everything had been carefully planned, years in advance, as part of the International Astrophysical Decade. Here was a unique opportunity for a research ship to get within a mere seventeen million miles of the sun, protected from its fury by a two-mile-thick shield of rock and iron. In the shadow of Icarus, the ship could ride safely round the central fire which warmed all the planets, and upon which the existence of all life depended. As the Prometheus of legend had brought the gift of fire to mankind, so the ship that bore his name would return to Earth with other unimagined secrets from the heavens.

There had been plenty of time to set up the instruments and make the surveys before *Prometheus* had to take off and seek the permanent shade of night. Even then, it was still possible for men in the tiny self-propelled space-pods—miniature spaceships, only ten feet long—to work on the night side for an hour or so, as long as they were not overtaken by the advancing line of sunrise. That had seemed a simple-enough condition to meet, on a world where dawn marched forward at only a mile an hour; but Sherrard had failed to meet it, and the penalty was death.

He was still not quite sure what had happened. He had been replacing a seismograph transmitter at Station 145, unofficially known as Mount Everest because it was a full ninety feet above the surrounding territory. The job had been a perfectly straightforward one, even though he had to do it by remote control through the mechanical arms of his pod. Sherrard was an expert at manipulating these; he could tie knots with his metal fingers almost as quickly as with his flesh-and-bone ones. The task had taken little more than twenty minutes, and then the radioseismograph was on the air again, monitoring the tiny quakes and shudders that racked Icarus in ever-increasing numbers as the asteroid approached the sun. It was small satisfaction to know that he had now made a king-sized addition to the record.

After he had checked the signals, he had carefully replaced the sun screens around the instruments. It was hard to believe that two flimsy sheets of polished metal foil, no thicker than paper, could turn aside a flood of radiation that would melt lead or tin within seconds. But the first screen reflected more than ninety per cent of the sunlight falling upon its mirror surface and the second turned back most of the rest, so that only a harmless fraction of the heat passed through.

He had reported completion of the job, received an acknowledgment from the ship, and prepared to head for home. The brilliant floodlights hanging from *Prometheus*—without which the night side of the asteroid would have been in utter darkness—had been an unmistakable target in the sky. The ship was only two miles up, and in this feeble gravity he could have jumped that distance had he been wearing a planetary-type space suit with flexible legs. As it was, the low-powered microrockets of his pod would get him there in a leisurely five minutes.

He had aimed the pod with its gyros, set the rear jets at Strength Two, and pressed the firing button. There had been a violent explosion somewhere in the vicinity of his feet and he had soared away from Icarus—but not toward the ship. Something was horribly wrong; he was tossed to one side of the vehicle, unable to reach the controls. Only one of the jets was firing, and he was pinwheeling across the sky, spinning faster and faster under the off-balanced drive. He tried to find the cutoff, but the spin had completely disorientated aim. When he was able to locate the controls, his first reaction made matters worse—he pushed the throttle over to full, like a nervous driver stepping on the accelerator instead of the brake. It took only a second to correct the mistake and kill the jet, but by then he was spinning so rapidly that the stars were wheeling round in circles.

Everything had happened so quickly that there was no time

for fear, no time even to call the ship and report what was happening. He took his hands away from the controls; to touch them now would only make matters worse. It would take two or three minutes of cautious jockeying to unravel his spin, and from the flickering glimpses of the approaching rocks it was obvious that he did not have as many seconds. Sherrard remembered a piece of advice at the front of the *Spaceman's Manual* "When you don't know what to do, *do nothing.*" He was still doing it when Icarus fell upon him, and the stars went out.

It had been a miracle that the pod was unbroken and that he was not breathing space. (Thirty minutes from now he might be glad to do so, when the capsule's heat insulation began to fail. . . .) There had been some damage, of course. The rear-view mirrors, just outside the dome of transparent plastic that enclosed his head, were both snapped off, so that he could no longer see what lay behind him without twisting his neck. This was a trivial mishap; far more serious was the fact that his radio antennas had been torn away by the impact. He could not call the ship, and the ship could not call him. All that came over the radio was a faint crackling, probably produced inside the set itself. He was absolutely alone, cut off from the rest of the human race.

It was a desperate situation, but there was one faint ray of hope. He was not, after all, completely helpless. Even if he could not use the pod's rockets—he guessed that the starboard motor had blown back and ruptured a fuel line, something the designers said was impossible—he was still able to move. He had his arms.

But which way should he crawl? He had lost all sense of location, for though he had taken off from Mount Everest, he might now be thousands of feet away from it. There were no recognizable landmarks in his tiny world; the rapidly sinking star of *Prometheus* was his best guide, and if he could keep the ship in view he would be safe. It would only be a matter of minutes before his absence was noted, if indeed it had not been discovered already. Yet without radio, it might take his colleagues a long time to find him; small though Icarus was, its fifteen square miles of fantastically rugged no man's land could provide an effective hiding place for a ten-foot cylinder. It might take an hour to locate him—which meant that he would have to keep ahead of the murderous sunrise.

He slipped his fingers into the controls that worked his mechanical limbs. Outside the pod, in the hostile vacuum that surrounded him, his substitute arms came to life. They reached down, thrust against the iron surface of the asteroid, and levered the pod from the ground. Sherrard flexed them, and the capsule jerked forward, like some weird, two-legged insect . . . first the right arm, then the left, then the right. . . .

It was less difficult than he had feared, and for the first time he felt his confidence return. Though his mechanical arms had been designed for light precision work, it needed very little pull to set the capsule moving in this weightless environment. The gravity of Icarus was ten thousand times weaker than Earth's: Sherrard and his space-pod weighed less than an ounce here, and once he had set himself in motion he floated forward with an effortless, dreamlike ease.

Yet that very effortlessness had its dangers. He had traveled several hundred yards, and was rapidly overhauling the sinking star of the *Prometheus,* when overconfidence betrayed him. (Strange how quickly the mind could switch from one extreme to the other; a few minutes ago he had been steeling himself to face death—now he was wondering if he would be late for dinner.) Perhaps the novelty of the movement, so unlike anything he had ever attempted before, was responsible for the catastrophe; or perhaps he was still suffering from the after-effects of the crash.

Like all astronauts, Sherrard had learned to orientate himself in space, and had grown accustomed to living and working when the Earthly conceptions of up and down were meaningless. On a world such as Icarus, it was necessary to pretend that there was a real, honest-to-goodness planet "beneath" your feet, and that when you moved you were traveling over a horizontal plain. If this innocent self-deception failed, you were heading for space vertigo.

The attack came without warning, as it usually did. Quite suddenly, Icarus no longer seemed to be beneath him, the stars no longer above. The universe tilted through a right angle; he was moving straight *up* a vertical cliff, like a mountaineer scaling a rock face, and though Sherrard's reason told him that this was pure illusion, all his senses screamed that it was true. In a moment gravity must drag him off this sheer wall, and he would drop down mile upon endless mile until he smashed into oblivion.

Worse was to come; the false vertical was still swinging like a compass needle that had lost the pole. Now he was on the *underside* of an immense rocky roof, like a fly clinging to a ceiling; in another moment it would have become a wall again—but this time he would be moving straight down it, instead of up. . . .

He had lost all control over the pod, and the clammy sweat that had begun to dew his brow warned him that he would soon lose control over his body. There was only one thing to do; he clenched his eyes tightly shut, squeezed as far back as possible into the tiny closed world of the capsule, and pretended with all his might that the universe outside did not exist. He did not even allow the slow, gentle crunch of his second crash to interfere with his self-hypnosis.

When he again dared to look outside, he found that the pod had come to rest against a large boulder. Its mechanical arms had broken the force of the impact, but at a cost that was more than he could afford to pay. Though the capsule was virtually weightless here, it still possessed its normal five hundred pounds of inertia, and it had been moving at perhaps four miles an hour. The momentum had been too much for the metal arms to absorb; one had snapped, and the other was hopelessly bent.

When he saw what had happened, Sherrard's first reaction was not despair, but anger. He had been so certain of success when the pod had started its glide across the barren face of Icarus. And now this, all through a moment of physical weakness! But space made no allowance for human frailties or emotions, and a man who did not accept that fact had no right to be here.

At least he had gained precious time in his pursuit of the ship; he had put an extra ten minutes, if not more, between himself and dawn. Whether that ten minutes would merely prolong the agony or whether it would give his shipmates the extra time they needed to find him, he would soon know.

Where were they? Surely they had started the search by now! He strained his eyes toward the brilliant star of the ship, hoping to pick out the fainter lights of space-pods moving toward him—but nothing else was visible against the slowly turning vault of heaven.

He had better look to his own resources, slender though they were. Only a few minutes were left before the *Prometheus* and her trailing lights would sink below the edge of the asteroid and leave him in darkness. It was true that the darkness would be all too brief, but before it fell upon him he might find some shelter against the coming day. This rock into which he had crashed, for example. . . .

Yes, it would give some shade, until the sun was halfway up the sky. Nothing could protect him if it passed right overhead, but it was just possible that he might be in a latitude where the sun never rose far above the horizon at this season of Icarus' four-hundred-and-nine-day year. Then he might survive the brief period of daylight; that was his only hope, if the rescuers did not find him before dawn.

There went *Prometheus* and her lights, below the edge of the world. With her going, the now-unchallenged stars blazed forth with redoubled brilliance. More glorious than any of them—so lovely that even to look upon it almost brought tears to his eyes—was the blazing beacon of Earth, with its companion moon beside it. He had been born on one, and had walked on the other; would he see either again?

Strange that until now he had given no thought to his wife and children, and to all that he loved in the life that now seemed so far away. He felt a spasm of guilt, but it passed swiftly. The ties of affection were not weakened, even across the hundred million miles of space that now sundered him from his family. At this moment, they were simply irrelevant. He was now a primitive, self-centered animal fighting for his life, and his only weapon was his brain. In this conflict, there was no place for the heart; it would merely be a hindrance, spoiling his judgment and weakening his resolution.

And then he saw something that banished all thoughts of his distant home. Reaching up above the horizon behind him, spreading across the stars like a milky mist, was a faint and ghostly cone of phosphorescence. It was the herald of the sun—the beautiful, pearly phantom of the corona, visible on Earth only during the rare moments of a total eclipse. When the corona was rising, the sun would not be far behind, to smite this little land with fury.

Sherrard made good use of the warning. Now he could judge with some accuracy the exact point where the sun would rise. Crawling slowly and clumsily on the broken stumps of his metal arms, he dragged the capsule round to the side of the boulder that should give the greatest shade. He had barely reached it when the sun was upon him like a beast of prey, and his tiny world exploded into light.

He raised the dark filters inside his helmet, one thickness after another, until he could endure the glare. Except where the broad shadow of the boulder lay across the asteroid, it was like looking into a furnace. Every detail of the desolate land around him was revealed by that merciless light; there were no greys, only blinding whites and impenetrable blacks. All the shadowed cracks and hollows were pools of ink, while the higher ground already seemed to be on fire, as it caught the sun. Yet it was only a minute after dawn.

Now Sherrard could understand how the scorching heat of a

billion summers had turned Icarus into a cosmic cinder, baking the rocks until the last traces of gas had bubbled out of them. Why should men travel, he asked himself bitterly, across the gulf of stars at such expense and risk—merely to land on a spinning slag heap? For the same reason, he knew, that they had once struggled to reach Everest and the Poles and the far places of the Earth—for the excitement of the body that was adventure, and the more enduring excitement of the mind that was discovery. It was an answer that gave him little consolation, now that he was about to be grilled like a joint on the turning spit of Icarus.

Already he could feel the first breath of heat upon his face. The boulder against which he was lying gave him protection from direct sunlight, but the glare reflected back at him from those blazing rocks only a few yards away was striking through the transparent plastic of the dome. It would grow swiftly more intense as the sun rose higher; he had even less time than he had thought, and with the knowledge came a kind of numb resignation that was beyond fear. He would wait —if he could—until the sunrise engulfed him and the capsule's cooling unit gave up the unequal struggle; then he would crack the pod and let the air gush out into the vacuum of space.

Nothing to do but to sit and think in the minutes that were left to him before his pool of shadow contracted. He did not try to direct his thoughts, but let them wander where they willed. How strange that he should be dying now, because back in the nineteen-forties—years before he was born—a man at Palomar had spotted a streak of light on a photographic plate and had named it so appropriately after the boy who flew too near the sun.

One day, he supposed, they would build a monument here for him on this blistered plain. What would they inscribe upon it? "Here died Colin Sherrard, astronics engineer, in the cause of Science." That would be funny, for he had never understood half the things that the scientists were trying to do.

Yet some of the excitement of their discoveries had communicated itself to him. He remembered how the geologists had scraped away the charred skin of the asteroid, and had polished the metallic surface that lay beneath. It had been covered with a curious pattern of lines and scratches, like one of the abstract paintings of the Post-Picasso Decadents. But these lines had some meaning; they wrote the history of Icarus, though only a geologist could read it. They revealed, so Sherrard had been told, that this lump of iron and rock had not always floated alone in space. At some remote time in the past, it had been under enormous pressure—and that could mean only one thing. Billions of years ago it had been part of a much larger body, perhaps a planet like Earth. For some reason that planet had blown up, and Icarus and all the thousands of other asteroids were the fragments of that cosmic explosion.

Even at this moment, as the incandescent line of sunlight came closer, this was a thought that stirred his mind. What Sherrard was lying upon was the core of a world—perhaps a world that had once known life. In a strange, irrational way it comforted him to know that his might not be the only ghost to haunt Icarus until the end of time.

The helmet was misting up; that could only mean that the cooling unit was about to fail. It had done its work well; even now, though the rocks only a few yards away must be glowing a sullen red, the heat inside the capsule was not unendurable. When failure came, it would be sudden and catastrophic.

He reached for the red lever that would rob the sun of its prey—but before he pulled it, he would look for the last time upon Earth. Cautiously, he lowered the dark filters, adjusting them so that they still cut out the glare from the rocks, but no longer blocked his view of space.

The stars were faint now, dimmed by the advancing glow of the corona. And just visible over the boulder whose shield would soon fail him was a stub of crimson flame, a crooked finger of fire jutting from the edge of the sun itself. He had only seconds left.

There was the Earth, there was the moon. Good-bye to them both, and to his friends and loved ones on each of them. While he was looking at the sky, the sunlight had begun to lick the base of the capsule, and he felt the first touch of fire. In a reflex as automatic as it was useless, he drew up his legs, trying to escape the advancing wave of heat.

What was that? A brilliant flash of light, infinitely brighter than any of the stars, had suddenly exploded overhead. Miles above him, a huge mirror was sailing across the sky, reflecting the sunlight as it slowly turned through space. Such a thing was utterly impossible; he was beginning to suffer from hallucinations, and it was time he took his leave. Already the sweat was pouring from his body, and in a few seconds the capsule would be a furnace.

He waited no longer, but pulled on the Emergency Release with all his waning strength, bracing himself at the same moment to face the end.

Nothing happened; the lever would not move. He tugged it again and again before he realized that it was hopelessly jammed. There was no easy way out for him, no merciful death as the air gushed from his lungs. It was then, as the true terror of his situation struck home to him, that his nerve finally broke and he began to scream like a trapped animal.

When he heard Captain McClellan's voice speaking to him, thin but clear, he knew that it must be another hallucination. Yet some last remnant of discipline and self-control checked his screaming; he clenched his teeth and listened to that familiar, commanding voice.

"Sherrard! Hold on, man! We've got a fix on you—but keep shouting!"

"Here I am!" he cried, "but hurry, for God's sake! I'm burning!"

Deep down in what was left of his rational mind he realized what had happened. Some feeble ghost of a signal was leaking through the broken stubs of his antennas, and the searchers had heard his screams—as he was hearing their voices. That meant they must be very close indeed, and the knowledge gave him sudden strength.

He stared through the steaming plastic of the dome, looking once more for that impossible mirror in the sky. There it was again—and now he realized that the baffling perspectives of space had trickled his senses. The mirror was not miles away, nor was it huge. It was almost on top of him, and it was moving fast.

He was still shouting when it slid across the face of the rising sun, and its blessed shadow fell upon him like a cool wind that had blown out of the heart of winter, over leagues of snow and ice. Now that it was so close, he recognized it at once; it was merely a large metal-foil radiation screen, no doubt hastily snatched from one of the instrument sites. In the safety of its shadow, his friends had been searching for him.

A heavy-duty, two-man capsule was hovering overhead, holding the glittering shield in one set of arms and reaching for him with the other. Even through the misty dome and the haze of heat that still sapped his senses, he recognized Captain McClellan's anxious face, looking down at him from the other pod.

So this was what birth was like, for truly he had been reborn.

He was too exhausted for gratitude—that would come later—but as he rose from the burning rocks his eyes sought and found the bright star of Earth. "Here I am," he said silently. "I'm coming back."

Back to enjoy and cherish all the beauties of the world he had thought was lost forever. No—not all of them.

He would never enjoy summer again.

SPACE MAN

BABETTE DEUTSCH

Jetted like the circus's
Human bullet, he'll face
A public privacy
For the space of his throttled jaunt.
Returning,
Will he be implacably displaced,
Haunted by earthlessness?
Craving the unknown, he endures,
Abides its brood of dangers,
Even this one of being
Always a stranger
To those riding at our planet's pace only around
The simple sun.

I AM A

LENORE MARSHALL

Cosmonaut
Cradled in dangers
Orbiting a garden universe
Snipping cosmos, probing Venus,
Sighting summer's end blindly,
Weightily weightless
Spinning out of reach,
            out
              of
                reach
Signaling strangers.

OFF COURSE

EDWIN MORGAN

the golden flood the weightless seat
the cabin song the pitch black
the growing beard the floating crumb
the shining rendezvouz the orbit wisecrack
the hot spacesuit the smuggled mouth-organ
the imaginary somersault the visionary sunrise
the turning continents the space debris
the golden lifeline the space walk
the crawling deltas the camera moon
the pitch velvet the rough sleep
the crackling headphone the space silence
the turning earth the lifeline continents
the cabin sunrise the hot flood
the shining spacesuit the growing moon
the crackling somersault the smuggled orbit
the rough moon the visionary rendezvouz
the weightless headphone the cabin debris
the floating lifeline the pitch sleep
the crawling camera the turning silence
the space crumb the crackling beard
the orbit mouth-organ the floating song

ORBITER 5 SHOWS HOW EARTH LOOKS FROM THE MOON

There's a woman in the earth, sitting on
her heels. You see her from the back, in three-
quarter profile. She has a flowing pigtail. She's
holding something
in her right hand—some holy jug. Her left arm is thinner,
in a gesture like a dancer. She's the Indian Ocean. Asia is
light swirling up out of her vessel. Her pigtail points to Europe
and her dancer's arm is the Suez Canal. She is a woman
in a square kimono,
bare feet tucked beneath the tip of Africa. Her tail of long hair is
the Arabian Peninsula.

A woman in the earth.

A man in the moon.

MAY SWENSON

THE FLIGHT OF APOLLO

STANLEY KUNITZ

I

Earth was my home, but even there I was a
stranger. This mineral crust. I walk like a
swimmer. What titanic bombardments in those old
astral wars! I know what I know: I shall never
escape from strangeness or complete my journey.
Think of me as nostalgic, afraid, exalted. I am
your man on the moon, a speck of megalomania, restless for the leap towards island universes pulsing
beyond where the constellations set. Infinite
space overwhelms the human heart, but in the middle
of nowhere life inexorably calls to life. Forward
my mail to Mars. What news from the Great Spiral
Nebula in Andromeda and the Magellanic Clouds?

II

I was a stranger on earth.
Stepping on the moon, I begin
the gay pilgrimage to new
Jerusalems
in foreign galaxies
Heat. Cold. Craters of silence.
The Sea of Tranquillity
rolling on the shores of entropy.
And, beyond,
the intelligence of the stars.

VOYAGE TO THE MOON

WILLIAM DICKEY

Of that world, having returned from it, I may say
There is no romance there, no air being present
To carry the sound of compliment. The inhabitants
Cannot smell one another, even when the sun
At long midday heats them beyond our temperature.

It is therefore a nation of pure philosophy
Without sin or absolution. The swift works
Of their brains show through their crystal faces
With absolute consonance. The pattern of their thoughts
Is like that of pleased clocks agreeing on an hour.

They are advanced in mathematics. The closest thing
To affection I could observe among them was
The appreciation of a theorem shared by two
Investigators. The emotion was expressed
By a formal, rapid exchanging of prime numbers.

The air of earth would surely be fatal to them,
Our sounds shatter, our perfumes corrode them. But
What would bring them, I think, most entirely to a stop
Would be to watch our explosions of hate and love
Which may serve as armament for the next expedition.

AFTERWARDS

EDWARD LUCIE-SMITH

Inhospitable.
            Another bald
Barren lump spinning in a thin shawl
Of unbreathable gas. I see it
From my narrow window, from what these
Hovering needles tell me in their
Too truthful gauges. I might descend,
Opening the airlock, adjusting my
Cumbersome helmet, hands gloved thick
Against the cold, or heat, or acid,
Strapping upon my back the light slim
Canister of my own atmosphere—
And each breath links me again with what,
The further I travel seems stranger:
Greenness, water, movement, a sphere not
Sufficient unto itself, but once
Happy to feed and lodge an itchy
Parasite.
            Now inhospitable.

A PROJECTION

REED WHITTEMORE

I wish they would hurry up their trip to Mars,
Those rocket gentlemen.
We have been waiting too long; the fictions of little men
And canals,
And of planting and raising flags and opening markets
For beads, cheap watches, perfume and plastic jewelry—
All these begin to be tedious; what we need now
Is the real thing, a thoroughly bang-up voyage
Of discovery.

Led by Admiral Byrd
In the *Nina, Pinta* and *Santa Maria*
With a crew of hundreds of experts
In physics, geology, war and creative writing,
The expedition should sail with a five-year supply
Of Pemmican, Jello, Moxie,
Warm woolen socks and jars of Gramma's preserves.

Think of them out there,
An ocean of space before them, using no compass,
Guiding themselves by speculative equations,
Looking,
Looking into the night and thinking now
There are no days, no seasons, time
Is only on watches,
                    and landing on Venus
Through some slight error, bearing
Proclamations of friendship,
Declarations of interstellar faith,
Acknowledgments of American supremacy,
And advertising matter.

I wonder,
Out in the pitch of space, having worlds enough,
If the walled-up, balled-up self could from its alley
Sally.
I wish they would make provisions for this,
Those rocket gentlemen.

WE'LL ALL BE SPACEMEN BEFORE WE DIE

MIKE EVANS

We'll all be spacemen before we die
flying in purple ships
to the sun
like children
on their first trip
to the sea.

We'll all be spacemen before we die
striding across
blue meadows
the rain
under our feet.

We'll all be spacemen before we die
sleeping
between black velvet sheets
woken
only by the moon

MOONSHOT SONNET

MARY ELLEN SOLT

THE ENCHANTED VILLAGE

A. E. VAN VOGT

Explorers of a new frontier they had been called before they left for Mars.

For a while after the ship crashed into a Martian desert, killing all on board except—miraculously—this one man, Bill Jenner spat the words occasionally into the constant, sand-laden wind. He despised himself for the pride he had felt when he first heard them.

His fury faded with each mile that he walked, and his black grief for his friends became a gray ache. Slowly he realized that he had made a ruinous misjudgment.

He had underestimated the speed at which the rocketship had been traveling. He'd guessed that he would have to walk three hundred miles to reach the shallow, Polar sea he and the others had observed as they glided in from outer space. Actually, the ship must have flashed an immensely greater distance before it hurtled down out of control.

The days stretched behind him, seemingly as numberless as the hot, red, alien sand that scorched through his tattered clothes. This huge scarecrow of a man kept moving across the endless, arid waste. He would not give up.

By the time he came to the mountain, his food had long been gone. Of his four waterbags, only one remained; and that was so close to being empty that he merely wet his cracked lips and swollen tongue whenever his thirst became unbearable.

Jenner climbed high before he realized that it was not just another dune that had barred his way. He paused, and as he gazed up at the mountain that towered above him, he cringed a little. For an instant, he felt the hopelessness of this mad race he was making to nowhere—but he reached the top. He saw that below him was a depression surrounded by hills as high or higher than the one on which he stood. Nestled in the valley they made was a village.

He could see trees, and the marble floor of a courtyard. A score of buildings were clustered around what seemed to be a central square. They were mostly low-constructed, but there were four towers pointing gracefully into the sky. They shone in the sunlight with a marble luster.

Faintly, there came to Jenner's ear a thin, high-pitched whistling sound. It rose, fell, faded completely, then came up again clearly and unpleasantly. Even as Jenner ran toward it, the noise grated on his ears, eerie and unnatural.

He kept slipping on smooth rock, and bruised himself when he fell. He rolled halfway down into the valley. The buildings remained new and bright, when seen from nearby. Their walls flashed with reflections. On every side was vegetation—reddish-green shrubbery—yellow-green trees laden with purple and red fruit.

With ravenous intent, Jenner headed for the nearest fruit tree. Close up, the tree looked dry and brittle. The large red fruit he tore from the lowest branch, however, was plump and juicy.

As he lifted it to his mouth, he remembered that he had been warned during his training period to taste nothing on Mars until it had been chemically examined. But that was meaningless advice to a man whose only chemical equipment was in his own body.

Nevertheless, the possibility of danger made him cautious. He took his first bite gingerly. It was bitter to his tongue, and he spat it out hastily. Some of the juice which remained in his mouth seared his gums. He felt the fire of it, and he reeled from nausea. His muscles began to jerk, and he lay down on the marble to keep himself from falling. After what seemed like hours to Jenner, the awful trembling finally went out of his body, and he could see again. He looked up despisingly at the tree.

The pain finally left him, and slowly he relaxed. A soft breeze rustled the dry leaves. Nearby trees took up that gentle clamor, and it struck Jenner that the wind here in the valley was only a whisper of what it had been on the flat desert beyond the mountain.

There was no other sound now. Jenner abruptly remembered the high-pitched, ever-changing whistle he had heard. He lay very still, listening intently, but there was only the rustling of the leaves. The noisy shrilling had stopped. He wondered if it had been an alarm, to warn the villagers of his approach.

Anxiously, he climbed to his feet and fumbled for his gun. A sense of disaster shocked through him. It wasn't there. His mind was a blank, and then he vaguely recalled that he had first missed the weapon more than a week before. He looked around him uneasily, but there was not a sign of creature life. He braced himself. He couldn't leave, as there was nowhere to go. If necessary, he would fight to the death to remain in the village.

Carefully Jenner took a sip from his water bag, moistening his cracked lips and his swollen tongue. Then he replaced the cap and started through a double line of trees toward the nearest building. He made a wide circle to observe it from several vantage points. On one side a low, broad archway opened into the interior. Through it, he could dimly make out the polished gleam of a marble floor.

Jenner explored the buildings from the outside, always keeping a respectful distance between him and any of the entrances. He saw no sign of animal life. He reached the far side of the marble platform on which the village was built and turned back decisively. It was time to explore interiors.

He chose one of the four-tower buildings. As he came within a dozen feet of it, he saw that he would have to stoop low to get inside.

Momentarily, the implications of that stopped him. These buildings had been constructed for a life form that must be very different from human beings.

He went forward again, bent down, and entered reluctantly, every muscle tensed.

He found himself in a room without furniture. However, there were several low, marble fences projecting from one marble wall. They formed what looked like a group of four wide, low stalls. Each stall had an open trough carved out of the floor.

The second chamber was fitted with four inclined planes of marble, each of which slanted up to a dais. Altogether, there were four rooms on the lower floor. From one of them, a circular ramp mounted up, apparently to a tower room.

Jenner didn't investigate the upstairs. The earlier fear that he would find alien life was yielding to the deadly conviction that he wouldn't. No life meant no food, nor chance of getting any. In frantic haste, he hurried from building to building, peering into the silent rooms, pausing now and then to shout hoarsely.

Finally, there was no doubt. He was alone in a deserted village on a lifeless planet, without food, without water—except for the pitiful supply in his bag—and without hope.

He was in the fourth and smallest room of one of the tower buildings when he realized that he had come to the end of his search. The room had a single "stall" jutting out from one wall. Wearily, Jenner lay down in it. He must have fallen asleep instantly.

When he awoke, he became aware of two things, one right

after the other. The first realization occurred before he opened his eyes—the whistling sound was back, high and shrill; it wavered at the threshold of audibility.

The other was that a fine spray of liquid was being directed down at him from the ceiling. It had an odor, of which Technician Jenner took a single whiff. Quickly he scrambled out of the room, coughing, tears in his eyes, his face already burning from chemical reaction.

He snatched his handkerchief and hastily wiped the exposed parts of his body and face.

He reached the outside, and there paused, striving to understand what had happened.

The village seemed unchanged.

Leaves trembled in a gentle breeze. The sun was poised on a mountain peak. Jenner guessed from its position that it was morning again, and that he had slept at least a dozen hours. The glaring white light suffused the valley. Half hidden by trees and shrubbery, the buildings flashed and shimmered.

He seemed to be in an oasis in a vast desert. It was an oasis all right, Jenner reflected grimly, but not for a human being. For him, with its poisonous fruit, it was more like a tantalizing mirage.

He went back inside the building, and cautiously peered into the room where he had slept. The spray of gas had stopped, not a bit of odor lingered, and the air was fresh and clean.

He edged over the threshold, half-inclined to make a test. He had a picture in his mind of a long-dead Martian creature lazing on the floor in the "stall" while a soothing chemical sprayed down on its body. The fact that the chemical was deadly to human beings merely emphasized how alien to man was the life that had spawned on Mars. But there seemed little doubt of the reason for the gas. The creature was accustomed to taking a morning shower.

Inside the "bathroom," Jenner eased himself feet first into the stall. As his hips came level with the stall entrance, the solid ceiling sprayed a jet of yellowish gas straight down upon his legs. Hastily, Jenner pulled himself clear of the stall. The gas stopped as suddenly as it had started.

He tried it again, to make sure it was merely an automatic process. It turned on, then it shut off.

Jenner's thirst-puffed lips parted with excitement. He thought, "If there can be one automatic process, there may be others."

Breathing heavily, he raced into the outer room. Carefully he shoved his legs into one of the two stalls. The moment his hips were in, a steaming gruel filled the trough beside the wall.

He stared at the greasy looking stuff with a horrified fascination —food—and drink. He remembered the poison fruit and felt repelled, but he forced himself to bend down and put his finger into the hot, wet substance. He brought it up, dripping, to his mouth.

It tasted flat and pulpy, like boiled wood fiber. It trickled viscously into his throat. His eyes began to water, and his lips drew back convulsively. He realized he was going to be sick and ran for the outer door—but didn't quite make it.

When he finally got outside, he felt limp and unutterably listless. In that depressed state of mind, he grew aware again of the shrill sound.

He felt amazed that he could have ignored its rasping even for a few minutes. Sharply, he glanced about, trying to determine its source, but it seemed to have none. Whenever he approached a point where it appeared to be loudest, then it would fade, or shift, perhaps to the far side of the village.

He tried to imagine what an alien culture would want with a mind-shattering noise—although, of course, it would not necessarily have been unpleasant to them.

He stopped, and snapped his fingers as a wild but nevertheless plausible notion entered his mind. Could this be music?

He toyed with the idea, trying to visualize the village as it had been long ago. Here, a music-loving race had possibly gone about its daily tasks to the accompaniment of what was to them beautiful strains of melody.

The hideous whistling went on and on, waxing and waning. Jenner tried to put buildings between himself and the sound. He sought refuge in various rooms, hoping that at least one would be sound-proof. None were. The whistle followed him wherever he went.

He retreated into the desert and had to climb halfway up one of the slopes before the noise was low enough not to disturb him. Finally, breathless but immeasurably relieved, he sank down on the sand, and thought blankly:

What now?

The scene that spread before him had in it qualities of both heaven and hell. It was all too familiar now—the red sands, the stony dunes, the small, alien village promising so much and fulfilling so little.

Jenner looked down at it with his feverish eyes and ran his parched tongue over his cracked, dry lips. He knew that he was a dead man unless he could alter the automatic food-making machines that must be hidden somewhere in the walls and under the floors of the buildings.

In ancient days, a remnant of Martian civilization had survived here in this village. The inhabitants had died off but the village lived on, keeping itself clean of sand, able to provide refuge for any Martian who might come along. But there were no Martians. There was only Bill Jenner, pilot of the first rocketship ever to land on Mars.

He had to make the village turn out food and drink that he could take. Without tools, except his hands; with scarcely any knowledge of chemistry, he must force it to change its habits.

Tensely, he hefted his water bag. He took another sip, and fought the same grim fight to prevent himself from guzzling it down to the last drop. And, when he had won the battle once more, he stood up and started down the slope.

He could last, he estimated, not more than three days. In that time, he must conquer the village.

He was already among the trees when it suddenly struck him that the "music" had stopped. Relieved, he bent over a small shrub, took a good, firm hold of it—and pulled.

It came up easily, and there was a slab of marble attached to it. Jenner stared at it, noting with surprise that he had been mistaken in thinking the stalk came up through a hole in the marble. It was merely stuck to the surface. Then he noticed something else—the shrub had no roots. Almost instinctively, Jenner looked down at the spot from which he had torn the slab of marble along with the plant. There was sand there.

He dropped the shrub, slipped to his knees, and plunged his fingers into the sand. Loose sand trickled through them. He reached deep, using all his strength to force his arm and hand down—sand—nothing but sand.

He stood up, and frantically tore up another shrub. It also came easily, bringing with it a slab of marble. It had no roots, and where it had been was sand.

With a kind of mindless disbelief, Jenner rushed over to a fruit tree and shoved at it. There was a momentary resistance, and then the marble on which it stood split and lifted slowly into the air. The tree fell over with a swish and a crackle as its dry branches and leaves broke and crumbled in a thousand pieces. Underneath where it had been, was sand.

Sand everywhere. A city built on sand. Mars, planet of sand. That was not completely true, of course. Seasonal vegetation had been observed near the polar icecaps. All but the hardiest of it died with the coming of summer. It had been intended that the rocketship land near one of those shallow, tideless seas.

By coming down out of control, the ship had wrecked more than itself. It had wrecked the chances for life of the only survivor of the voyage.

Jenner came slowly out of his daze. He had a thought then. He picked up one of the shrubs he had already torn loose, braced his foot against the marble to which it was attached and tugged, gently at first, then with increasing strength.

It came loose finally, but there was no doubt that the two were part of a whole. The shrub was growing out of the marble.

Marble? Jenner knelt beside one of the holes from which he had torn a slab, and bent over an adjoining section. It was quite porous —calciferous rock, most likely, but not true marble at all. As he reached toward it, intending to break off a piece, it changed color. Astounded, Jenner drew back. Around the break, the stone was turning a bright orange-yellow. He studied it uncertainly, then tentatively he touched it.

It was as if he had dipped his fingers into searing acid. There was a sharp, biting, burning pain. With a gasp, Jenner jerked his hand clear.

The continuing anguish made him feel faint. He swayed and moaned, clutching the bruised members to his body. When the agony finally faded, and he could look at the injury, he saw that the skin had peeled, and that already blood blisters had formed. Grimly, Jenner looked down at the break in the stone. The edges remained bright orange-yellow.

The village was alert, ready to defend itself from further attacks.

Suddenly weary, he crawled into the shade of a tree. There was only one possible conclusion to draw from what had happened, and it almost defied common sense. This lonely village was alive.

As he lay there, Jenner tried to imagine a great mass of living substance growing into the shape of buildings, adjusting itself to suit another life form, accepting the role of servant in the widest meaning of the term.

If it would serve one race, why not another? If it could adjust to Martians, why not to human beings?

There would be difficulties, of course. He guessed wearily that essential elements would not be available. The oxygen for water could come from the air . . . thousands of compounds could be made from sand . . . though it meant death if he failed to find a solution, he fell asleep even as he started to think about what they might be.

When he awoke, it was quite dark. Jenner climbed heavily to his feet. There was a drag to his muscles that alarmed him. He wet his mouth from his water bag, and staggered toward the entrance of the nearest building. Except for the scraping of his shoes on the "marble," the silence was intense.

He stopped short—listened, and looked. The wind had died away. He couldn't see the mountains that rimmed the valley, but the buildings were still dimly visible, black shadows in a shadow world.

For the first time, it seemed to him that, in spite of his new hope, it might be better if he died. Even if he survived, what had he to look forward to? Only too well he recalled how hard it had been to rouse interest in the trip and to raise the large amount of money required. He remembered the colossal problems that had had to be solved in building the ship, and some of the men who had solved them were buried somewhere in the Martian desert.

It might be twenty years before another ship from Earth would try to reach the only other planet in the solar system that had shown signs of being able to support life.

During those uncountable days and nights, those years, he would be here alone. That was the most he could hope for—if he lived. As he fumbled his way to a dais in one of the rooms, Jenner considered another problem:

How did one let a living village know that it must alter its processes? In a way, it must already have grasped that it had a new tenant. How could he make it realize he needed food in a different chemical combination than that which it had served in the past; that he liked music, but on a different scale system; and that he could use a shower each morning—of water, not of poison gas?

He dozed fitfully, like a man who is sick rather than sleepy. Twice, he wakened, his lips on fire, his eyes burning, his body bathed in perspiration. Several times he was startled into consciousness by the sound of his own harsh voice crying out in anger and fear at the night.

He guessed, then, that he was dying.

He spent the long hours of darkness tossing, turning, twisting, befuddled by waves of heat. As the light of morning came, he was vaguely surprised to realize that he was still alive. Restlessly, he climbed off the dais, and went to the door.

A bitingly cold wind blew, but it felt good to his hot face. He wondered if there was enough *pneumococcus* in his blood for him to catch pneumonia. He decided not.

In a few moments he was shivering. He retreated back into the house, and for the first time noticed that, despite the doorless doorway, the wind did not come into the building at all. The rooms were cold, but not draughty.

That started an association: Where had this terrible body heat come from? He teetered over to the dais where he had spent the night. Within seconds, he was sweltering in a temperature of about a hundred and thirty.

He climbed off the dais, shaken by his own stupidity. He estimated that he had sweated at least two quarts of moisture out of his dried-up body on that furnace of a bed.

This village was not for human beings. Here, even the beds were heated for creatures who needed temperatures far beyond the heat comfortable for men.

Jenner spent most of the day in the shade of a large tree. He felt exhausted, and only occasionally did he even remember that he had a problem. When the whistling started, it bothered him at first, but he was too tired to move away from it. There were long periods when he hardly heard it, so dulled were his senses.

Late in the afternoon, he remembered the shrubs and the tree he had torn up the day before, and wondered what had happened to them. He wet his swollen tongue with the last few drops of water in his bag, climbed lackadaisically to his feet, and went to look for the dried-up remains.

There weren't any. He couldn't even find the holes where he had torn them out. The living village had absorbed the dead tissue into itself and repaired the breaks in its "body."

That galvanized Jenner. He began to think again . . . about

mutations, genetic readjustment, life forms adapting to new environments. There'd been lectures on that before the ship left Earth, rather generalized talks designed to acquaint the explorers with the problems men might face on an alien planet. The important principle was quite simple: adjust or die.

The village had to adjust to him. He doubted if he could seriously damage it, but he could try. His own need to survive must be placed on as sharp and hostile a basis as that.

Frantically, Jenner began to search his pockets. Before leaving the rocket, he had loaded himself with odds and ends of small equipment. A jackknife, a folding metal cup, a printed radio, a tiny superbattery that could be charged by spinning an attached wheel—and for which he had brought along, among other things, a powerful electric fire lighter.

Jenner plugged the lighter into the battery and deliberately scraped the red-hot end along the surface of the "marble." The reaction was swift. The substance turned an angry purple this time. When an entire section of the floor had changed color, Jenner headed for the nearest stall trough, entering far enough to activate it.

There was a noticeable delay. When the food finally flowed into the trough, it was clear that the living village had realized the reason for what he had done. The food was a pale, creamy color, where earlier it had been murky gray.

Jenner put his finger into it, but withdrew it with a yell, and wiped his finger. It continued to sting for several moments. The vital question was: had it deliberately offered him food that would damage him, or was it trying to appease him without knowing what he could eat?

He decided to give it another chance, and entered the adjoining stall. The gritty stuff that flooded up this time was yellower. It didn't burn his finger, but Jenner took one taste, and spat it out. He had the feeling that he had been offered a soup made of a greasy mixture of clay and gasoline.

He was thirsty now with a need heightened by the unpleasant taste in his mouth. Desperately, he rushed outside and tore open the water bag, seeking the wetness inside. In his fumbling eagerness, he spilled a few precious drops onto the courtyard. Down he went on his face and licked them up.

Half a minute later, he was still licking, and there was still water.

The fact penetrated suddenly. He raised himself and gazed

wonderingly at the droplets of water that sparkled on the smooth stone. As he watched, another one squeezed up from the apparently solid surface, and shimmered in the light of the sinking sun.

He bent and with the tip of his tongue sponged up each visible drop. For a long time, he lay with his mouth pressed to the "marble," sucking up the tiny bits of water that the village doled out to him.

The glowing white sun disappeared behind a hill. Night fell like the dropping of a black screen. The air turned cold, then icy. He shivered as the wind keened through his ragged clothes. But what finally stopped him was the collapse of the surface from which he had been drinking.

Jenner lifted himself in surprise, and in the darkness gingerly felt over the stone. It had genuinely crumbled. Evidently the substance had yielded up its available water and had disintegrated in the process. Jenner estimated that he had drunk altogether an ounce of water.

It was a convincing demonstration of the willingness of the village to please him, but there was another, less satisfying implication. If the village had to destroy a part of itself every time it gave him a drink, then clearly the supply was not unlimited.

Jenner hurried inside the nearest building, climbed onto a dais —and climbed off again hastily, as the heat blazed up at him. He waited, to give the Intelligence a chance to realize he wanted a change, then lay down once more. The heat was as great as ever.

He gave that up because he was too tired to persist, and too sleepy to think of a method that might let the village know he needed a different bedroom temperature. He slept on the floor with an uneasy conviction that it could *not* sustain him for long. He woke up many times during the night, and thought: "Not enough water. No matter how hard it tries—" then he would sleep again, only to wake once more, tense and unhappy.

Nevertheless, morning found him briefly alert; and all his steely determination was back—that iron willpower that had brought him at least five hundred miles across an unknown desert.

He headed for the nearest trough. This time, after he had activated it, there was a pause of more than a minute; and then about a thimbleful of water made a wet splotch at the bottom.

Jenner licked it dry, then waited hopefully for more. When none came, he reflected gloomily that somewhere in the village, an entire group of cells had broken down and released their water for him.

Then and there he decided that it was up to the human being, who could move around, to find a new source of water for the village, which could not move.

In the interim, of course, the village would have to keep him alive, until he had investigated the possibilities. That meant, above everything else, he must have some food to sustain him while he looked around.

He began to search his pockets. Toward the end of his food supply, he had carried scraps and pieces wrapped in small bits of cloth. Crumbs had broken off into the pocket and he had searched often during those long days in the desert. Now by actually ripping the seams, he discovered tiny particles of meat and bread, little bits of grease and other unidentifiable substances.

Carefully, he leaned over the adjoining stall, and placed the scrapings in the trough there. The village would not be able to offer him more than a reasonable facsimile. If the spilling of a few drops on the courtyard could make it aware of his need for water, then a similar offering might give it the clue it needed as to the chemical nature of the food he could eat.

Jenner waited, then entered the second stall and activated it. About a pint of thick, creamy substance trickled into the bottom of the trough. The smallness of the quantity seemed evidence that perhaps it contained water.

He tasted it. It had a sharp, musty flavor and a stale odor. It was almost as dry as flour—but his stomach did not reject it.

Jenner ate slowly, acutely aware that at such moments as this the village had him at its mercy. He could never be sure that one of the food ingredients was not a slow acting poison.

When he had finished the meal, he went to a food trough in another building. He refused to eat the food that came up, but activated still another trough. This time he received a few drops of water.

He had come purposefully to one of the tower buildings. Now, he started up the ramp that led to the upper floor. He paused only briefly in the room he came to, as he had already discovered that they seemed to be additional bedrooms. The familiar dais was there in a group of three.

What interested him was that the circular ramp continued to wind on upward. First, to another, smaller room that seemed to have no particular reason for being. Then it wound on up to the top of the tower, some seventy feet above the ground. It was high enough for him to see beyond the rim of all the surrounding hilltops. He had thought it might be but he had been too weak to make the climb before. Now, he looked out to every horizon. Almost immediately, the hope that had brought him up, faded.

The view was immeasurably desolate. As far as he could see was an arid waste, and every horizon was hidden in a mist of wind-blown sand.

Jenner gazed with a sense of despair. If there was a Martian sea out there somewhere, it was beyond his reach.

Abruptly, he clenched his hands in anger against his fate, which seemed inevitable now. At the very worst, he had hoped he would find himself in a mountainous region. Seas and mountains were generally the two main sources of water. He should have known, of course, that there were very few mountains on Mars. It would have been a wild coincidence if he had actually run into a mountain range.

His fury faded, because he lacked the strength to sustain any emotion. Numbly, he went down the ramp.

His vague plan to help the village ended as swiftly and finally as that.

The days drifted by, but as to how many he had no idea. Each time he went to eat, a smaller amount of water was doled out to him. Jenner kept telling himself that each meal would have to be his last. It was unreasonable for him to expect the village to destroy itself when his fate was certain now.

What was worse, it became increasingly clear that the food was not good for him. He had misled the village as to his needs by giving it stale, perhaps even tainted samples, and prolonged the agony for himself. At times after he had eaten, Jenner felt dizzy for hours. All too frequently, his head ached, and his body shivered with fever.

The village was doing what it could. The rest was up to him, and he couldn't even adjust to an approximation of Earth food.

For two days, he was too sick to drag himself to one of the troughs. Hour after hour, he lay on the floor. Some time during the second night, the pain in his body grew so terrible that he finally made up his mind.

"If I can get to a dais," he told himself, "the heat alone will kill me; and in absorbing my body, the village will get back some of its lost water."

He spent at least an hour crawling laboriously up the ramp of the nearest dais, and when he finally made it, he lay as one already dead. His last waking thought was: "Beloved friends, I'm coming."

The hallucination was so complete that, momentarily, he seemed to be back in the control room of the rocketship, and all around him were his former companions.

With a sigh of relief, Jenner sank into a dreamless sleep.

He woke to the sound of a violin. It was a sad-sweet music that told of the rise and fall of a race long dead.

Jenner listened for a while, and then with abrupt excitement realized the truth. This was a substitute for the whistling—the village had adjusted its music to him!

Other sensory phenomena stole in upon him. The dais felt comfortably warm, not hot at all. He had a feeling of wonderful physical well-being.

Eagerly, he scrambled down the ramp to the nearest food stall. As he crawled forward, his nose close to the floor, the trough filled with a steamy mixture. The odor was so rich and pleasant that he plunged his face into it, and slopped it up greedily. It had the flavor of thick, meaty soup and was warm and soothing to his lips and mouth. When he had eaten it all, he did not need a drink of water for the first time.

"I've won!" thought Jenner, "The village has found a way!"

After a while, he remembered something, and crawled to the bathroom. Cautiously, watching the ceiling, he eased himself backward into the shower stall. The yellowish spray came down, cool and delightful.

Ecstatically, Jenner wriggled his four-foot tail and lifted his long snout to let the thin streams of liquid wash away the food impurities that clung to his sharp teeth.

Then he waddled out to bask in the sun and listen to the timeless music.

PRISONERS OF PARADISE

DAVID REDD

Shaamon was an artist, and she herself was a work of art. Her towering body had the same indefinable appealing quality as a sparkling jewel. She resembled a misty veil wound around itself to form a vertical cylinder of milky light, over thirty feet tall. The luminous gauze curtains within her body were in constant rippling motion, matching the aurorae that shimmered in the dark evening sky. Under a strong light she would have looked no more a work of art than a dusty cobweb, but in the eternal twilight she was truly beautiful.

Other veils were all around her, standing on the slopes of the mountain range, forming a forest of light. They seemed motionless, but they were working hard, slowly grinding away the rock where they stood. A veil's sharp cutting edges could eat through anything, given time. So the glowing veils spent their lives, making their pilgrimages to the mountains and patiently engraving their patterns on the stone.

Withdrawing her mind from the golden thoughtweb of ceaseless telepathic conversation, Shaamon glided to the edge of her circular engraving and stood at its perimeter. Solemnly she examined her work for any imperfections. Inside the circle, a strange series of dots and twisting lines had been carved into the limestone. Each mark had a definite relationship to the others, and even the depth of the grooves had a special significance.

It was complete. The balance of the curves around the center had taken far longer than the rest of the pattern, but the labor had been worthwhile. Everything was perfect.

A huge glowing column of milky light, staring at a weird design etched on to the rock—was that any different from a human artist studying his latest creation? Perhaps. Shaamon did not call her friends to admire her work, for art was a personal affair, and engravings were made for individual satisfaction, not for the pleasure of others. The carvings were simply an outlet for the creative impulses present in all worker females.

Shaamon let her thoughts spill into the open once more, altering the flavor of the telepathic mindpool. Every contributing veil was aware of her return.

Savoring the golden oneness for a moment, Shaamon informed the other veils that she had finished her engraving and was returning to her Nest. A great gust of farewell emotion from her friends flowed over her; she bowed before it in grateful acceptance. Rather reluctantly, she cut herself off from the golden mindpool and was alone in her own pale self. Then she tensed herself and leaped into the air, uncurling as she rose. Before she could fall, she had spread out to her natural shape, a circular veil so thin as to be almost two-dimensional. She rippled her body and floated away from the hill, rising slowly. It was nice to fly again. She did not mind having to fold herself into a cylinder to work, but it had meant she could not fly while she was carving her pattern on the shadowy hillside.

Gaining speed, Shaamon soared through the air. Navigation was no problem, for the Nests were in direct line between the limestone hills and Elethe. She had just left the hills, and beyond the distant granite mountains was the dim blue radiance of Elethe, forever peering at her from behind the horizon.

Elethe was the sun, and if the veils had been astronomers they would have known it was dying.

Shaamon flew on towards her Nest at her customary speed. Above her the aurorae painted the dark sky with vivid fire, concealing all but the brightest stars. No clouds formed to hide the aurorae, for clouds needed warmth to exist, and warmth was something the failing sun could no longer send. The last snows lay where they had fallen a million years ago. And somewhere in the sky was the pale ghost of an aged moon.

Below Shaamon the landscape was tinted blue by the feeble rays of Elethe. The fiery aurorae sent strangely colored shadows racing over the snows. Shaamon saw hints of green and purple, haunting shades rarely seen except when some other light combined with that of Elethe. For the thousandth time she wished she could capture them and delight in them always, instead of having to see them flicker and vanish. But there was no way of engraving colors onto stone. Only her memory could preserve them.

Several luminous blue spires towered up from the ground below. Colonies of tiny communal animals lived in the spires, controlled by a race mind. By themselves the individual animals were completely unintelligent. Nearly all the world's surviving species had once been communal, and the veils themselves still lived in the routine of their forebears, although they were no longer a single multicreature—they had separated eventually, and now the voluntary mindpools were the last vestiges of the veil race minds. Shaamon wondered whether the creatures beneath her would evolve in the same way. She sent a thought of greeting lancing down to the shining spires, and the race mind replied with a brief mental wave of friendly emotion.

The distant mountains were appreciably closer. Shaamon had no sense of time, living in a timeless world, so she felt no desire to speed up and reach the Nest sooner. She had no fear of predators to spur her on: they had become extinct so long ago that even the memory of them had disappeared.

Other memories had disappeared too. As she passed over a sparkling crystal forest she saw huge shapes slowly circling round a clearing. The clumsy amoeboids were taking part in one of their meaningless rituals.

The amoeboids had once been the world's greatest people. Their ancestors had visited the moon, in the days when Elethe shone brightly, but now they could only shamble through the gleaming crystals and ponderously dance beneath the blazing aurorae. They did not remember. They were no longer intelligent.

This was merely a part of the greater tragedy. Elethe was imperceptibly fading, century by century, and the planets were dying with their sun.

Shaamon and the other veils knew nothing of this. Only scientists could have read the signs and told them, and science was something their world no longer possessed.

She soared on over the snow, rippling gracefully, gliding silently through the thin air. The faint glow from her body was visible from the ground, but now there were none to see her. Shaamon was passing over a great empty desert of blue-white dunes, where the only forms of life were grotesque, stunted half-plants that could hardly be called alive. She did not like this part of the homeward journey, but it was the last stage before coming within range of the Nest mindpool. Joining that magnificent golden thoughtweb was a moment to look forward to . . .

Something was happening.

Strange little vibrations came tingling through the atmosphere, impinging on her upper surface. This was sound, of a degree she had never experienced before, and the intensity was increasing rapidly. In the sky above her, a glowing red dot had appeared in the aurorae. It too was growing, rushing down towards her. Shaamon had heard of meteorites, had even seen one fall, but this was something different.

Frightened, Shaamon curled up into cylindrical form, letting herself fall to the blue-shadowed dunes below. The vibrations were disrupting her external nervous system, making it difficult to think. And what was that red dot flaming in the sky?

Approaching the ground, she opened out to break her fall, curled up again and dropped lightly on to the pearly-hued mixture of dust and snow. The vibrations were very powerful now, pounding into her helpless body. She instinctively retreated into a mindless state, waiting for the sound to cease. If it continued, she might even have to destroy her personality and encyst.

The noise suddenly boomed twice as loud and stopped altogether. She was grasped and hurled across the dunes, battered by the most terrible shock she had ever received. Somehow she survived, and found herself falling in a shower of sand and snow. Half the desert was in the air with her.

Unthinkingly she opened out to slow her fall, and was pelted by flying debris. Pain seared through her. Rippling frantically, she fought her way up into clear air and hovered there, grateful to be alive. She had received several painful gashes and bruises, but no serious injuries.

And the alien thoughts poured into her mind. In that instant Shaamon learned that the red falling star had been a *ship,* a tough shell which protected the soft thick body of its misshapen occupant. But the shell was broken, and the helpless creature inside was dying.

Where had this deformed monster come from? There was nothing like it in her experience. Quickly Shaamon inserted herself into the rushing thought-stream of the dying monster. Her aching wounds were forgotten as she struggled to absorb the kaleidoscope of thought and emotion flowing over her. But the ideas were incomprehensible, and the bright color-filled pictures were too strange for her to understand. Watching the mental chaos was no good. She would have to enter mindpool with the monster and pray that she could break the contact before it died.

Shaamon hesitantly began merging personalities, forcing herself to open out to the alien mind. However, the creature did not respond; it made no effort to complete the linkage. This was terrible! She could not let it die without finding out anything more—she did not even know its name! Hurriedly, for the monster's thoughts were appreciably weaker, she projected an image of herself into its mind.

"Christ, a bloody beer mat!" The response was in a stylised sound-based framework, although the previous thoughts had been mainly visual and emotional.

Shaamon sensed that she had been compared with some object or animal known to the creature; a faint mental image was visible for a moment among the rapidly fading thoughts. She concentrated on that picture, setting off fiery little association-chains in the alien memory. Instinctively she sampled each chain.

There were peculiar designs on the "beer-mat" objects, and they had not been engraved. Permanent colors had been fixed to their surfaces!

The monster's thoughts had the dull red flavor of a creature very near death. Shaamon desperately searched through the flickering alien memories, sending up flurries of association-chains and pouncing on each one as it appeared. She followed the idea of reproduced pictures into the dead-end of microfilm, then discovered the art-form of painting. She almost lost it again before she realized what she had found. *Colored substances could be used to form pictures!*

Suddenly Total Awareness of Death cascaded out from the alien brain, blotting out the monster's remaining thoughts and almost engulfing her. Clutching her new knowledge, Shaamon tore away, fleeing lest her own mind be destroyed as well.

And then Shaamon was alone once more, a shimmering veil hovering silently above the pearly dunes in the familiar dim blue light of Elethe, with the swirling aurorae blazing above her. She gazed out over the desert. Far away, half buried in an immense crater, was the dark bulk of the shell that had become a tomb.

Rippling gently, without the energy to fly faster, Shaamon slowly resumed the journey to her Nest. She was limp after her mental exertions, but very satisfied. Although she had not learned the creature's origin, she had gained something far more important. *Painting . . .*

She happily wondered what new forms art would take, with color as an added medium. It would seem very difficult at first, but artists of the future would use color and think nothing of it. Why, it would add a whole new dimension to engraving! Shaamon could imagine patterns where grooves of the same depth would contain different colors. She was dazzled by the enormous possibilities opening before her.

And even the problem of finding colors was no problem at all.

The mining veils had often found colored minerals in their quest for salt. She had seen some yellow metal herself, and surely there must be other colors in the ground somewhere, judging by the thoughts of the dead monster. Yes, it would be easy enough to find the materials for painting. She wondered why nobody had ever thought of it before.

While she was still gliding over the desert, happy and excited with her new discovery, a brilliant golden mind touched hers. It was the Nest mindpool.

Her sisters began the usual recognition pattern—then stopped. Abruptly they withdrew, without giving her a chance to join. It was impossible—but it had happened!

Puzzled, dismayed, horribly frightened by the unthinkable rebuff, Shaamon sent a pleading thought into her sisters. "Why? What have I done?"

"You have changed," the mindpool answered. "You are not normal." The veils had sensed her mental turmoil in that momentary contact and retreated for fear of contamination. A single insane mind could infect hundreds of others—had done, in the past.

"I have not changed! Let me in!" Shaamon replied angrily.

"We dare not. There is something peculiar about you. You are not the Shaamon who departed for the mountains. There was a violent shock wave before you arrived, and you were nearer to its source than we. If you have been injured you must not join us. The safety of the Nest comes first."

"I am not injured!" They had been referring to mental wounds, not physical damage. "This is what happened. Listen!" And Shaamon told her sisters how she had discovered the dying monster and searched its mind.

". . . It contained so much knowledge I could never have learned it," Shaamon concluded. "I was lucky to find something we could understand, let alone something we need.

"And now that we know about painting, we can easily insert colored materials into our engravings, and then our art will include relationships of color as well as form . . ."

There was no detectable emotion from the mindpool, only the mere fact of its presence. It was apparently examining the possibilities of the situation, thinking on a level far above that of the individuals comprising it. Knowing this, Shaamon felt a ripple of fear. Through sheer instinct, the mindpool sometimes acted like the race mind it had once been, especially in times of stress, and she had an uncomfortable feeling she was responsible for a sudden tension in the thoughtweb. If her sisters were sufficiently worried about the effects of her discovery, they might revert to the habits of their ancestors—

Suddenly a burst of blinding energy flashed out from the mindpool. Caught by the terrible power from ten thousand veils, Shaamon was sucked into what had been the mindpool. Conscientiously, the race mind made her body continue gliding towards the Nest, just as She controlled all the other workers. The latent guardian of the veils had come into being once more.

"No difficulty about this affair," She mused. There had been similar cases in the past, when individual veils had stumbled on odd discoveries or thought up crazy ideas. "It's the old story all over again. This painting is innocent in itself, but it will lead to implements. And if the workers had tools they'd go soft and useless."

Quickly She went through Her memories of Shaamon's encounter, removing all ideas of painting and substituting a suitably edited version of events. At the same time She renewed the mental block against bringing metals out of the ground—the conditioning had grown weak with age.

A brief mental effort, and the task was done. All thoughts of painting had vanished forever. The race mind instantly separated into Her component entities. The veils returned to normal.

Shaamon and her sisters were in golden mindpool, discussing her adventures.

"You had a lucky escape, Shaamon," thought one. "The shock wave could have killed you as well as the monster."

"I felt sorry for that creature," Shaamon thought sadly. " I never learned what it was called, nor where it came from."

"We'll have to find out," her sisters told her. "We'll send out an expedition."

"That's a good idea," Shaamon replied, gliding down towards the friendly towers of the Nest. "A very good idea. I wonder what we'll find."

A.D. 2267

JOHN FREDERICK NIMS

Once on the gritty moon (burnt earth hung far
In the black, rhinestone sky—lopsided star),
Two gadgets, with great fishbowls for a head,
Feet clubbed, hips loaded, shoulders bent. She said,
"Fantasies haunt me. A green garden. Two
Lovers aglow in flesh. The pools so blue!"
He whirrs with masculine pity, "Can't forget
Old superstitions? The earth-legend yet?"

GHOST CRABS

TED HUGHES

At nightfall, as the sea darkens,
A depth darkness thickens, mustering from the gulfs and
the submarine badlands,
To the sea's edge. To begin with
It looks like rocks uncovering, mangling their pallor.
Gradually the laboring of the tide
Falls back from its productions,
Its power slips back from glistening nacelles, and they
are crabs.
Giant crabs, under flat skulls, staring inland
Like a packed trench of helmets.
Ghosts, they are ghost crabs.
They emerge
An invisible disgorging of the sea's cold
Over the man who strolls along the sands.
They spill inland, into the smoking purple
Of our woods and towns—a bristling surge
Of tall and staggering spectres
Gliding like shocks through water.
Our walls, our bodies, are no problem to them.
Their hungers are homing elsewhere.
We cannot see them or turn our minds from them.
Their bubbling mouths, and their eyes
In a slow mineral fury
Press through our nothingness where we sprawl on our beds,
Or sit in our rooms. Our dreams are ruffled maybe.
Or we jerk awake to the world of possessions
With a gasp, in a sweat burst, brains jamming blind
Into the bulb-light. Sometimes, for minutes, a sliding
Staring
Thickness of silence
Presses between us. These crabs own this world.

All night, around us or through us,
They stalk each other, they fasten on to each other,
They mount each other, they tear each other to pieces,
They utterly exhaust each other.
They are the powers of this world.
We are their bacteria,
Dying their lives and living their deaths.

At dawn, they sidle back under the sea's edge.
They are the turmoil of history, the convulsion
In the roots of the blood, in the cycles of concurrence.
To them, our cluttered countries are empty battleground.
All day they recuperate under the sea.
Their singing is like a thin sea-wind flexing in the rocks
of a headland,
Where only crabs listen.
They are God's only toys.

RAY BRADBURY

Oh, it was to be so jolly! What a game! Such excitement they hadn't known in years. The children catapulted this way and that across the green lawns, shouting at each other, holding hands, flying in circles, climbing trees, laughing. Overhead the rockets flew, and beetle cars whispered by on the streets, but the children played on. Such fun, such tremulous joy, such tumbling and hearty screaming.

Mink ran into the house, all dirt and sweat. For her seven years she was loud and strong and definite. Her mother, Mrs. Morris, hardly saw her as she yanked out drawers and rattled pans and tools into a large sack.

"Heavens, Mink, what's going on?"

"The most exciting game ever!" gasped Mink, pink-faced.

"Stop and get your breath," said her mother.

"No, I'm all right," gasped Mink. "Okay I take these things, Mom?"

"But don't dent them," said Mrs. Morris.

"Thank you, thank you!" cried Mink, and boom! she was gone, like a rocket.

Mrs. Morris surveyed the fleeing tot. "What's the name of the game?"

"Invasion!" said Mink. The door slammed.

In every yard on the street children brought out knives and forks and pokers and old stovepipes and can-openers.

It was an interesting fact that this fury and bustle occurred only among the younger children. The older ones, those ten years and more, disdained the affair and marched scornfully off on hikes or played a more dignified version of hide-and-seek on their own.

Meanwhile, parents came and went in chromium beetles. Repair men came to repair the vacuum elevators in houses, to fix fluttering television sets or hammer upon stubborn food-delivery tubes. The adult civilization passed and repassed the busy youngsters, jealous of the fierce energy of the wild tots, tolerantly amused at their flourishings, longing to join in themselves.

"This and this and *this*," said Mink, instructing the

others with their assorted spoons and wrenches. "Do that, and bring *that* over here. No! *Here,* ninny! Right. Now, get back while I fix this." Tongue in teeth, face wrinkled in thought. "Like that. See?"

"Yayyy!" shouted the kids.

Twelve-year-old Joseph Connors ran up.

"Go away," said Mink straight at him.

"I wanna play," said Joseph.

"Can't!" said Mink.

"Why not?"

"You'd just make fun of us."

"Honest, I wouldn't."

"No. We know *you.* Go away or we'll kick you."

Another twelve-year-old boy whirred by on little motor skates. "Hey, Joe! Come on! Let them sissies play!"

Joseph showed reluctance and a certain wistfulness. "I *want* to play," he said.

"You're old," said Mink firmly.

"Not *that* old," said Joe sensibly.

"You'd only laugh and spoil the Invasion."

The boy on the motor skates made a rude lip noise. "Come on, Joe! Them and their fairies! Nuts!"

Joseph walked off slowly. He kept looking back, all down the block.

Mink was already busy again. She made a kind of apparatus with her gathered equipment. She had appointed another little girl with a pad and pencil to take down notes in painful, slow scribbles. Their voices rose and fell in the warm sunlight.

All around them the city hummed. The streets were lined with good green and peaceful trees. Only the wind made a conflict across the city, across the country, across the continent. In a thousand other cities there were trees and children and avenues, business men in their quiet offices taping their voices or watching televisors. Rockets hovered like darning needles in the blue sky. There was the universal, quiet conceit and easiness of men accustomed to peace, quite certain there would never be trouble again. Arm in arm, men all over earth were a united front. The perfect weapons were held in equal trust by all nations. A situation of incredibly beautiful balance had been brought about. There were no traitors among men, no unhappy ones, no disgruntled ones; therefore the world was based upon a stable ground. Sunlight illumined half the world and the trees drowsed in a tide of warm air.

Mink's mother, from her upstairs window, gazed down.

The children. She looked upon them and shook her head. Well, they'd eat well, sleep well, and be in school on Monday. Bless their vigorous little bodies. She listened.

Mink talked earnestly to someone near the rose bush—though there was no one there.

These odd children. And the little girl, what was her name? Anna? Anna took notes on a pad. First, Mink asked the rose bush a question, then called the answer to Anna.

"Triangle," said Mink.

"What's a tri," said Anna with difficulty, "angle?"

"Never mind," said Mink.

"How you spell it?" asked Anna.

"T-r-i——" spelled Mink slowly, then snapped, "Oh, spell it yourself!" She went on to other words. "Beam," she said.

"I haven't got tri," said Anna, "angle down yet!"

"Well, hurry, hurry!" cried Mink.

Mink's mother leaned out of the upstairs window. "A-n-g-l-e," she spelled down at Anna.

"Oh, thanks, Mrs. Morris," said Anna.

"Certainly," said Mink's mother and withdrew, laughing, to dust the hall with an electro-duster magnet.

The voices wavered on the shimmery air. "Beam," said Anna. Fading.

"Four-nine-seven-A-and-B-and-X," said Mink, far away, seriously. "And a fork and a string and a—hex-hex-agony—hexagon*al!*"

At lunch Mink gulped milk at one toss and was at the door. Her mother slapped the table.

"You sit right back down," commanded Mrs. Morris. "Hot soup in a minute." She poked a red button on the kitchen butler, and ten seconds later something landed with a bump in the rubber receiver. Mrs. Morris opened it, took out a can with a pair of aluminum holders, unsealed it with a flick, and poured hot soup into a bowl.

During all this Mink fidgeted. "Hurry, Mom! This is a matter of life and death! Aw——"

"I was the same way at your age. Always life and death. I know."

Mink banged away at the soup.

"Slow down," said Mom.

"Can't," said Mink. "Drill's waiting for me."

"Who's Drill? What a peculiar name," said Mom.

"You don't know him," said Mink.

"A new boy in the neighborhood?" asked Mom.

"He's new all right," said Mink. She started on her second bowl.

"Which one is Drill?" asked Mom.

"He's around," said Mink evasively. "You'll make fun. Everybody pokes fun. Gee, darn."

"Is Drill shy?"

"Yes. No. In a way. Gosh, Mom, I got to run if we want to have the Invasion!"

"Who's invading what?"

"Martians invading Earth. Well, not exactly Martians. They're—I don't know. From up." She pointed with her spoon.

"And *inside,*" said Mom, touching Mink's feverish brow.

Mink rebelled. "You're laughing! You'd kill Drill and everybody."

"I didn't mean to," said Mom. "Drill's a Martian?"

"No. He's—well—maybe from Jupiter or Saturn or Venus. Anyway, he's had a hard time."

"I imagine." Mrs. Morris hid her mouth behind her hand.

"They couldn't figure a way to attack Earth."

"We're impregnable," said Mom in mock seriousness.

"That's the word Drill used! Impreg—— That was the word, Mom."

"My, my, Drill's a brilliant little boy. Two-bit words."

"They couldn't figure a way to attack, Mom. Drill says—he says in order to make a good fight you got to have a new way of surprising people. That way you win. And he says also you got to have help from your enemy."

"A fifth column," said Mom.

"Yeah. That's what Drill said. And they couldn't figure a way to surprise Earth or get help."

"No wonder. We're pretty darn strong." Mom laughed, cleaning up. Mink sat there, staring at the table, seeing what she was talking about.

"Until, one day," whispered Mink melodramatically, "they thought of children!"

"Well!" said Mrs. Morris brightly.

"And they thought of how grown-ups are so busy they never look under rose bushes or on lawns!"

"Only for snails and fungus."

"And then there's something about dim-dims."

"Dim-dims?"

"Dimens-shuns."

"Dimensions?"

"Four of 'em! And there's something about kids under nine and imagination. It's real funny to hear Drill talk."

Mrs. Morris was tired. "Well, it must be funny. You're keeping Drill waiting now. It's getting late in the day, and if you want to have your Invasion before your supper bath, you'd better jump."

"Do I have to take a bath?" growled Mink.

"You do! Why is it children hate water? No matter what age you live in children hate water behind the ears!"

"Drill says I won't have to take baths," said Mink.

"Oh, he does, does he?"

"He told all the kids that. No more baths. And we can stay up till ten o'clock and go to two television shows on Saturday 'stead of one!"

"Well, Mr. Drill better mind his p's and q's. I'll call up his mother and——"

Mink went to the door. "We're having trouble with guys like Pete Britz and Dale Jerrick. They're growing up. They make fun. They're worse than parents. They just won't believe in Drill. They're so snooty, 'cause they're growing up. You'd think they'd know better. They were little only a coupla years ago. I hate them worst. We'll kill them *first."*

"Your father and me last?"

"Drill says you're dangerous. Know why? 'Cause you don't believe in Martians! They're going to let *us* run the world. Well, not just us, but the kids over in the next block, too. I might be queen." She opened the door.

"Mom?"

"Yes?"

"What's lodge-ick?"

"Logic? Why, dear, logic is knowing what things are true and not true."

"He *mentioned* that," said Mink. "And what's im-pres-sion-able?" It took her a minute to say it.

"Why, it means——" Her mother looked at the floor, laughing gently. "It means——to be a child, dear."

"Thanks for lunch!" Mink ran out, then stuck her head back in. "Mom, I'll be sure you won't be hurt much, really!"

"Well, thanks," said Mom.

Slam went the door.

At four o'clock the audio-visor buzzed. Mrs. Morris flipped the tab. "Hello, Helen!" she said in welcome.

"Hello, Mary. How are things in New York?"

"Fine. How are things in Scranton? You look tired."

"So do you. The children. Underfoot," said Helen.

Mrs. Morris sighed. "My Mink too. The super-invasion."

Helen laughed. "Are your kids playing that game, too?"

"Lord, yes. Tomorrow it'll be geometrical jacks and motorized hopscotch. Were we this bad when we were kids in '48?"

"Worse. Japs and Nazis. Don't know how my parents put up with me. Tomboy."

"Parents learn to shut their ears."

A silence.

"What's wrong, Mary?" asked Helen.

Mrs. Morris's eyes were half closed; her tongue slid slowly, thoughtfully, over her lower lip. "Eh?" She jerked. "Oh, nothing. Just thought about *that.* Shutting ears and such. Never mind. Where were we?"

"My boy Tim's got a crush on some guy named—*Drill,* I think it was."

"Must be a new password. Mink likes him too."

"Didn't know it had got as far as New York. Word of mouth, I imagine. Looks like a scrap drive. I talked to Josephine and she said her kids—that's in Boston—are wild on this new game. It's sweeping the country."

At this moment Mink trotted into the kitchen to gulp a glass of water. Mrs. Morris turned. "How're things going?"

"Almost finished," said Mink.

"Swell," said Mrs. Morris. "What's *that?"*

"A yo-yo," said Mink. "Watch."

She flung the yo-yo down its string. Reaching the end it——

It vanished.

"See?" said Mink. "Ope!" Dibbling her finger, she made the yo-yo reappear and zip up the string.

"Do that again," said her mother.

"Can't. Zero hour's five o'clock. 'Bye!" Mink exited, zipping her yo-yo.

On the audio-visor, Helen laughed. "Tim brought one of those yo-yos in this morning, but when I got curious he said he wouldn't show it to me, and when I tried to work it, finally, it wouldn't work."

"You're not *impressionable,"* said Mrs. Morris.

"What?"

"Never mind. Something I thought of. Can I help you, Helen?"

"I wanted to get that black-and-white cake recipe——"

The hour drowsed by. The day waned. The sun lowered in the peaceful blue sky. Shadows lengthened on the green lawns. The laughter and excitement continued. One little girl ran away, crying. Mrs. Morris came out the front door.

"Mink, was that Peggy Ann crying?"

Mink was bent over in the yard, near the rose bush. "Yeah. She's a scarebaby. We won't let her play, now. She's getting too old to play. I guess she grew up all of a sudden."

"Is that why she cried? Nonsense. Give me a civil answer, young lady, or inside you come!"

Mink whirled in consternation, mixed with irritation. "I can't quit now. It's almost time. I'll be good. I'm sorry."

"Did you hit Peggy Ann?"

"No, honest. You ask her. It was something—well, she's just a scaredy pants."

The ring of children drew in around Mink where she scowled at her work with spoons and a kind of square-shaped arrangement of hammers and pipes. "There and there," murmured Mink.

"What's wrong?" said Mrs. Morris.

"Drill's stuck. Half-way. If we could only get him all the way through it'd be easier. Then all the others could come through after him."

"Can I help?"

"No'm, thanks. I'll fix it."

"All right. I'll call you for your bath in half an hour. I'm tired of watching you."

She went in and sat in the electric relaxing chair, sipping a little beer from a half-empty glass. The chair massaged her back. Children, children. Children and love and hate, side by side. Sometimes children loved you, hated you—all in half a second. Strange children, did they ever forget or forgive the whippings and the harsh, strict words of command? She wondered. How can you ever forget or forgive those over and above you, those tall and silly dictators?

Time passed. A curious, waiting silence came upon the street, deepening.

Five o'clock. A clock sang softly somewhere in the house in a quiet musical voice: "Five o'clock—five o'clock. Time's a-wasting. Five o'clock," and purred away into silence.

Zero hour.

Mrs. Morris chuckled in her throat. Zero hour.

A beetle car hummed into the driveway. Mr. Morris. Mrs. Morris smiled. Mr. Morris got out of the beetle, locked it, and called hello to Mink at her work. Mink ignored him. He laughed and stood for a moment watching the children. Then he walked up the front steps.

"Hello, darling."

"Hello, Henry."

She strained forward on the edge of the chair, listening. The children were silent. Too silent.

He emptied his pipe, refilled it. "Swell day. Makes you glad to be alive."

Buzz.

"What's that?" asked Henry.

"I don't know." She got up suddenly, her eyes widening. She was going to say something. She stopped it. Ridiculous. Her nerves jumped. "Those children haven't anything dangerous out there, have they?" she said.

"Nothing but pipes and hammers. Why?"

"Nothing electrical?"

"Heck, no," said Henry. "I looked."

She walked to the kitchen. The buzzing continued. "Just the same, you'd better go tell them to quit. It's after five. Tell them——"

Her eyes widened and narrowed. "Tell them to put off their Invasion until tomorrow." She laughed, nervously.

The buzzing grew louder.

"What are they up to? I'd better go look, all right."

The explosion!

The house shook with dull sound. There were other explosions in other yards on the streets.

Involuntarily, Mrs. Morris screamed. "Up this way!" she cried senselessly, knowing no sense, no reason. Perhaps she saw something from the corners of her eyes; perhaps she smelled a new odor or heard a new noise. There was no time to argue with Henry to convince him. Let him think her insane. Yes, insane! Shrieking, she ran upstairs. He ran after her to see what she was up to. "In the attic!" she screamed. "That's where it is!" It was only a poor excuse to get him in the attic in time. Oh, God—in time!

Another explosion outside. The children screamed with delight, as if at a great fireworks display.

"It's not in the attic!" cried Henry. "It's outside!"

"No, no!" Wheezing, gasping, she fumbled at the attic door. "I'll show you. Hurry! I'll show you!"

They tumbled into the attic. She slammed the door, locked it, took the key, threw it into a far cluttered corner.

She was babbling wild stuff now. It came out of her. All the subconscious suspicion and fear that had gathered secretly all afternoon and fermented like a wine in her. All the little revelations and knowledges and sense that had bothered her all day and which she had, logically and carefully and sensibly, rejected and censored. Now it exploded in her and shook her to bits.

"There, there," she said, sobbing against the door. "We're safe until tonight. Maybe we can sneak out. Maybe we can escape!"

Henry blew up too, but for another reason. "Are you crazy? Why'd you throw that key away? Damn it, honey!"

"Yes, yes, I'm crazy, if it helps, but stay here with me!"

"I don't know how in hell I *can* get out!"

"Quiet. They'll hear us. Oh, God, they'll find us soon enough———"

Below them, Mink's voice. The husband stopped. There was a great universal humming and sizzling, a screaming and giggling. Downstairs the audio-televisor buzzed and buzzed insistently, alarmingly, violently. *Is that Helen calling?* thought Mrs. Morris. *And is she calling about what I think she's calling about?*

Footsteps came into the house. Heavy footsteps.

"Who's coming in my house?" demanded Henry angrily. "Who's tramping around down there?"

Heavy feet. Twenty, thirty, forty, fifty of them. Fifty persons crowding into the house. The humming. The giggling of the children. "This way!" cried Mink, below.

"Who's downstairs?" roared Henry. "Who's there?"

"Hush. Oh, nonononononono!" said his wife weakly, holding him. "Please, be quiet. They might go away."

"Mom?" called Mink. "Dad?" A pause. "Where are you?"

Heavy footsteps, heavy, heavy, very *heavy* footsteps, came up the stairs. Mink leading them.

"Mum?" A hesitation. "Dad?" A waiting, a silence.

Humming. Footsteps towards the attic. Mink's first.

They trembled together in silence in the attic, Mr. and Mrs. Morris. For some reason the electric humming, the queer cold light suddenly visible under the door crack, the strange odor and the alien sound of eagerness in Mink's voice finally got through to Henry Morris too. He stood, shivering, in the dark silence, his wife beside him.

"Mom! Dad!"

Footsteps. A little humming sound. The attic-lock melted. The door opened. Mink peered inside, tall blue shadows behind her.

"Peekaboo," said Mink.

Klee 1927.9.

GREEN PATCHES

ISAAC ASIMOV

He had slipped aboard the ship! There had been dozens waiting outside the energy barrier when it had seemed that waiting would do no good. Then the barrier had faltered for a matter of two minutes (which showed the superiority of unified organisms over life fragments) and he was across.

None of the others had been able to move quickly enough to take advantage of the break, but that didn't matter. All alone, he was enough. No others were necessary.

And the thought faded out of satisfaction and into loneliness. It was a terribly unhappy and unnatural thing to be parted from all the rest of the unified organism, to be a life fragment oneself. How could these aliens stand being fragments?

It increased his sympathy for the aliens. Now that he experienced fragmentation himself, he could feel, as though from a distance, the terrible isolation that made them so afraid. It was fear born of that isolation that dictated their actions. What but the insane fear of their condition could have caused them to blast an area, one mile in diameter, into dull-red heat before landing their ship? Even the organized life ten feet deep in the soil had been destroyed in the blast.

He engaged reception, listening eagerly, letting the alien thought saturate him. He enjoyed the touch of life upon his consciousness. He would have to ration that enjoyment. He must not forget himself.

But it could do no harm to listen to thoughts. Some of the fragments of life on the ship thought quite clearly, considering that they were such primitive, incomplete creatures. Their thoughts were like tiny bells.

Roger Oldenn said, "I feel contaminated. You know what I mean? I keep washing my hands and it doesn't help."

Jerry Thorn hated dramatics and didn't look up. They were still maneuvering in the stratosphere of Saybrook's Planet and he preferred to watch the panel dials. He said, "No reason to feel contaminated. Nothing happened."

"I hope not," said Oldenn. "At least they had all the

field men discard their spacesuits in the air lock for complete disinfection. They had a radiation bath for all men entering from outside. I *suppose* nothing happened."

"Why be nervous, then?"

"I don't know. I wish the barrier hadn't broken down."

"Who doesn't? It was an accident."

"I wonder." Oldenn was vehement. "I was here when it happened. My shift, you know. There was no reason to overload the power line. There was equipment plugged into it that had no damn business near it. None whatsoever."

"All right. People are stupid."

"Not that stupid. I hung around when the Old Man was checking into the matter. None of them had reasonable excuses. The armor-baking circuits, which were draining off two thousand watts, had been put into the barrier line. They'd been using the second subsidiaries for a week. Why not this time? They couldn't give any reason."

"Can you?"

Oldenn flushed. "No, I was just wondering if the men had been"—he searched for a word—"hypnotized into it. By those things outside."

Thorn's eyes lifted and met those of the other levelly. "I wouldn't repeat that to anyone else. The barrier was down only two minutes. If anything had happened, if even a spear of grass had drifted across, it would have shown up in our bacteria cultures within half an hour, in the fruit-fly colonies in a matter of days. Before we got back it would show up in the hamsters, the rabbits, maybe the goats. Just get it through your head, Oldenn, that nothing happened. Nothing."

Oldenn turned on his heel and left. In leaving, his foot came within two feet of the object in the corner of the room. He did not see it.

He disengaged his reception centers and let the thoughts flow past him unperceived. These life fragments were not important, in any case, since they were not fitted for the continuation of life. Even as fragments, they were incomplete.

The other types of fragments now—they were different. He had to be careful of them. The temptation would be great, and he must give no indication, none at all, of his existence on board ship till they landed on their home planet.

He focused on the other parts of the ship, marveling at the diversity of life. Each item, no matter how small, was sufficient to itself. He forced himself to contemplate this, until the unpleasantness of the thought grated on him and he longed for the normality of home.

Most of the thoughts he received from the smaller fragments were vague and fleeting, as you would expect. There wasn't much to be had from them, but that meant their need for completeness was all the greater. It was that which touched him so keenly.

There was the life fragment which squatted on its haunches and fingered the wire netting that enclosed it. Its thoughts were clear, but limited. Chiefly, they concerned the yellow fruit a companion fragment was eating. It wanted the fruit very deeply. Only the wire netting that separated the fragments prevented its seizing the fruit by force.

He disengaged reception in a moment of complete revulsion. *These fragments competed for food!*

He tried to reach far outward for the peace and harmony of home, but it was already an immense distance away. He could reach only into the nothingness that separated him from sanity.

He longed at the moment even for the feel of the dead soil between the barrier and the ship. He had crawled over it last night. There had been no life upon it, but it had been the soil of home, and on the other side of the barrier there had still been the comforting feel of the rest of organized life.

He could remember the moment he had located himself on the surface of the ship, maintaining a desperate suction grip until the air lock opened. He had entered, moving cautiously between the outgoing feet. There had been an inner lock and that had been passed later. Now he lay here, a life fragment himself, inert and unnoticed.

Cautiously, he engaged reception again at the previous focus. The squatting fragment of life was tugging furiously at the wire netting. It still wanted the other's food, though it was the less hungry of the two.

Larsen said, "Don't feed the damn thing. She isn't hungry; she's just sore because Tillie had the nerve to eat before she herself was crammed full. The greedy ape! I wish we were back home and I never had to look another animal in the face again."

He scowled at the older female chimpanzee frowningly and the chimp mouthed and chattered back to him in full reciprocation.

Rizzo said, "Okay, okay. Why hang around here, then? Feeding time is over. Let's get out."

They went past the goat pens, the rabbit hutches, the hamster cages.

Larsen said bitterly, "You volunteer for an exploration voyage. You're a hero. They send you off with speeches—and make a zoo keeper out of you."

"They give you double pay."

"All right, so what? I didn't sign up just for the money. They said at the original briefing that it was even odds we wouldn't come back, that we'd end up like Saybrook. I signed up because I wanted to do something important."

"Just a bloomin' bloody hero," said Rizzo.

"I'm not an animal nurse."

Rizzo paused to lift a hamster out of the cage and stroke it. "Hey," he said, "did you ever think that maybe one of these hamsters has some cute little baby hamsters inside, just getting started?"

"Wise guy! They're tested every day."

"Sure, sure." He muzzled the little creature, which vibrated its nose at him. "But just suppose you came down one morning and found them there. New little hamsters looking up at you with soft, green patches of fur where the eyes ought to be."

"Shut up, for the love of Mike," yelled Larsen.

"Little soft, green patches of shining fur," said Rizzo, and put the hamster down with a sudden loathing sensation.

He engaged reception again and varied the focus. There wasn't a specialized life fragment at home that didn't have a rough counterpart on shipboard.

There were the moving runners in various shapes, the moving swimmers, and the moving fliers. Some of the fliers were quite large, with perceptible thoughts; others were small, gauzy-winged creatures. These last transmitted only patterns of sense perception, imperfect patterns at that, and added nothing intelligent of their own.

There were the non-movers, which, like the non-movers at home, were green and lived on the air, water, and soil. These were a mental blank. They knew only the dim, dim consciousness of light, moisture, and gravity.

And each fragment, moving and non-moving, had its mockery of life.

Not yet. Not yet. . . .

He clamped down hard upon his feelings. Once before, these life fragments had come, and the rest at home had tried to help them —too quickly. It had not worked. This time they must wait.

If only these fragments did not discover him.

They had not, so far. They had not noticed him lying in the corner of the pilot room. No one had bent down to pick up and discard him. Earlier, it had meant he could not move. Someone might have turned and stared at the stiff wormlike thing, not quite six inches long. First stare, then shout, and then it would all be over.

But now, perhaps, he had waited long enough. The take-off was long past. The controls were locked; the pilot room was empty.

It did not take him long to find the chink in the armor leading to the recess where some of the wiring was. They were dead wires.

The front end of his body was a rasp that cut in two a wire of just the right diameter. Then, six inches away, he cut it in two again. He pushed the snipped-off section of the wire ahead of him packing it away neatly and invisibly into a corner of recess. Its outer covering was a brown elastic material and its core was gleaming, ruddy metal. He himself could not reproduce the core, of course, but that was not necessary. It was enough that the pellicle that covered him had been carefully bred to resemble a wire's surface.

He returned and grasped the cut sections of the wire before and behind. He tightened against them as his little suction disks came into play. Not even a seam showed.

They could not find him now. They could look right at him and see only a continuous stretch of wire.

Unless they looked very closely indeed and noted that, in a certain spot on this wire, there were two tiny patches of soft and shining green fur.

"It is remarkable," said Dr. Weiss, "that little green hairs can do so much."

Captain Loring poured the brandy carefully. In a sense, this was a celebration. They would be ready for the jump through hyper-space in two hours, and after that, two days would see them back on Earth.

"You are convinced, then, the green fur is the sense organ?" he asked.

"It is," said Weiss. Brandy made him come out in splotches, but he was aware of the need of celebration—quite aware. "The experiments were conducted under difficulties, but they were quite significant."

The captain smiled stiffly. " 'Under difficulties' is one way of phrasing it. I would never have taken the chances you did to run them."

"Nonsense. We're all heroes aboard this ship, all volunteers, all great men with trumpet, fife, and fanfarade. You took the chance of coming here."

"You were the first to go outside the barrier."

"No particular risk was involved," Weiss said. "I burned the ground before me as I went, to say nothing of the portable barrier that surrounded me. Nonsense, Captain. Let's all take our medals when we come back; let's take them without attempt at gradation. Besides, I'm a male."

"But you're filled with bacteria to here." The captain's hand made a quick, cutting gesture three inches above his head. "Which makes you as vulnerable as a female would be."

They paused for drinking purposes.

"Refill?" asked the captain.

"No, thanks. I've exceeded my quota already."

"Then one last for the spaceroad." He lifted his glass in the general direction of Saybrook's Planet, no longer visible, its sun only a bright star in the visiplate. "To the little green hairs that gave Saybrook his first lead."

Weiss nodded. "A lucky thing. We'll quarantine the planet, of course."

The captain said, "That doesn't seem drastic enough. Someone might always land by accident someday and not have Saybrook's insight, or his guts. Suppose he did not blow up his ship, as Saybrook did. Suppose he got back to some inhabited place."

The captain was somber. "Do you suppose they might ever develop interstellar travel on their own?"

"I doubt it. No proof, of course. It's just that they have such a completely different orientation. Their entire organization of life has made tools unnecessary. As far as we know, even a stone ax doesn't exist on the planet."

"I hope you're right. Oh, and, Weiss, would you spend some time with Drake?"

"The Galactic Press fellow?"

"Yes. Once we get back, the story of Saybrook's Planet will be released for the public and I don't think it would be wise to over-sensationalize it. I've asked Drake to let you consult with him on the story. You're a biologist and enough of an authority to carry weight with him. Would you oblige?"

"A pleasure."

The captain closed his eyes wearily and shook his head.

"Headache, Captain?"

"No. Just thinking of poor Saybrook."

He was weary of the ship. Awhile back, there had been a queer, momentary sensation, as though he had been turned inside out. It was alarming and he had searched the minds of the keen-thinkers for an explanation. Apparently the ship had leaped across vast stretches of empty space by cutting across something they knew as "hyper-space." The keen-thinkers were ingenious.

But—he was weary of the ship. It was such a futile phenomenon. These life fragments were skillful in their constructions, yet it was only a measure of their unhappiness, after all. They strove to find in the control of inanimate matter what they could not find in themselves. In their unconscious yearning for completeness, they built machines and scoured space, seeking, seeking . . .

These creatures, he knew, could never, in the very nature of things, find that for which they were seeking. At least not until such time as he gave it to them. He quivered a little at the thought.

Completeness!

These fragments had no concept of it, even. "Completeness" was a poor word.

In their ignorance they would even fight it. There had been the ship that had come before. The first ship had contained many of the keen-thinking fragments. There had been two varieties, life producers and the sterile ones. (How different this second ship was. The keen-thinkers were all sterile, while the other fragments, the fuzzy-thinkers and the no-thinkers, were all producers of life. It was strange.)

How gladly that first ship had been welcomed by all the planet! He could remember the first intense shock at the realization that the visitors were fragments and not complete. The shock had given way to pity, and the pity to action. It was not certain how they would fit into the community, but there had been no hesitation. All life was sacred and somehow room would have been made for them—for all of them, from the large keen-thinkers to the little multipliers in the darkness.

But there had been a miscalculation. They had not correctly analyzed the course of the fragments' ways of thinking. The keen-thinkers became aware of what had been done and resented it. They were frightened, of course; they did not understand.

They had developed the barrier first, and then, later, had destroyed themselves, exploding their ship to atoms.

Poor, foolish fragments.

This time, at least, it would be different. They would be saved, despite themselves.

John Drake would not have admitted it in so many words, but he was very proud of his skill on the photo-typer. He had a travel-kit model, which was a six-by-eight, featureless dark plastic slab, with cylindrical bulges on either end to hold the roll of thin paper. It fitted into a brown leather case, equipped with a beltlike contraption that held it closely about the waist and at one hip. The whole thing weighed less than a pound.

Drake could operate it with either hand. His fingers would flick quickly and easily, placing their light pressure at exact spots on the blank surface, and, soundlessly, words would be written.

He looked thoughtfully at the beginning of his story, then up at Dr. Weiss. "What do you think, Doc?"

"It starts well."

Drake nodded. "I thought I might as well start with Saybrook himself. They haven't released his story back home yet. I wish I could have seen Saybrook's original report. How did he ever get it through, by the way?"

"As near as I could tell, he spent one last night sending it through the sub-ether. When he was finished, he shorted the motors, and converted the entire ship into a thin cloud of vapor a millionth of a second later. The crew and himself along with it."

"What a man! You were in this from the beginning, Doc?"

"Not from the beginning," corrected Weiss gently. "Only since the receipt of Saybrook's report."

He could not help thinking back. He had read that report, realizing even then how wonderful the planet must have seemed when Saybrook's colonizing expedition first reached it. It was practically a duplicate of Earth, with an abounding plant life and a purely vegetarian animal life.

There had been only the little patches of green fur (how often had he used that phrase in his speaking and thinking!) which seemed strange. No living individual on the planet had eyes. Instead, there was this fur. Even the plants, each blade or leaf or blossom, possessed the two patches of richer green.

Then Saybrook had noticed, startled and bewildered, that there was no conflict for food on the planet. All plants grew pulpy appendages which were eaten by the animals. These were regrown in a matter of hours. No other parts of the plants were touched. It was as though the plants fed the animals as part of the order of nature. And the plants themselves did not grow in overpowering profusion. They might almost have been cultivated, they were spread across the available soil so discriminately.

How much time, Weiss wondered, had Saybrook had to observe the strange law and order on the planet?—the fact that insects kept their numbers reasonable, though no birds ate them; that the rodent-like things did not swarm, though no carnivores existed to keep them in check.

And then there had come the incident of the white rats.

That prodded Weiss. He said, "Oh, one correction, Drake. Hamsters were not the first animals involved. It was the white rats."

"White rats," said Drake, making the correction in his notes.

"Every colonizing ship," said Weiss, "takes a group of white rats for the purpose of testing any alien foods. Rats, of course, are very similar to human beings from a nutritional viewpoint. Naturally, only female white rats are taken."

Naturally. If only one sex was present, there was no danger of unchecked multiplication in case the planet proved favorable. Remember the rabbits in Australia.

"Incidentally, why not use males?" asked Drake.

"Females are hardier," said Weiss, "which is lucky, since that gave the situation away. It turned out suddenly that all the rats were bearing young."

"Right. Now that's where I'm up to, so here's my chance to get some things straight. For my own information, Doc, how did Saybrook find out they were in a family way?"

"Accidentally, of course. In the course of nutritional investigations, rats are dissected for evidence of internal damage. Their condition was bound to be discovered. A few more were dissected; same results. Eventually, all that lived gave birth to young—with *no* male rats aboard!"

"And the point is that all the young were born with little green patches of fur instead of eyes."

"That is correct. Saybrook said so and we corroborate him. After the rats, the pet cat of one of the children was obviously affected. When it finally kittened, the kittens were not born with closed eyes but with little patches of green fur. There was no tomcat aboard.

"Eventually Saybrook had the women tested. He didn't tell them what for. He didn't want to frighten them. Every single one of them was in the early stages of pregnancy, leaving out of consideration those few who had been pregnant at the time of embarkation. Saybrook never waited for any child to be born, of course. He knew they would have no eyes, only shining patches of green fur.

"He even prepared bacterial cultures (Saybrook was a thorough man) and found each bacillus to show microscopic green spots."

Drake was eager. "That goes way beyond our briefing—or, at least, the briefing I got. But granted that life on Saybrook's Planet is organized into a unified whole, how is it done?"

"How? How are your cells organized into a unified whole? Take an individual cell out of your body, even a brain cell, and what is it by itself? Nothing. A little blob of protoplasm with no more capacity for anything human than an amoeba. Less capacity, in fact, since it couldn't live by itself. But put the cells together and you have something that could invent a spaceship or write a symphony."

"I get the idea," said Drake.

Weiss went on, "*All* life on Saybrook's Planet is a *single* organism. In a sense, all life on Earth is too, but it's a fighting dependence, a dog-eat-dog dependence. The bacteria fix nitrogen; the plants fix carbon; animals eat plants and each other; bacterial decay hits everything. It comes full circle. Each grabs as much as it can, and is, in turn, grabbed.

"On Saybrook's Planet, each organism has its place, as each

cell in our body does. Bacteria and plants produce food, on the excess of which animals feed, providing in turn carbon dioxide and nitrogenous wastes. Nothing is produced more or less than is needed. The scheme of life is intelligently altered to suit the local environment. No group of life forms multiplies more or less than is needed, just as the cells in our body stop multiplying when there are enough of them for a given purpose. When they don't stop multiplying, we call it cancer. And that's what life on Earth really is, the kind of organic organization we have, compared to that on Saybrook's Planet. One big cancer. Every species, every individual doing its best to thrive at the expense of every other species and individual."

"You sound as if you approve of Saybrook's Planet, Doc."

"I do, in a way. It makes sense out of the business of living. I can see their viewpoint toward us. Suppose one of the cells of your body could be conscious of the efficiency of the human body as compared with that of the cell itself, and could realize that this was only the result of the union of many cells into a higher whole. And then suppose it became conscious of the existence of free-living cells, with bare life and nothing more. It might feel a very strong desire to drag the poor thing into an organization. It might feel sorry for it, feel perhaps a sort of missionary spirit. The things on Saybrook's Planet—or the thing; one should use the singular—feels just that, perhaps."

"And went ahead by bringing about virgin births, eh, Doc? I've got to go easy on that angle of it. Post-office regulations, you know."

"There's nothing ribald about it, Drake. For centuries we've been able to make the eggs of sea urchins, bees, frogs, et cetera develop without the intervention of male fertilization. The touch of a needle was sometimes enough, or just immersion in the proper salt solution. The thing on Saybrook's Planet can cause fertilization by the controlled use of radiant energy. That's why an appropriate energy barrier stops it; interference, you see, or static.

"They can do more than stimulate the division and development of an unfertilized egg. They can impress their own characteristics upon its nucleoproteins, so that the young are born with the little patches of green fur, which serve as the planet's sense organ and means of communication. The young, in other words, are not individuals, but become part of the thing on Saybrook's Planet. The thing on the planet, not at all incidentally, can impregnate any species—plant, animal, or microscopic."

"Potent stuff," muttered Drake.

"Totipotent," Dr. Weiss said sharply. "Universally potent. Any fragment of it is totipotent. Given time, a single bacterium from Saybrook's Planet can convert *all of Earth* into a single organism! We've got the experimental proof of that."

Drake said unexpectedly, "You know, I think I'm a millionaire, Doc. Can you keep a secret?"

Weiss nodded, puzzled.

"I've got a souvenir from Saybrook's Planet," Drake told him, grinning. "It's only a pebble, but after the publicity the planet will get, combined with the fact that it's quarantined from here on in, the pebble will be all any human being will ever see of it. How much do you suppose I could sell the thing for?"

Weiss stared. "A pebble?" He snatched at the object shown him, a hard, gray ovoid. "You shouldn't have done that, Drake. It was strictly against regulations."

"I know. That's why I asked if you could keep a secret. If you could give me a signed note of authentication——*What's the matter, Doc?*"

Instead of answering, Weiss could only chatter and point. Drake ran over and stared down at the pebble. It was the same as before——

Except that the light was catching it at an angle, and it showed up two little green spots. Look very closely; they were patches of green hairs.

He was disturbed. There was a definite air of danger within the ship. There was the suspicion of his presence aboard. How could that be? He had done nothing yet. Had another fragment of home come aboard and been less cautious? That would be impossible without his knowledge, and though he probed the ship intensely, he found nothing.

And then the suspicion diminished, but it was not quite dead. One of the keen-thinkers still wondered, and was treading close to the truth.

How long before the landing? Would an entire world of life fragments be deprived of completeness? He clung closer to the severed ends of the wire he had been specially bred to imitate, afraid of detection, fearful for his altruistic mission.

Dr. Weiss had locked himself in his own room. They were already within the solar system, and in three hours they would be landing.

He had to think. He had three hours in which to decide.

Drake's devilish "pebble" had been part of the organized life on Saybrook's Planet, of course, but it was dead. It was dead when he had first seen it, and if it hadn't been, it was certainly dead after they fed it into the hyper-atomic motor and converted it into a blast of pure heat. And the bacterial cultures still showed normal when Weiss anxiously checked.

That was not what bothered Weiss now.

Drake had picked up the "pebble" during the last hours of the stay on Saybrook's Planet—*after* the barrier breakdown. What if the breakdown had been the result of a slow, relentless mental pressure on the part of the thing on the planet? What if parts of its being waited to invade as the barrier dropped? If the "pebble" had not been fast enough and had moved only after the barrier was re-established, it would have been killed. It would have lain there for Drake to see and pick up.

It was a "pebble," not a natural life form. But did that mean it was not *some* kind of life form? It might have been a deliberate production of the planet's single organism—a creature deliberately designed to look like a pebble, harmless-seeming, unsuspicious. Camouflage, in other words—a shrewd and frighteningly successful camouflage.

Had any other camouflaged creature succeeded in crossing the barrier *before* it was re-established—with a suitable shape filched from the minds of the humans aboard ship by the mind-reading organism of the planet? Would it have the casual appearance of a paperweight? Of an ornamental brass-head nail in the captain's old-fashioned chair? And how would they locate it? Could they search every part of the ship for the telltale green patches—even down to individual microbes?

And why camouflage? Did it intend to remain undetected for a time? Why? So that it might wait for the landing on Earth?

An infection *after landing* could not be cured by blowing up a ship. The bacteria of Earth, the molds, yeasts, and protozoa, would go first. Within a year the non-human young would begin arriving by the uncountable billions.

Weiss closed his eyes and told himself it might not be such a bad thing. There would be no more disease, since no bacterium would multiply at the expense of its host, but instead would be satisfied with its fair share of what was available. There would be no more overpopulation; the hordes of mankind would decline to adjust themselves to the food supply. There would be no more wars, no crime, no greed.

But there would be no more individuality, either.

Humanity would find security by becoming a cog in a biological machine. A man would be brother to a germ, or to a liver cell.

He stood up. He would have a talk with Captain Loring. They would send their report and blow up the ship, just as Saybrook had done.

He sat down again. Saybrook had had proof, while he had only the conjectures of a terrorized mind, rattled by the sight of two green spots on a pebble. Could he kill the two hundred men on board ship because of a feeble suspicion?

He had to *think!*

He was straining. Why did he have to wait? If he could only welcome those who were aboard now. *Now!*

Yet a cooler, more reasoning part of himself told him that he could not. The little multipliers in the darkness would betray their new status in fifteen minutes, and the keen-thinkers had them under continual observation. Even one mile from the surface of their planet would be too soon, since they might still destroy themselves and their ship out in space.

Better to wait for the main air locks to open, for the planetary air to swirl in with millions of the little multipliers. Better to greet each one of them into the brotherhood of unified life and let them swirl out again to spread the message.

Then it would be done! Another world organized, complete!

He waited. There was the dull throbbing of the engines working mightily to control the slow dropping of the ship; the shudder of contact with planetary surface, then——

He let the jubilation of the keen-thinkers sweep into reception, and his own jubilant thoughts answered them. Soon they would be able to receive as well as himself. Perhaps not these particular fragments, but the fragments that would grow out of those which were fitted for the continuation of life.

The main air locks were about to be opened——

And all thought ceased.

Jerry Thorn thought, Damn it, something's wrong *now.*

He said to Captain Loring, "Sorry. There seems to be a power breakdown. The locks won't open."

"Are you sure, Thorn? The lights are on."

"Yes, sir. We're investigating it now."

He tore away and joined Roger Oldenn at the air-lock wiring box. "What's wrong?"

"Give me a chance, will you?" Oldenn's hands were busy. Then he said, "For the love of Pete, there's a six-inch break in the twenty-amp lead."

"What? That can't be!"

Oldenn held up the broken wires with their clean, sharp, sawn-through ends.

Dr. Weiss joined them. He looked haggard and there was the smell of brandy on his breath.

He said shakily, "What's the matter?"

They told him. At the bottom of the compartment, in one corner, was the missing section.

Weiss bent over. There was a black fragment on the floor of the compartment. He touched it with his finger and it smeared, leaving a sooty smudge on his finger tip. He rubbed it off absently.

There might have been something taking the place of the missing section of wire. Something that had been alive and only looked like wire, yet something that would heat, die, and carbonize in a tiny fraction of a second once the electrical circuit which controlled the air lock had been closed.

He said, "How are the bacteria?"

A crew member went to check, returned and said, "All normal, Doc."

The wires had meanwhile been spliced, the locks opened, and Dr. Weiss stepped out into the anarchic world of life that was Earth.

"Anarchy," he said, laughing a little wildly. "And it will stay that way."

MUSHROOMS

SYLVIA PLATH

Overnight, very
Whitely, discreetly,
Very quietly

Our toes, our noses
Take hold on the loam,
Acquire the air.

Nobody sees us,
Stops us, betrays us;
The small grains make room.

Soft fists insist on
Heaving the needles,
The leafy bedding,

Even the paving.
Our hammers, our rams,
Earless and eyeless,

Perfectly voiceless,
Widen the crannies,
Shoulder through holes. We

Diet on water,
On crumbs of shadow,
Bland-mannered, asking

Little or nothing.
So many of us!
So many of us!

We are shelves, we are
Tables, we are meek,
We are edible,

Nudgers and shovers
In spite of ourselves.
Our kind multiplies:

We shall by morning
Inherit the earth.
Our foot's in the door.

MUSHROOMS

MIKE EVANS

Mushrooms grew
Overnight
like they always did
Only this time
there was
nobody
to
pick them

SOME BEINGS OUT THERE JUST MAY BE LISTENING

JOHN NOBLE WILFORD

Most scientists today assume that life is not unique to Earth and that around some of the countless stars in the universe there must be planets where civilizations have evolved, some of which could be more advanced than Earth's. Accordingly, a small but inspired effort has been under way for years to locate these extraterrestrial beings and to let them know someone is here. It is a fascinating exercise born of curiosity and cosmic loneliness.

The latest attempt to make extraterrestrial contact is a long shot if there ever was one. It is a recorded message, called "Sounds of Earth," carried by the two Voyager spacecraft. One of the robot vehicles was launched August 20, 1977, and the other was scheduled to embark the next day.

Unlike nearly all other spacecraft, which never leave the solar system, the Voyagers are to reconnoiter the outer planets and then make their way out into the galaxy, silent wanderers in space and time. Therefore, on the off chance that some other spacefaring civilization might intercept one of the Voyagers, Dr. Carl Sagan of Cornell University got the idea of enclosing a message from Earth like "a bottle cast into the cosmic ocean."

In preparing a message designed to enable extraterrestrial beings thousands or millions of years hence to put together some picture of twentieth-century Earth, its inhabitants, cultures, and technology, Dr. Sagan and a committee of scientists, musicians, and artists had to make certain assumptions. First, they assumed that whoever intercepted the spacecraft would be from a civilization as advanced technologically as this one, or even more so, for they would probably be on an expedition far from their native world. Second, it was assumed that the interceptors would have a visual imaging system, not necessarily an optical system like that of humans, but some ability to sense light. Finally, Dr. Sagan's group assumed the creatures would have a sense of hearing, though the varying electrical voltages carrying the sounds might be intelligible through other sensory organs.

Then Dr. Sagan and the committee had to try to describe Earth in two hours of sights and sounds recorded on a twelve-inch copper disk to be played at sixteen and two-thirds revolutions per minute. A sequence of 116 pictures and diagrams was selected and recorded in electronic form. The sequence starts with a view of the solar system and moves to pictures of Earth taken from space. Life is described with drawings of basic biology and pictures of a fetus, a birth, a nursing mother, a group of children, and a family. Then there are pictures of a leaf, a snowflake, insects, fish, birds, elephants, and people of different races and cultures. To portray human technology, there are pictures of houses (African and New England); cities (Oxford and Boston); the United Nations building and the Sydney, Australia, opera house; a microscope and a radio telescope and a rocket launching.

After oral greetings in fifty-five languages, an "essay in sound" includes natural sounds (rain and surf, crickets and frogs and dogs and whales) and man-made sounds (sawing, tractor, riveter, train whistle and Saturn 5 lift-off). The final sequence is a selection of music, from Bach and Beethoven to Louis Armstrong and Chuck Berry, from Mexican mariachi and Peruvian pan pipes to an Indian raga and a Navajo night chant.

No one living now will ever know if the Voyager message is delivered. If the spacecraft follow their intended courses, according to calculations, they are not likely to come near another star for about 40,000 years. And should someone encounter it, could they decipher the message?

Some of the engineers who built the Voyagers at the Jet Propulsion Laboratory in Pasadena, California, believe the spacecraft are decipherable messages in themselves. Some extraterrestrial Sherlock Holmes could, for example, deduce from the thumb screws in the craft that its builders had fingers and from the printing on some of the parts that they had some kind of optical systems. An analysis of the metals might give the finders some idea about Earth—that it is a planet that has had a molten period, has a magnetic field, is volcanic and, consequently, has an atmosphere. The nuclear power system on board, even if it had long since died out, could provide further clues to the stage of Earth's twentieth-century technology.

Meanwhile, the most promising approach toward communicating with extraterrestrial beings lies in radio astronomy, not phonograph records on spacecraft. Some radio telescopes in the United States and the Soviet Union monitor the sky routinely for any radio signals that appear unnatural and might be from a distant civilization. So far, it has been a modest effort, and to no avail.

But Dr. Frank Drake, director of the National Astronomy and Ionosphere Center, foresees an expanded and improved search in the next few years, following a strategy emerging from studies at the Ames Research Center of the National Aeronautics and Space Administration. The initial steps in the strategy, Dr. Drake said, include having the agency's deep-space tracking antenna at Goldstone, California, join in a more systematic listening program, and improving the radio receivers so they could monitor one million channels simultaneously. Eventually, the study recommends placing a huge radio telescope in Earth orbit, further improving the range and resolution of the search.

A CLOSE ENCOUNTER WITH ARTHUR C. CLARKE

MARK DAVIDSON and
NIRMALI PONNAMPERUMA

Nobody could be more pleased about the science fiction resurgence inspired by *Star Wars* and *Close Encounters of the Third Kind* than Arthur C. Clarke. Clarke, whose nearly fifty books of science fiction and fact have sold some twenty million copies in more than thirty languages, welcomes this newest competition for his own science fiction blockbuster, the much-revived Stanley Kubrick epic, *2001: A Space Odyssey.*

"The popularity of science fiction can be very beneficial in terms of the future of all humanity," Clarke said in a recent interview for *Science Digest* in the study of his large, two-story home in Colombo, capital city of Sri Lanka (formerly Ceylon). Wearing his usual attire of shirt, sarong, and sandals—he enumerated three reasons for his seemingly extravagant praise of science fiction:

"In the first place, science fiction benefits humanity by spawning some of our most dedicated scientists. I know an awful lot of scientists who originally were turned on by science fiction, and I'm rather proud of the fact that I know several astronauts who became astronauts through reading my books.

"Secondly, science fiction tends to increase interest in science among the general public. Also, the more the public knows about science, the more likely they'll go along with political leaders who support important scientific projects.

"Finally, I think science fiction serves humanity's mental health. So many movies and novels nowadays are pessimistic, but science fiction usually is optimistic. In the science fiction area, you have the feeling that the future can be better than the past, that we can do something about the future, that we don't have to wait until it comes and clobbers us."

One of the most exciting prospects for humanity's future, in Clarke's view, is communication with extraterrestrial intelligence. He believes that momentous event is inevitable, if nations such as the United States adequately fund radio astronomy probes. "It is preposterous to think that we are the only intelligent creatures in a cosmos of a hundred million galaxies. Our own galaxy must be an absolute Babel of conversation, and it is surely only a matter of time before we can hear our neighbors.

"The British cosmologist Fred Hoyle expresses the view that there may be a kind of galactic communications network, linking thousands of millions of worlds. Someday we may be clever enough to plug ourselves into that circuit, and the things we could learn might change our own society beyond recognition. It would be as if Abraham Lincoln's America could have found a way to tune in on today's American television."

Speaking of encounters with superior beings, an interviewer wondered if Clarke had given much thought as to what we might learn from them.

"No fair!" he replied. "You've stumbled on the subject of my next novel!"

In that case, would Clarke at least narrow his answer down to this: What questions would *he* ask if he were the first human to place a long-distance call to the stars?

"Of course, I'd want to ask the obvious practical questions, like how to cure cancer and how to harness the energy of atomic fusion. But then I'd want to know if other planets have gods. And I'd ask if they knew if time and space are limited. And I'd ask if death is universal."

Clarke conceded that such profound questions might not be answerable, at least in the beginning, because of difficulties in transmission and translation.

"But even if our cosmic conversation never rose above the 'Me Tarzan, You Jane' level, such contact would be extremely valuable because it would be proof that other intelligent races do exist."

Why, he was asked, does he think such proof is important to humanity?

"Well, we no longer would feel so alone in an apparently hostile universe. More importantly, perhaps, knowledge that other beings had safely passed their nuclear crises would give us renewed hope for our own future. It would help to dispel present nagging doubts about the survival value of intelligence. We have, as yet, no definite proof that too much brain, like too much armor, is not one of those unfortunate evolutionary accidents that leads to the annihilation of its possessors."

But suppose our galactic neighbors turn out to be Bug Eyed Monsters? Maybe we should think twice about calling attention to ourselves?

"I don't buy that. The insanely malevolent invaders beloved by the horror comics have little plausibility. That's because they would have destroyed themselves long before they got to us. Any race intelligent enough to conquer interstellar space must have conquered its own inner demons."

Is it possible that space beings already have visited our planet —or are cruising around right now?

"It's not *im*possible. But I must say that I've become completely bored with all those fraudulent or downright insane books about aerial crockery. And, incidentally, I have the same utter disdain for supposedly factual books about antediluvian astronauts, emotional cabbages, and Bermuda hexagons. My interest is in science and science fiction, not sham."

ACKNOWLEDGMENTS

Forrest J. Ackerman and A. E. Van Vogt: For "The Enchanted Village" by A. E. Van Vogt from *Other World's Science Stories;* copyright © 1951 by Clark Publishing Company. Lurton Blassingame: For "And He Built a Crooked House" by Robert A. Heinlein from *Astounding Science Fiction;* copyright © 1940 by Street & Smith Publications, Inc. Brandt & Brandt: For "By the Waters of Babylon" from *Selected Works of Stephen Vincent Benét,* Holt, Rinehart & Winston, Inc.; copyright 1937 by Stephen Vincent Benét; copyright renewed © 1965 by Rachel Benét Lewis, Stephanie Benét Mahin, and Thomas C. Benét. Communications Research Machines, Inc.: For "And It Will Serve Us Right" by Isaac Asimov, reprinted from *Psychology Today* Magazine, April 1969; copyright © Communications Research Machines, Inc. Delacorte Press: For "Harrison Bergeron" from *Welcome to the Monkey House* by Kurt Vonnegut, Jr., a Seymour Lawrence book for Delacorte Press; originally appeared in *Fantasy and Science Fiction;* copyright © 1961 by Kurt Vonnegut, Jr. Mike Evans: For "We'll All Be Spacemen Before We Die" and "Mushrooms" from *Holding Your Eight Hands,* edited by Edward Lucie-Smith. Doubleday & Company, Inc.: For "Green Patches" from *Nightfall and Other Stories* by Isaac Asimov; copyright 1950 by World Editions, Inc. For "Electronic Concert" from *Collected Poems of Babette Deutsch;* copyright © 1963 by Babette Deutsch. For "Space Man" from *Collected Poems of Babette Deutsch;* copyright © 1969 by Babette Deutsch. Harper & Row Publishers, Inc.: For "Ghost Crabs" from *Wodwo* by Ted Hughes; copyright © 1966 by Ted Hughes. Indiana University Press: For "Moonshot Sonnet" from *Concrete Poetry* by Mary Ellen Solt. Alfred A. Knopf, Inc.: For "Mushroom" from *The Colossus and Other Poems* by Sylvia Plath; copyright © 1960 by Sylvia Plath. Little, Brown and Company: For "The Flight of Apollo" from *The Testing Tree: Poems by Stanley Kunitz;* copyright © 1969 by Stanley Kunitz. Harold Matson Company, Inc.: For "A Sound of Thunder" by Ray Bradbury; copyright 1952 by Ray Bradbury. For "Litterbug" by Tony Morphett; copyright 1969 by Tony Morphett. For "Zero Hour" from *The Martian Chronicles* by Ray Bradbury; copyright 1951 by Ray Bradbury. For "Of Missing Persons" from *The Third Level* by Jack Finney; copyright 1957 by Jack Finney. University of Minnesota Press: For "A Projection" from *Poems: New and Selected* by Reed Whittemore; copyright © 1967 by Reed Whittemore. Henry Morrison, Inc. and Donald E. Westlake: For "The Winner" by Donald E. Westlake; copyright © 1970 by Harry Harrison for *Nova I.* W. W. Norton and Company, Inc.: For "I Am A" from *Latest Will, New and Selected Poems* by Lenore Marshall; copyright © 1969 by Lenore Marshall. Oxford University Press: For "Afterwards" from *Confessions and Histories* by Edward Lucie-Smith; © 1964 by Oxford University Press. Theron Raines and Henry Slesar: For "Victory Parade" by Henry Slesar; originally appeared in *Playboy* magazine; copyright 1957 by *Playboy.* For "Chief" by Henry Slesar: originally appeared in *Playboy* magazine; copyright © 1960 by Henry Slesar. Rutgers University Press: For "A.D. 2267" from *Of Flesh and Bone* by John Frederick Nims, 1967. Scott Meredith Literary Agency and David Redd: For "Prisoners of Paradise" by David Redd; copyright 1966 by David Redd. Scott Meredith Literary Agency and Rog Phillips: For "The Yellow Pill" by Rog Phillips from *Astounding Science Fiction.* Scott Meredith Literary Agency and Arthur C. Clarke: For "The Sentinel" from *The Nine Billion Names of God* by Arthur C. Clarke; copyright 1951 by Avon Periodicals, Inc. For "Summertime on Icarus" by Arthur C. Clarke, reprinted from *Vogue* Magazine; © 1960 by Condé Nast Publications. Scott Meredith Literary Agency, Inc. and E. G. Von Wald: For "Hemeac" by

E. G. Von Wald from *Galaxy* magazine; copyright 1968 by Galaxy Publishing Corporation. Charles Scribner's Sons: For "Orbiter Five Shows How Earth Looks from the Moon" from *Iconographs* by May Swenson; originally appeared in *The Southern Review;* copyright © 1969 by May Swenson. Something Else Press: For "Off Course" by Edwin Morgan from *An Anthology of Concrete Poetry,* edited by Emmett Williams; copyright © 1967 by Something Else Press. University of Texas Press and William Dickey: For "Voyage to the Moon" by William Dickey from Vol. VII, No. 3 of *Texas Quarterly;* copyright © 1964 by University of Texas Press. For "Some Beings Out There Just May Be Listening" by John Noble Wilford; copyright © 1977 by The New York Times Company; reprinted by permission. *Science Digest:* For "A Close Encounter with Arthur C. Clarke" by Mark Davidson and Nirmali Ponnamperuma; copyright © 1978 by The Hearst Corporation. The authors and editors have made every effort to trace the ownership of all copyrighted selections in this book and to make full acknowledgment for their use.

ILLUSTRATION

Roger Hane, cover; courtesy of Marlborough Galleries, 8, 108; private collection, 23; M. C. Escher, 24, 46, 59; Museum of Modern Art, 45, 60, 90, 168, 181; Galerie Mathias Fels, 70; The Hamlyn Group, 89; Abrams, 92, 206, 229; courtesy of Marthe Prévot, 118; Philadelphia Museum of Art, 125; courtesy of Ronald S. Lauder, 126; Boymansvan Boyningnen Museum, 140; Whitney Museum of American Art, 144; courtesy of *Art News,* 146; courtesy of Harry Torczyner, 158; courtesy of Bernard Childs, 179; Galerie Lambert, 190; courtesy of Mr. and Mrs. William Mazer, 205; courtesy of Mr. and Mrs. Joseph R. Shapiro, 215; private collection, 218; courtesy of John L. Loeb, Jr., 230; courtesy of the National Air and Space Museum, 248, 251.

80 81 82 83 / 10 9 8 7 6 5 4 3 2